THE JOVIAN SIGNAL

Space Hotel Daedalus

PADA BATOS

With a special thanks to my wife.

Dedicated to all who have aspirations for our bright future on Earth, on the Moon and beyond in our Solar system.

The Assignment

The midsummer traffic on the road to Quito gets denser the closer you get. Heat, dust, and the smell of asphalt have driven Veronica into a roadside restaurant used as resting stop by the truckers moving lumber to the port of Quito. She regrets leasing an open car, the sun, and dust just make driving a thing you need to overcome as fast as possible. Compared to the dusty road the restaurant seems nicer despite the constant humming from the ceiling fans, refrigerators, and the news blasting from the wall-screen. The bar desk flanks the backside of the aisle, and a row of wooden benches and tables faces the windows viewing the road. At the far side of the road the tall trees rise as a wall of green vegetation blocking further sight.

Veronica gazes at the trees while in the middle of her call "...but they closed Hotel Daedalus for maintenance?" she thinks impatiently.

"Yes anyway, we already have occupancy for you up there, and arranged everything for your arrival next week. This long assignment comes with an 10,000 upfront payment and all expenses covered on your account here at Thai News. Please confirm if you accept the contract, Miss Wieeloff" the AI operator replies.

She knows she needs a job badly to pay the bills not to mention the credit. Without reading the contract she nods with a confident smile "Yes, I'll go to Daedalus. Please book me a flight from Quito to the Spaceport. Where do I go from?" she asks in her mind and takes a sip of her ice-tea.

The Operator continues "It will depart from Singapore. I'll let the Thai News Board know about your decision and mail your tickets."

"Thank you" Veronica thinks and commands her mind assistant to end the call before the Operator begins on the goodbye sequence.

With a self-satisfied smile, she thinks, 'Hey, I will go to the Moon'. She closes her eyes and asks her mind assistant for the job-file she just received, her mind displays a visual image of the document, and some kind of coded file. The job assignment explains she has to meet Dr. Marc Sheehaus at Hotel Daedalus and hand him the code. He will give her the details about the story she has to write about. 'Odd' she thinks 'why not let me know right away, so I can get started?' The file has no photo of Marc, but she remembers him from a reception at the Thai News.

Dr. Sheehaus was a *boring* retired astrology professor, short, gray haired and always wearing a plain quilt-coat and holding a glass of whiskey. It makes her laugh to herself. Veronica opens her eyes and looks through the window without focusing on anything and in a glimpse sees her own reflection in the window glass. She closes her eyes and continues to read the file. It says, Dr. Marc Sheehaus worked on a science project onboard Daedalus, something about a probe for Ceres. 'But... he retired years ago?' she thinks, and remembers the reception in Bangkok. A colleague made a short introduction to him, and she had to use all her charm just to drag a smile out of the man. He saluted kindly and then looked the other way. She had to move in front of him to get his attention, she made a joke followed by her dashing smile "Did you discover the Halley's Comet, Dr. Sheehaus?"

Sheehaus looked at her roughly with a vague smile "Miss Wieeloff, if you have anything thoughtful on your mind please let me know" he then left toward the bar.

'I hope he is in a better mood' she thinks, and moves a bit shyly on the bench. She remembers the news article she had read about the Daedalus Space hotel. The hotel closed one year ago for major maintenance and reconstruction works.

A Chinese mining company built Daedalus to transport minerals and equipment to and from the Moon. Years later they moved the mining to another location on the Moon and sold Daedalus.

A tourist company from Singapore turned it into a luxury space-hotel. They added two new habitat ring-sections, with a third section still under construction.

As in a dream she imagines the many advertisements she had seen about vacations at Hotel Daedalus. This beautiful metallic blue-gray cylindrical space station that reflects the sunlight like the Sun's twin star, with its spacey hotel rooms. The fancy restaurants not to forget the casino, and the shopping deck where The Gala Salon stands out as the most booked diner on the Space Hotel. The Glamorous Gala Salon has a large window front giving a view of spaceships arriving and the spectacular sight of the Moon and Earth.

The station even has a garden or biosphere in a separate ring-section. They also offer guided trips to the Moon. Groups go down with the elevator and then travel by the mining company's track to the new busy mining site for lunch and then back.

Veronica returns from her daydreaming with a sense of thrill and continues to read. Further the file says she has to socialize with a man named Ray Barton who has an inheritance claim in her name for a property on Daedalus. The property was sold in petto to a company called Mohann Inc. they acquired it for a fraction of its value. She gets the money from the sale as payment for the job. 'What job?' She wonders and reads further, Dr. Sheehaus will let her in on the job. 'Oh, with that old fool the job can't be hard. Finally, a jackpot' She feels a rush down her spine.

'*Look at this*' The file has a photo of Ray, he has dark-blond hair with a fringe falling on his left side. He has a cute nose and dark blue eyes 'Handsome, looks like I will enjoy this one', she thinks and continues reading the profile on Ray. Thirty-four years old and unmarried, he has a private interest in mountain climbing and works as a legal insurance inspector now freelance. Ray used to work at the Huang Shipping Insurance Inc. with headquarters in Singapore. 'Uh, that sounds boring, if he gets my money then he will do.' He had spent three years with his father on the station then moved back to Earth, working at Huang. 'Well, he looks in good shape, a mountain climber sounds strong and daring.' She figures.

With a sense of confidence she turns her head, opens her eyes and focuses right away on her reflection in the window. She looks satisfied at her perfect curves with every proportion right, her straight dark-brown hair matches the light brown eyes and honey bronze colored skin. She is so thankful for her mother who had her made perfect from conception. She looks one hundred percent like her mother, who conceived her from her own stem cells. They then genetically screened her one cell embryo, enhanced and corrected it, making her smarter, healthier and more beautiful than her creator, her mother.

Veronica throws her head back, ready to go and catch that man Ray, 'He is a lucky one' she knows all she needs is her sex.

The waitress gets Veronica's attention when she asks a second time and this time louder, if she has finished her cake?

"**Yes**, you can give me the bill, please" Veronica replies in a sharp tone, she just can't stand interruptions.

"*Well*, who the one sleeping, *dear*" the waitress responds snappily as she hands out the payment card. The mind assistant does the payment transfer with the new account number from Thai News.

She got her mind-implant 6 years ago, as a 22-year birthday gift from her mother. The best gift she ever had, now 8 months have passed with the new upgrade. The implant comes with the newest quantum entanglement communicator, with instant data transfer.

A tiny time crystal records all her thoughts, senses, emotions, and any external data she receives.

She can see documents and videos when closing her eyes. The assistant organizes the storage for her, finds any information she asks for, makes voice calls, and helps her solve problems etc. Most essential, it never misinterprets her intentions. Now the mind-assistant has become her best friend, and she cannot imagine how to live without it.

Veronica gets up from the bench leaning forward as she stands up, very confident, showing off what is inside the half open jacket. She walks toward the exit with a daring look as she says to the trucker sitting at the next table in front of her, busy eating his meal "Hi Alligator *Now* you can stop looking... *Got your ears on?*" Zipping up the pink leather jacket, it tightens around her breasts as she sends him a kiss with a catwalk for the door. The tight leather skirt curves nicely around her butt.

The truck driver looks speechless over his shoulder as she leaves, asking the man sitting at the rail "What happened to her?"

The drive to the hotel gets deadly dangerous for everyone on the road. With several nearly fatal overtakes, she sounds the horn as if it would save her from a frontal shock. Passing a warning sign: Radar Mind your speed. She shouts "*Send the bill to the rental*" as she waves at the camera.

At her hotel she slams the door behind her. "Never again" she scoffs and throws the car keys on the small table next to the entrance door. She heads straight for the shower, undressing the few items she wears on the way. The simple hotel room has a bed and a small bathroom. Nothing fancy about it, not to mention the lack of view. This trip she had to pay for by herself, and the finances got low, till now.

In the shower the mind–assistant announces an incoming call. "I'll take it" she thinks a bit ignored.

"Hello Sweet Cat, did they send you the data?" the man asks anxiously.

"Yes, I got it, and the *job* – I didn't expect a job that tremendous" she thinks, while soaping her body with the soft sponge.

"Don't forget your birth certificate and dress like a lady for once, you can't throw this one away" the man says with a firm voice.

"I just need one hand for the money, and the other for you, my dear" she thinks in response.

"Ha, ha, yeah, you better hold on, Sweet Cat" the man hangs up.

'What a jerk' Veronica thinks to herself as she turns up the hot water. The vapor mixed with coconut oil makes her feel good. She starts to sing a few phrases from a happy song she heard on her drive back from the citizen office.

Swift, on the other side of the Pacific. Ray has just closed yet another dispute between a shipping company and its client, this time about some damaged goods. He sits in his office with a cup of coffee and feels relieved, free from that nagging client, and pleased to have received his payment in hand. Most of his work involves trivial, small cases about lost shipping containers, trivial shipping accidents at port docking not to mention wrong or faulty equipment etc. etc.

When settling disputes, at best, they meet in port-offices or at the lawyer's office. More often they meet in nightclubs or restaurants depending on what it takes to get the clients to ease-up.

Ray never went to court with a case, he worked as a go-between. If he failed to sign a deal with the client, he handed the case over to the insurance company's legal department.

'No new cases, I wonder if Huang has any jobs for me?' Ray thinks on his way out to the hall. He shares the front desk and lavatory with six other companies. They replaced the front desk receptionist with a coffee machine to pay their monthly rent, all seven needed to cut back on expenses.

As he returns to his office with a refill he sees a classy dressed man reading in his comfortable armchair. "*Wang*" Ray blaze heartfelt as he stares amazedly at Mr. Wang, "How long since last time?" They salute with a firm handshake.

"Glad to see you too, Ray" Wang respond, smiling. He continues "You still work in insurance I see" as he returns a document back into its envelope.

"Sure, we all need to live in one way or another" Ray respond as he walks over to the desk with his coffee "Would you like a cup?" he encourages.

Wang looks straight at Ray "No, thanks, if you haven't got anything stronger" he says with a simple nod toward the archive.

"You cannot fool an old fox" Ray reply laughing as he opens the archive. Ray pulls out two glasses and a bottle of ordinary whiskey.

He pours the drinks and asks a little tense "What brings you to this part of the world?"

"I got a new case for you on Daedalus, all expenses on me." Wang says and hand Ray the envelope as he continues "I got a claim on an apartment there, a job straightforward. A young woman inherits her uncle's apartment and need some legal advice as the old man has committed suicide. She is a charming young lady named Veronica Wieeloff, she works as a journalist, freelance just like you. I ask you to do this for me, I never flew to the Moon. You know your way on Daedalus you stayed there half of your life" Wang looks seriously at Ray, as if the case matters life and death for him.

Ray shakes his head looking out the window at the large office building across the street.

"I quit domestic cases years ago, and on Daedalus, forget about it" He feels a sudden dryness and bottoms the glass.

"You *can't* say no to me, Ray. I taught you everything you know, how to find evidence of misplaced goods at the terminals, how to find evidence of client fraud, how to make the client to accept and settle a dispute, you name it. I made you the man you have become." Wang takes the first sip of his drink and looks hard at Ray "I even taught you how to beat down a rustler."

Ray looks back at him in a sad kind of way "Yeah, but I just make the clients agree to a deal, you make them pay for it" he laments.

"Well, you know the law is the law. I need your help Ray, especially on Hotel Daedalus, I want you to make it up to me." Wang has kind of softened his voice looking down at the glass.

Ray takes a step back "*No Not ever!* I do not mix my work with the work of the police." He slides the envelope unto the desk toward Wang.

Wang look very serious at Ray "Let me remind you of the good old times, Ray. When a young man messed it up and lost the big client and Wang had to put all his prestige in at the Boss for him to have a career after the biggest blow in the company's history. The cold sweated young man after the fiasco say no matter what you ask for, just let me know, and I'll pay you back. You remember that, don't you? Well, your payback time have arrived, Ray I tell you. You got the call!"

Ray nods with a solemn look on his face. 'I know this man always collects' he thinks with a heavy heart as he sits down at his desk and start reading the document. Straightforward, a claim by Veronica Wieeloff on the apartment with content owned by Henrik Hoffman on Daedalus. It's worth about 50 million, 'a lot of money, but also a trivial case with all in its order...' Ray thinks as he gets interrupted by Wang's pad ringing.

After listening to the caller for a short moment Wang looks at Ray and gets his attention by pointing at the pad. "I'll project this call, for my associate to view in. Please excuse me for a minute" he says tactfully to the caller. The screen projects onto the wall. The image has all the same faults as the wall with its holes and marks from before Ray rented the office two years ago.

"*Nikki*" Ray shouts in surprise seeing her projected onto the wall, "you know Mr. Wang?" Ray asks, even more surprised than when he found Wang in his office a moment ago.

"Hi Ray, hello Mr. Wang, *Nikki Navarro*" Nikki salutes with a big smile.

Wang smiles back at the young attractive woman "I see you two know each other. They told me an employee from Daedalus would call me regarding our booking of rooms, and a shuttle schedule" Wang say with a light blush.

"Sorry Mr. Wang, I didn't know You and Ray do business together" Nikki say with a hand gesture. She continues with her soft voice "Ray and I go back when he stayed here with his father a couple of years ago."

Ray feel happy to see Nikki and smile without saying a word. He observes as she moves a hair lock away from her praline face.

After an embarrassing pause Wang take the word "And... when can we shuttle up to meet you, Nikki?"

"Yes, I've got two Crew Cabins for you, as all the hotel rooms were booked. With all the preparations going on, as you know... The Crew Cabins compared to the hotel pay off in privacy, I can assure you." She says with an easy nod, she looks down at the terminal and continue "The shuttle departs from Singapore airport tomorrow. They normally take off in the morning. Let me look it up for you, Mr. Wang, just a moment."

Nikki looks down on her terminal and search for the travel plan, the conventional Daedalus uniform give her an appearance of authority.

"Lovely bird" Wang say to Ray in a low voice.

"Yes a lot" Ray reply as discrete as possible.

Nikki looks back onto the camera "It will depart 9:30 in the morning, you need check-in one hour before, and I'll transfer the boarding pass to you after our call, Mr. Wang. *So Ray... you will go too?*" she asks eagerly.

Ray moves a bit closer "Yes, I've got to handle this case here" he lifts the documents up from the table.

"You promised me you would come back, remember?" Nikki asks with a bright smile.

"Well, yes of course I do. I will make it up to you" Ray respond sending her a happy smile back. The screen turn blank, and the call end.

"You sure look like one of these old light bulbs" Wang says with a big grin and continue "Do you feel all right? Let's celebrate our trip to the Moon, shall we?" he asks cheerful and cast a glance in direction of the archive.

Next day on the taxi ride to the airport Ray notice a man acting strange, like if he tries to follow them on his eBike. He shakes the idea off his mind 'So many people go to the airport every day'. They chat about the Oil slump. "You can't run your old bike anymore" Ray say to Wang with a nod toward the electric bike passing their Cab.

"Nor the Buick" Wang reply with a sad expression and continue "I remember a man from Atlanta who made the synthetic oil, they just took all away from him. No one can run an old gas car anymore, they will not let you."

"They beam energy down to earth from the orbit power plant, and it powers the shuttle, did you know?" Ray asks with a look of fascination on his face.

"*Yeah*, I hatched before you, you know, I just don't like they shoot that laser at us." Wang laugh and look up at the sky though the Caps roof window.

"Who run the Station?" Wang change subject as all the technical stuff dulls him.

"The same who runs things elsewhere, the rich and crooked... The Saymora Corporation owns Daedalus, you know" Ray responds as he looks out the window at the eBike, as it passes for the second time, he notices the dark-red silk neckerchief flapping in the wind.

In the spaceport terminal they check in their luggagel, Wang suddenly bend down and opens his suitcase. "A fellow at 3 o'clock follow us, let's lose him, we split and meet at the gate just in time to get aboard."

Ray look directly to his right as he walks away from Wang. A strange man with a red neckerchief look observing at them as he pass. Ray walk fast down the shopping section a distance in front of the man, he mingles into a large group of travelers and then enters a gift shop. In the shop Ray stand fingering with a flowerpot as he looks out the shop-window.

"The Garden Mum flower purifies the air" the shop attendant say with a smile, getting Rays attention she continues "do you want it in a box?" Ray narrow his eyes as he tries to recognize the woman.

"Do I want it in a box?" Ray asks uncertain.

"*The flowerpot*" the shop attendant says with a gesture at the flower in Rays hands.

Back in the hall Ray walks to the arrival area as he looks for a man in leather dress. 'Where did he go?' he thinks as he studies all the people reflected in the large front windows.

A shuttle glide into the runway and taxi to the terminal. '*There*' He follows one dressed in leather walking decisive to the arrival gate, a man arrives, they hug each other warmly. Ray stops as he runs his hand through his hair '*Oh, a woman*'.

The last call for his boarding sound on the speakers. Ray runs all the way back to the departure gate where Wang waits "...*yes, I assure you, he will come any moment.*" Wang says to the Steward, at the same time he sees Ray down the corridor and call at him "*Come on Ray, hurry up!*"

Ray snap for his breath as they get aboard. "Do you know who this spook reminds me of?" Wang ask Ray as they walk on the idle looking for their seats.

"No, who?" Ray have regained his breath.

Wang continues "The creep from the Perth case."

"*Aha yeah*, you right, Ben from Perth..." The Stewardess interrupt Ray with a gesture and ask them to fasten the belt tight as the first part of the flight get a bit shaky.

Ray fold his arms across his chest "Did you see the fellow again in the airport?" he asks as he focuses at Wang.

"No, I went to the Cafe and had breakfast, why?" Wang asks.

Ray look upset at Wang, by the fact, that he had not had any breakfast and run around the airport terminal for one hour.

The shuttle start to shake a little, as the engines take in air. They move forward and lift off from the ground smoothly and start to ascend faster and faster in a curve inclining upward.

"You know Wang, Right now they point the energy beam from the ground on the shuttle's belly receiver" Ray says with a thrill.

"Seriously, when will they stop pointing that thing at us?" Wang ask anxiously and hold his breath.

"When we get out of the atmosphere, shortly, relax Wang" Ray say thrilled by the acceleration. He looks out the side window with a sensation of fascination, seeing the earths' horizon start to bend as they continue to climb. After a while the sound and vibration from the engines stop and stuff start float in the cabin. "Wang, we are up, you can relax now, they have switched to ion-mode."

A Steward come floating down the idle and Wang grab the man's jacket "Can I have a straight whiskey, *Please*" he asks with a firm voice.

"No alcohol allowed on the shuttles, Sir. Can I bring you a bottle of spring water with a straw?" Wang looks perplexed at the Steward without saying a word, then nod with a helpless hand gesture. Wang looks at Ray for some sympathy, but Ray stare out the window, absorbed by the sight of the huge blue horizon curving more and more.

The Caption announces on the intercom that they have left Earths atmosphere and not to remove the safety belt, just loss the belt to cruse position. On the rest of the trip a relay satellite will power the shuttle.

Ray taps on the screen in front of him, and chose a News channel he knows from the list. Wang interrupt him "How can you look at that rubbish, Ray?"

Ray slide deeper into the chair "We have a long flight ahead of us, so you better get distracted with something" he put on the ear plugs.

"Was it 15 hours?" Wang asks trying to keep the conversation going.

"No, 16 hours... take a look at the information here." Ray push the button on Wang's display, after reading a while Wang look at Ray for some more guidance with the screen, but Ray has fallen asleep.

The Signal

Ray watch for Daedalus. He stiffens when a reflection from the sun suddenly flash from behind the Moon and hit him in his eyes. He shades the view till the light fade in intensity. The Space Hotel moves steadily into sight as a small Star rising on the Moon's horizon. The closer they get, the more impressive the view. Daedalus hang motionless in wires from the Moons backside, the Moon get so close as it seems like you can touch it.

Ray gets breathless, and the blood rush through his arms. In slow motion the blue-gray silver cylinder gets bigger and bigger, he feels graceful.

They approach the dock on the Space Hotel next to the four wires going down to the Moon. Ray shades his eyes to get a better look at the construction workers and crawler-drones installing engines on the back edge of the shield. An elevator returns, and cover his sight, it moves steady up the cables till it connect with the station.

His eyes sparkle from excitement. A small Helium-pot come floating back to the elevator where it docks for its return to the process plant on the Moon.

Ray looks down on the Moon, seeing the craters up close is so fascinating. He wonders if there will be time for a Moon walk at the end of the trip. A moving reflection capture his attention on the shadow side. Some faint lights glow close to where the elevator cables end 'It must be the elevators moon port' he thinks. They get closer to the Elevator, and it blocks his view of the moon. He studies the shiny metal tiles that make up the shield of the station. Now and then small engines light up to maintain the station in place. He remembers how his old man had explained him all about the Elevator from when they started construction to how they operated it.

The shield look like a tin-can hanging still in space. A cylinder open in one end facing deep space and closed in the other end toward the Moon. The closed end of the shield have the docking-port and elevator section. Inside the shield rotates the station, like a stack of donuts rotating giving it normal gravity.

They build the station to take empty helium-pots down to the moon for refilling, and then lanced them back into space by the centrifugal launcher.

Earth get 80% of its energy from the fusion reactors in earth orbit. Big business for the mining company, now richer than any single nation on earth.

The shuttle dock and chaos arise as everybody and everything float around in the cabin. The first-timers make it hard for the rest as they move out of control. The stewards do there best to get the repeaters out first, telling the first-timers to stay strapped in their seats, but with little luck.

"*I've lost the envelope*" Ray shout desperate, as he looks below his seat with his feet upside down "*I just read it a while ago.*"

"Come on, let's go" Wang says impatient, unstrapping his seatbelt he flows away in an off angle. He looks delirious as he tumbles down the idle facing the ceiling.

"*Meet me at the Botanic Club if we get lost*" Ray shouts and lose eye contact with Wang. Ray dives below the seats looking for the envelope.

Wang don't know how to move in weightlessness and in his attempt to move forward he flows backward in the shuttle.

The steward ask Ray to exit straightaway and guide him down the idle together with the other Repeaters, the line moves slowly forward. At the exit in front of him, a man with red neckerchief look straight at him. 'It is him' Ray thinks, instead of the bike-dress he now wears a dark gray garb with his red neckerchief tightly knot. 'He must have taken the envelope' Ray think frustrated, as the man disappear into the airlock. Ray push back with all his strength and set off to the exit. The airlock door closes just in front of him, and he smash into the door and bunch back.

"*Did you make it in time?*" one angry Lady scoff at Ray.

An upset man roars "*You just pushed me in the face, ruddy.*"

Ray feel his ears and chin getting hot as he waits for the people to get out of the airlock on the other side. And more waiting till the door open again on his side. Time seems forever disembarking the shuttle.

Once through, he makes his way down the corridor into the port terminal, he sees the back of the man entering the second airlock. Ray pushes back on the wall and gain distance floating toward the man but loose him again as the door close. The second airlock lead into the rotating lobby of the Oeuvre-section. There are two transporters, diagonal to one and another, one for Crew only, and the other marked Hotel Daedalus with large golden letters.

Ray back away as all the guest fill the Hotel transporter, he studies the info-gram on top of the transporter: Second floor, First floor and Service deck, for each ring sections Oeuvre, Crew, Bio and Hotel. 'Did he go to the Crew section, or the Hotel section?' he wonders and pushes himself into the Crew transporter and select the Second floor, the spacious transporter move fast and silent. He fell his weight toward the floor grow as he moves away from the center outward on the Oeuvre-section.

Ray step out of the transporter and stand passive in the middle of the narrow corridor. He studies the sign above a door >Crew Office< 'Why did this man steal the testament? Or maybe I lost it in the shuttle?' Ray thinks.

A man pardons, so he can pass on the narrow corridor.
Ray decides to enter the Crew Office and announce the envelope lost, at least he will get it back if they find it on the shuttle. At the Crew Administration Office he files theenvelope lost and ask a few questions about Henrik Hoffman "...so Mr. Hoffman died her onDaedalus two weeks ago you say?"

"Yes, he committed suicide in his apartment, at least, so they say. You might talk to Dr. O'Barley on Sickbay he has the medical journal" the skinny office clerk explain.

"Right, thank you, you have helped me a lot" Ray reply with a slow smile, 'at least someone looks for that envelope' he thinks relieved.

Ray take his pad out of his pocket and open the Boarding confirmation: Cabin Nº 237 on the corridor 1C. With the pad in his hand he gives Wang a call, but there is no answer. 'He takes a nap after the trip' he imagines and decide to visit him later. Down on first floor, the corridor is stuffy from crew walking to and from work. Ray find his Cabin, the room-assistant welcome him and start to explain its function as voice assisted Control. Ray tell it to stop as he knows the speech too well.

His luggage haven't arrived yet, so the shower have to wait. He takes a seat and look at the panoramic view displayed on the large screen next to him. A small text says 'Hotel Daedalus 2104-06-28-01.53301 UMT SW-Live'. The image has no movements, the steady-image show the cables going down to the anchor on the Moon, he remembers Dad had explained how the elevator worked. The weight of the long cables balance, so they don't pull the station down to the moon. He smiles at the Universal Metric Time, so odd compared to the time at home.

Ray studies the screen and wonders what angle the camera have. With his own orientation sitting in the sofa facing toward the entrance door but discard the thought as he remembers they rotate and the camera not.

The crew cabin have a small entrance with a mini kitchen leading directly into the living room. Fitted with a working desk, and a small sofa group, next is the bedroom and bathroom. No windows just wall-screens in the two main rooms. The walls have leather coating in a light gray color and on the floor a carpet. 'The carpet smell new, better than at home' Ray think as he stretch his legs on the sofa. The excitement of returning to the Station keep him in the past when Dad... Zzz

Ray wakes up by the room-assistant announcing a delivery waiting outside his door. He tells the assistant to open the door as he stands-up. A self-driving Service-wagon enters with his luggage followed by Nikki.

Ray gives Nikki a warmhearted hug "*Hello Nikki*, how wonderful to see you again" his heart pound, and he feels hot.

"*Hey Ray*, you look handsome with that shirt" Nikki reply and keep smiling as she looks around "old cabin, it needs renovation..." she quakes.

They unload the luggage in the middle of the room, and the wagon leave.

Ray looks at Nikki 'She sure looks great', then looking in her bright eyes "Well, the cabin looks new to me, how great to see you again, Nikki" he breathes.

Nikki keep smiling "I'm happy to see you too, and that you join the voyage. How about going out tonight?" she asks with sparkling eyes.

Ray move his luggage into the bedroom "Sure, just need to pass by Wang first, have you talked to him?" He asks in a louder voice from the bedroom.

"No, not yet" Nikki reply quietly, a bit disappointed that Ray pay so little attention to her "I better go, see you tonight then... we can dine together in the Canteen?" she questions.

"Sure" Ray gush and come back from the bedroom with a small brown paper bag. He hands it to Nikki "a little something from mother earth" he says with a smile.

Nikki looks into the bag and with a little "whiii" sound of surprise takes out a small Garden Mum plant inside a transparent plastic box. "*You know you are not allowed to bring soil up here it can contaminate the whole place*" she looks serious at Ray.

Ray gazes at the flower box "Come on, don't you like it?" he shakes his head, "it removes toxic from the air, it's a pretty flower!"

Nikki put the flowerpot back into the bag and give Ray a kiss on his chin "Bye Ray" She says and leave the cabin, with the bag.

After the shower he dress for the evening in a dark blue suit, and gives Wang a second call but no answer and no message-box either. 'Well, I'll just have to look for him at the Botanic Club' he thinks and head for the door.

Ray walk relaxed down the corridor, making way for people passing now and then, he recalls last time he was up here and get a bit sentimental. Dad explained all details so vivid as if he had built the space station himself. 'The Atom-Assembler fabricate any material used to build the station, just from moon dust'. He reflects and feel as if Dad has said it.

The section airlock is open, so he walks straight into the Biological ring. The narrow corridors change wall color from a smooth iron gray to a scabby apricot. The door signs name food processing plants, and their offices. The place buss with crew, Ray walks a bit faster, he recalls the biosphere on the other side of the section and smile at the thought. 'How wonderful full of trees and bees with a fresh smell of dewy grass' he pictures all the greens and colorful flowers.

Passing the last airlock to the Hotel ring-sections give a sensation of exiting a crowded tunnel. Ray stop and look at the Grand-Dour of the Hotel sections, he just stands there impressed by the sumptuous size of everything.

The two new Hotel rings don't have any airlocks between them. The open space give Ray the sensation of walking outside, like down on earth. At the end of the station he sees crawler-drones moving on the wall of the fifth ring in construction, a luxury apartment section.

Ray recall he has to meet Wang at the Botanic Club 'A half circles walk to the Biosphere'. A sentimental inspiration get to him, he decides to take a little d-tour to have a look at the stars at the Star Lounge.

The entrance is discrete with stairs leading up to a low third floor. The place sounds half empty some low voices and porcelain clinging come from the obscured tables. The familiar smell of muffins and tea make him relax, with a sense of coming home. He orders what come close to a cup of coffe on the station. A Green Tea and enjoy the view of the stars in almost darkness. He recalls when his old man sat just here, and pointed out all the constellations he knew about.

Ray look out into the dark until his eyes adapt to the low light. He recognizes it immediately. The Water Bearer with the Aquarii stars forming the shoulders, and next to it The Eagle easy to see with the bright Aquilae star pointing it out. 'Wang must be at the Botanic Club' Ray recall and empty his cup.

Two men wait for Ray at a bench next to the Star Lounge as Ray comes out from the dark Lounge they get up and walk up to him. The lights in the large corridor at first seem so bright, Ray cannot see clear and wonder who they are.

"*Hello Ben?*" still trying to see who come toward him. As the two men get closer and Rays sight get better he recognizes them. "You could have brought a friend with you" Ray says in a disgraceful tone to Ben.

"I don't choose my colleges" Ben respond with a hand gesture.

"Hello Mr. Mark" Ray salute with a half felt smile.

Mr. Mark turn on a foul grin "*What bring you up here?*" he command.

Ray look discontent at his uniform as he replies "On business with a friend, just don't know where he went."

"Oh, can we help you find him for you?" Ben asks cocky. Ray rise his shoulders doubtful.

Mr. Mark walk around Ray *"Are you asking for help?"* he adds sarcastic and continue, *"you are in the wrong environment, earthling."*

Ray look at Mr. Mark "I didn't know you had sealed the Station off from Earth?"

Mr. Mark look surprised at Ray "Yes, it will be, very soon. And what do you know about that?" he questions.

Ray get tired of Mr. Mark's silly remarks and turn to Ben "Ben, did you see this friend of mine. I have called him but no answer. He's in his mid-fifty's, tall, silver-gray hair and mustache with a blue striped coat?"

"Another earthling" Mr. Mark add with a wide grin.

Ben laugh along. *"No!* That sounds like one out of many here in the Hotel..."

Mr. Mark interrupt Ben *"And* what does your friend do here on Daedalus?" as he nods his head to the side.

"Meeting with a girl" Ray reply trivial.

"Ha, ha, then you know where to find him, don't you?" Ben says with a foul smile on his face.

Mr. Mark look displeased at Ben then pointing a finger at Ray "Are your friend here on Business?" he rants.

Ray looks down at the ground "Sort of..." he heckles.

Mr. Mark fixes his eyes on Ray *"Big Business?"* he asks pushy.

Ray get uncomfortable with the way Mr. Mark press on "Maybe, maybe not" he responds while lifting his shoulders.

Mr. Mark scratch himself at the back of his head as he looks at Ben "What a story, do you get it Ben?" Ben look back and shake his head. Mr. Mark fix his eyes at Ray again *"Ray,* do the girl by any chance have a name?"

"Miss Wieeloff, Veronica Wieeloff" Ray respond with a feeling of unease. He closes his eyes and take a deep breath with a desire to get going.

Mr. Mark get upset, he looks to both sides and race his hands and explode *"I say, your friend are in the wrong Business. So are you if you make her your company. Here is a little advice, take the next shuttle home, Ray, it is your last chance"* He turns as he gives Ben a nod, and they walk away.

Ray looks down at the floor as he rethinks what just happen, he calmly walks down the shopping corridor on second floor. Ray looks at all the happy people enjoying themselves. A laugh comes from a bar table, others look occupied eating and drinking. Or come out of the shops chatting and smiling with their hands full of bags with stuff made on Daedalus, most likely from Moon material.

A sense of relax come back from watching the felicity in the people all around. Ray notices a plain man following him, by the clumsy way the man sneak along the walls. He stops and seeks his empty pockets, in an instant he makes a turnaround and surprise the man as they suddenly stand face to face, "*What?*" Ray yell directly into the man's face.

"Hello Mr. Barton" the man salute as he takes half a step backward "you are Mr. Ray Barton, am I right?" he asks kindly.

Ray looks down on the short, gray haired man "*Yes, that's me*" he fumes.

"I saw your name on the boarding list in the Crew Office." He stretch his hand out and salute "Dr. Marc Sheehaus" they shake hands and Dr. Sheehaus continue tense "I'm truly happy to have found you" he rambles.

"*Yeah*, you just look people up and then follow them around, *right?*" Ray ask upset.

Dr. Sheehaus get even more nervous "Well you see, the man you came with..."

"You mean Mr. Wang?" Ray interrupt.

"Yes that's him, I..." Dr. Sheehaus hold his hands tight.

"How do you know Mr. Wang?" Ray interrupt again.

Dr. Sheehaus clear his throat "I have a matter for him" he stutters edgily.

Ray stare incredulous at Dr. Sheehaus "*A matter?*" he gasps and study Dr. Sheehaus's old fashion quilt-coat and don't know what to make out of it "Well... you surely show up in time, come with me, I'm going to meet him at the Crew Club" he suggests.

They walk through the air-lock and into the Biological ring, turn the corner, and a bit down the corridor to the old Crew Club. An old fashion neon-sign light up the entrance: Botanic Club. "*Hurry up*" Ray wait for Dr. Sheehaus as he holds the door.

They walk up to the Bar, The energetic bartender recognize Ray on the spot "**Hello Ray**, you are back with us again?" he salutes louder than the music.

"Passing by" Ray say and salute with a nod "have you seen my friend, he's old, gray haired and in a classy blue coat?"

"No, all younger people here tonight, can I give you anything?" The bartender asks.

"No, thanks, but thank you for your help." Ray takes a walk round the Club, the place buzz of laughter and hooting from all the young people enjoying themselves. He pass between the tables, now and then a bright smile get his attention or the smell of a daring perfume, but no sight of Mr. Wang. He returns to the bar where Dr. Sheehaus sit on a bar stool with a glass in his hand. Relieved to see Ray return, he makes a questionable gesture with the hand. "He will be here any time now" Ray say to calm Dr. Sheehaus down, and continue "can I help you with your matter for Mr. Wang?"

Dr. Sheehaus lean closer to Ray "It is actually an astrological observation that go back some years now, you cannot trust anybody in this matter. It is about the Signal..." he hesitates.

Ray's pad interrupt their conversation, as he answers the call, he gives Dr. Sheehaus a hand gesture to pause the conversation. He walks away from the bar for a little privacy "Yes, yes, I'm on my way. Bye Nikki" Ray reply fast and end the call. A minor headache arise as he tries to focus his mind 'And Wang, why don't he call me? Best to go meet Nikki first, then I'll find him later' he concludes and walks back to the bar.

'Where is Dr. Sheehaus?' he thinks as he runs his hand through his hair, looking around... nowhere. 'Great, just great, he got missing too' Ray think and rush out of the Bar.

Out on the corridor Ray look indecisive to each side of the corridor then start to walk calmly to the Biosphere. As he enters the park a wonderful humid air freshen his skin, so differen from the rest of the Station. The smell of stodgy air mix with the green vegetation bring a vivid recall of the forest back home. He closes his eyes and takes a deep breath recalling sitting on the veranda at home. Then looking at all the differen plants and butterflies in different colors of yellow, white and blue. The sound of bumblebees summing around make him turn his head. In a small group of people Ray see a man turn fast as soon as he spot Ray. He wears a red neckerchief and now facing toward an information board as if he studies it.

Ray walk determent over to the man and stand just behind him "No Kidding! You know how to hide, don't you? Reading that board just make you invisible, why don't you fly round disguised like the bumblebees there. Now I got you, give me back my envelope"

The man turn his head and look very angry at Ray "I don't have any of your stuff, but I can tell you one thing. I'm gonna zip you up   scumbag, get   closer, and I'll slice you right away." The people next to the man look disgusted at him.

Ray step away and point at the information board "It is in French" he laughs, the man turnaround and look at the board...

Ray walk fast across the Canteen floor between the crowded tables. Caching for his breath from running "Sorry I'm late, Nikki" he begs.

"You surely start as a gentleman" Nikki sobs "I have been sitting here for some time, even from before I called you" she gives Ray a long sore look.

Ray sit half hidden behind the menu card "I was cutup with that business of Wang's... let's eat" he murmurs with an eager to change subject he looks up from the menu card "what have you been doing today?" he smiles awkwardly.

Nikki looks serious at him "I've spent the whole afternoon in the laboratory where I had the Garden Mum flower cleaned from the dirty soil and its roots sterilized. I planted it in our sterile grain substance and gave it some nutrient, now it is healthy!... And the soil, by the way, is disposed in the toxic dump container and will be sent toward the Sun for disintegration in do time." She points out.

Ray, lack words "Good", he returns to the menu card as he lean back in the chair, looking at it without reading much.

"You got plenty of time to make it right to me, as we have to spend the next eight or ten years together" Ray look perplexed at her, 'what is she talking about?' he thinks and move uncomfortable on the chair.

"Are you going to Earth?" Ray asks as he stares at her and drop the menu card on the table.

"*You don't know?*" Nikki stiffen,   they look each other in the eyes.

"*I don't know what? Please let me know*" Ray pull his chair closer to the table, his heart beat heavier in his chest.

"*Look at your Boarding pass*" Nikki command jabbing a finger, "checkout the return date" she insists.

Ray takes the pad out and find the Boarding pass, he turns on a satisfied grin "It is Open. I can return any date I like" he shows her his pad.

Nikki smiles back as one smile to someone who don't understand a thing "You are going on a long, long trip my friend" she nods affirmative.

"Well... *how come?*" he asks quietly and remember reading about the closure of the Hotel, and the reformation works and now. 'Why install these huge engines on a stationary space hotel?' Ray thinks looking down at the table.

Nikki sees that Ray are completely lost. She lean forward and take his hand "The last shuttle return to Earth tomorrow morning, and the last booking was this afternoon. I know, I work as an administration volunteer in the weekends. They asked for extra help a month ago to ease the burden before we go" she says with a half-shrug.

Ray look tense at Nikki "*Go? Go where? Where do we go, Nikki?*" he pulls his hands back and dry them in the napkin with a fluttering feeling getting to his stomach.

Nikki reaches out and take Rays hand, she holds it tight as she starts to explain in a calm tone. "A radio telescope on Earth picked up a faint signal from Jupiter, five years ago. A year later or so, they sent a probe from the moon's Centrifugal Launcher. When the probe arrived at Jupiter it confirmed the signal, and they say the probe have located the source of the signal. They have not told us much, and asked us not to talk about it to anyone from Earth.

But now, what differenc dos it makes? Besides, you are coming with us" she rejoices.

Ray tries to smile as he looks past Nikki "*We are going to Jupiter?... **To Jupiter?***" They start looking at the menu cards again. Ray gazes to the side looking at nothing, 'Who will pay my rent at home?' he wonders.

Nikki takes the order for Ray and herself "Two Seafood salads with Lime sprinkle water." They eat quietly the dim light in the Canteen make a good companion hiding the feelings.

Ray rub his hands to get some circulation back as he looks toward the exit "Right then, thank you for now... I think I'll go to my cabin and rest, a long trip you know..." he excuses.

They leave quietly and stay outside the Canteen door for a moment. Nikki rub Ray kindly on his back "I'm sorry, sure you will find your place here, see you tomorrow. Goodnight" she coos.

"Goodnight" Ray muse and leave. Nikki stands for a while looking at him walking down the corridor till he disappears among the people behind the ceiling.

Walking past the transporter, Ray decides to go visit Wang. The transporter sounds like an electric scooter as it gets in motion. After a short ride the doors open at Crew level 2 and Ray get out on the hectic corridor.

Besides from the light purplish wall color, first and second floor crew corridors look the same. Ray passes two doors and find cabin 2C46. The room-assistant respond to his call on the doorbell "Mr. Wang is not available right now, can I take a message?"

'Wang have told the assistant to be undisturbed, or he is out' Ray think and tell the assistant to tell Wang to call him as soon as he can.

Back in his cabin Ray lay down on the sofa, with a spinning head from this crazy day. He narrow his gaze at a cloudy distance 'Did Wang know about the voyage to Jupiter? Surly this whole mess is his fault' Ray hug a pillow then throw it into the armchair next to him, 'and without telling me anything... how could he do such a thing? What is so important about that signal from Jupiter? Who took the envelope with the testament, and why? Who is the man following them? And what did Dr. Sheehaus want to talk with Wang about? Why was Mr. Mark so upset? What should he do for 10 years in a tin-can floating in space and, and ?' he feels uncomfortable hot and look for the window...

Ray pull himself up from the sofa 'Maybe I didn't look properly?' he searches for the envelope in his luggage a second time, nothing. 'What can

I do?' he thinks, and make himself a cup of tea at the mini kitchen. Back in the armchair he thinks through the conversation with Wang at the Office. His thoughts start to mix with a dream about climbing a mountain on the moon, and he falls asleep in the chair.

Departure

The News host talk about the Voyage to Jupiter and all the preparations they do on Hotel Daedalus making it into an Interplanetary Spaceship. Ray stop and watch the screen, a closeup show the new engines made on Daedalus by the Oeuvre-section. He listens with great interest and have both screens turned on as he moves from room to room organizing his new home.

The reporter explains how a mix of countries, companies and tourists finance the voyage as a science trip. The Saymora Corporation who owns the Hotel has paid the largest part of the whole endeavor. Ray wonder how they can afford to pay for a trip like this.

All guests and personal have boarded. From now on, only supply ships can dock. The travel time is less than 3 years to Jupiter and 3 to 4 years back to Earth depending on the return date.

The Station have been refurnished with engines, and some scientific equipment coming from Earth. Lots of materials have been coming up from the Moon too, like fuel for the fusion reactor, aluminum and other metals for maintenance.

The speaker announce a big Departure Party at The Gala Salon to celebrate the moment of disconnecting the elevator-cables from the moon. Ray recall he was to meet with Nikki at the party later tonight. He feels sad and wonder how to pay for his stay on Daedalus... the room-assistant throttle down the sound on the screens and announce that Dr. Sheehaus are at the door, Ray asks on what occasion?

"Dr. Sheehaus with an urgent visit", the guest reply to the doorbell speaker.

'That silly man again' Ray think upset. He open the door in a haste and stand face to face with Dr. Sheehaus who is surprised to see Ray direct in the doorway. **"Why are you following me around?"** Ray booms into his face.

Dr. Sheehaus rub his quilt-coat insecurely "Please let me explain, it will only take a minute" he trembles.

"I do not have time for your gossip. Talk straight, what is it you want?" Ray buss vigorously and let Dr. Sheehaus enter.

"I was just looking for Mr Wang maybe he can help me find Miss Wieeloff, we have a business in common... look." Dr. Sheehaus hand Ray his pad with the photo of Veronica Wieeloff. Ray walks over to the sofa as he looks at the picture, discretely he sends a copy to his room-assistant as a doorbell message.

Dr. Sheehaus rub his hands "Beautiful girl, ain't she? And very clever too" he rush as he follows just behind Ray.

Ray gazes down at the floor "And what is that all about?" he questions and turns around, handing the pad back to Sheehaus.

Dr. Sheehaus try to find his words "You see, she is very important to me and some other people" he exclaims.

Ray freeze "What is so important about her?" he hesitates pointing his finger at Sheehaus's pad, he feels so puzzled by the whole matter.

Dr. Sheehaus look back at the exit "Tell Mr. Wang that I want to see her again" he sobs and walk toward the door.

"Again? Is she here on Hotel Daedalus?" Ray quake, as he spread his hands out in sheer disarray.

Dr. Sheehaus grind his teeth *"Your friend need to know he can end up dead if he doesn't stop playing around"* he hisses bitterly, **"This is last warning"** he yells and rush out the door.

Ray falls into the armchair and glance at the door 'What was that all about?' He asks the room-assistant for the last doorbell messages. The picture of the young beautiful woman appear on the wall-screen he copies the photo to his pad. Indeed, Veronica is an attractive woman wearing a classic knee short skirt, she has long brown hair, bronze colored skin and a dashing smile... his pad calls.

"*Yes, Wang.* Where are you?" Ray are happy to see Wang calling.

"I am in the Casino at the Saymora Hotel. Search for Henrik Hoffman on the Station News channel, will you? I have to go looking for the girl..." Wang disconnects the call.

Ray asks the room-assistant to search for Hoffman on the local channel. Not much come up, just an official statement that he had passed away, they said it was ruled as suicide by the autopsy. Further it said that Mr. Hoffman was in the Helium-3 business where the market had worked against his investments according to a friend of the Hoffman family, Thomas T. Brogan who sends his condolences.

Ray remembers the Crew Office had mentioned that Hoffman was still at Sickbay... a second thought awake him, he has to meet Nikki at the Departure Party in The Gala Salon within half an hour. He turns the wall-screen off and hurry dressing for the party.

On his way to the party he decides to take a swing past the Casino, just to see if Wang is around.

The Casino is celebrating too, Ray make his way toward the Chip Exchange. "*Hello Ray*" a balled man salute as he passes the Black Jack table "*Ray, there's a hand free*" the man cant and point at the empty chair next to him. "*Later Li*" Ray salute with a smile as he pass.

At the Chip Exchange the dressed up woman with a large blue hairspring recognize Ray at the spot. "Hello my dear, how handsome you are today, how much can I give you?" she cheers.

Ray give her a big smile and get straight to the point "I'm looking for a friend of mine, Mr. Wang. He normally plays the wheel and have a taste for older whiskey and younger women" he smirks.

The woman open her mouth in a makeup surprise "*Well Ray,* you just described 99% of our male guests. Let me give Lizzy a call she makes the books, you know..." she hesitates.

Ray sees the man with the red neckerchief at the entrance. The man spot Ray and starts to make his way through the crowd to get to him at the Exchange Boot.

The woman fix her gaze at Ray as she makes her call "Hi Lizzy, can you see if a Mr. Wang have made any payments in the Casino today?" She thew her gum ecstatically as she waits for an answer... "Yes I know they record all transactions... right... I see, Thank you anyway." She hangs up.

Just from her look Ray know that Wang haven't been here. She continues "We have no records of pleasure, no exchange, no drinks, no tips. I'm sorry Ray" she laments.

"Thank you, see you soon" Ray salute with a hand kiss and walk fast down the idle leading to the staff exit. He tries the door and find it open.

The man with the neckerchief follows fast behind into the staff quarters, it is dark inside. At the end of the corridor a faint light lit from the crack of a closed door. There is a loud sound of things falling when the man run into some buckets and stuff placed on the floor in his way. *"You little creep, I gonna get you. You are history"* the man blasts aggressively.

At the Departure Party in The Gala Salon, Nikki stand on the top stair in the entrance hallway, waiting for Ray. She is looking at the stage where a man elegantly dressed in gala talk about the big transformation Station Daedalus have overcome. From Mining enterprise to Luxury Hotel and now, its final transformation into an Interplanetary Spaceship. "Quite an endeavor" the man announce as Ray arrive and give Nikki a kiss on her neck.

Just enough tenderness to make Nikki forgive Ray for being late, again. *"You are late"* Nike gushes with a light blush from the kiss.

Ray check his shirt sleeves "Just had to attend that business of Wang's..." he smiles and feel Nikki's tenseness.

He takes her hand and step back studding her precious long gala dress she looks wonderful in black, and with a gesture he continues "Let's go to the party."

They go find the table that Nikki have reserved for them. Not the best spot to see the window view but a more discrete location. Besides everybody can see the same view on the big wall-screen.

As they salute with a drink the announcement come "We will detach from the Moon in a few seconds... we will begin to move out of our geostationary orbit, above the lunar port, and leave Lagrange point 2 in the earth-moon system." the man on the stage explain.

They look up at the wall-screen, one half of the image is seen from Daedalus and down toward the Moon. It is zoomed in on the Moon port where the elevator-cables are anchored. The other half of the screen show the view from a camera on the Moon with the cables going up and fainting away in the dark. Daedalus shines as the brightest star in the Milky Way.

The man at the Stage make a jump and with a loud voice announce *"We have detached!* We are now on our trajectory to Jupiter. *Full head!"* he cheers. People stand up and applaud thundering, every one is so excited and salute each other. The wall-screen change the bottom text from: Hotel Daedalus, to Interplanetary Explorer Daedalus 2104-06-29-09.25380 UMT SW-Live.

"It is just like New Year's Eve" Ray say and smile at Nikki who are very emotional too. She was born on Daedalus and had lived her whole life here... attached to the Moon, and now, they were letting go of the Moon and of Earth, a tear fall on her chin. She felt it like saying goodbye to her hometown, even though she felt safe and at home on Daedalus.

Ray hand her his handkerchief with a polite smile "What an adventure..." An loud high-pitched sound disrupts the celebration. Everybody looks at the window and the screen, some sit down.

"*Don't worry*" the man at the stage say and race his hand "it is the cables pulling in. They have told me that they sound in the beginning till they get into their track. You will hear this sound now and then the next couple of months as the cables retrieve." The *eerie* sound stop and everyone relaxes. On the wall-screen a ray of light shine through a crack between the platform and the Port on the Moon as they detach. The music starts, and a Lady enter the stage dressed in a long classic silver dress. She starts to sing a beautiful ballad as the light slightly dim.

"Can you feel anything?" Ray ask.
"No, we are accelerating on due course. We will never feel any movement" Nikki explain.

"*Aha*" Ray fell relived to know, as he continues "I just saw these huge engines when we arrived, they looked very potent..." he hesitates.

Nikki smiles at Ray "The new Engines are big because of the large surface the magnets need" she explains prudishly.

Ray know what Nikki talk about but can't quite follow her "But, ion-engines are two weak to push a large station, sorry *ship*, like this" he points out.

Nikki smiles comfortable at Ray as she continues "They are not the kind of ion-engines you think of. These engines generate by oscillation a large antiparallel electromagnetic field behind the ship in a dense diamagnetic-plasma that are constantly ejected from the engine at supersonic speed. They push against a wall of plasma, if you will. Or rather the moving magnetic field create eddy currents in the diamagnetic cloud that provide an opposing magnetic field as push back or counter thrust. The plasma behave just like a superconductor and are therefor very energy efficient. That's why they are so big" Nikki explain convincing.

Ray study Nikki's coaxing look for a while, "*Well*, you definitely got your science right. They use more or less the same technique to lift the cargo ships in the water, to reduce drag... you know..." he asserts and wondered where she had learned all that.

Nikki lean slightly over the table "They have explained a lot on the doc-channel for more than a year now. Besides we have been implementing so many new systems, you see?" she smiles, sip her fruit drink as she gazes at the singer on the stage.

A few couples debut the dance floor. Most people sit around their tables laughing and small talking. "What a wonderful party" Nikki gushes as she catches Ray's blue-eyes.

Ray notice how she glow, he gets up "Lets dance" he invites, she takes his hand with a gentle smile. They dance to a couple of oldies and get carried away. He catches the smile in her eyes and pull her closer to the breeze of a soft song drifting them over the dance floor.

The floor fills up to the catching music, they swing around not noting anything or anyone else around them. Ray hold Nikki tight and sense her heart beating 'She smells lovely...'

A couple dancing, bump into Ray from the back he almost falls over Nikki as it come as a complete surprise. The woman behind him fall and grab Ray in his arm he almost gets pulled down with her in the fall but manage to stay on foot. Ray bent down and give her a hand, helping her up, she falls back and can barely stand as her ankle twist.

"*O' I can't stand*, please help me over to the table, will you?" the young Lady ask. She holds on to Rays arm and limp beside him. Her dance partner leads the way back to their table.

Ray notices the sweet perfume, and her smooth skin as he helps her unto the chair.

"How kind of you. Please take a seat" she insists pointing at the empty chair next to her.

Ray looks toward the dance floor "Not at all, surely your ankle recover soon" he frets as he takes a polite look at the woman. "I need to get back to my table, thank you" he excuses.

The woman fix her sight on Ray "Thank you for saving me" she says warmhearted.

Ray feel a slight chill from her charming beauty as he falls into her brown eyes. He turnaround and walk straight back to their table.

Nikki gives Ray a happy smile as he returns to the table, her cheeks flush "You just left me alone on the dance floor" she sobs grumpy.

Ray look surprised at her "She needed help" Ray reply with a hand gesture in direction of the other table.

Nikki move restless on her seat "What a clumsy and selfish way to drag you off the dance floor." She insists with a slight angry gesture "*She did that on purpose*" she rants.

Ray lean back "Come on Nikki, why should she do anything like that?" he asks perplexed.

"*I just know she did*" Nikki say and look away "*... and you ogled at her*" she complains hurt.

As they sit looking at the dance floor, Ray wonder why that woman looked so familiar to him, did he know her from somewhere? He decides to go and take a second look at her.

"Let's have a second round, let me see if I can surprise you" Ray says with a smile as he gets up and walk toward the bar. On the way he takes a detour to get closer to the table where he left the Lady with the bruised ankle. No sight of her, now someone else occupies the table.

Ray comeback to Nikki empty-handed. He sits down without a word and look at the few people that remains on the dance floor. Most people stay at their tables talking and laughing.

Nikki looks thoughtful at Ray, she follows his sight to see if they know any of the couples dancing, but no.

A waiter ask permission and place two bowls of fruit and ice cream with a beautiful flower as decoration in each dessert. Sparklers light up the table in sparkly flashes.

Ray bright up in a big smile as he sees how happy the desert have made Nikki. She throws her arms in the air and smile at Ray *"Yes, I love ice cream"* she chants.

Time flies as they chat and laugh at each other, for a split second a small wobble move the liquid in Ray's glass. He looks up but no one seems to notice or care about it, and the party continue with small groups of people talking, laughing and dancing. ***"Did you see that?"*** he shouts.

Nikki lookup at the Wall-screen "See what?" she quizzes, the Moon have moved a bit further away, that's all.

Ray point at his glass of juice "The waves in the glass, the liquid wobbled, didn't you see it?" he insists.

Nikki shake her head slightly "No... maybe you kicked at the table leg?" she suggests and change subject.

Later an older man wearing the classic Daedalus Service Uniform come over to the table *"Hello Ray!* It is really you?" The man interrupts.

Ray lookup surprised to hear the familiar voice *"Bukari*, great to see you too" he bust out.

Bukari nod politely at Nikki and continue "Maintenance ask for you on an urgent matter" he pleads.

"Urgent? Yes of course" Ray responds to the man and stand-up easy. 'Something to do with Wang' he imagines, "Nikki, surely a short meeting, I'll call you" he asserts timid.

Nikki, left alone at the table in the Gala Salon, look down on the table with a heavy sight. To add to the ignoring situation a loud *"irrrrr"* sound make everybody look at the wall-screen. *"That's it"* she cries out and picks up her purse, kick the chair aside and walk straight to the exit.

Ray follows Bukari to the transporter, on there way out he sees a man observing them from the bar. Bukari is formal and dedicated "The Maintenance Department are at the other end, in the Oeuvre section" he explains as they enter the transporter.

Ray looks down at the floor "How can a girl get from earth to Daedalus without having a room reservation here? I say, it is impossible for her to get a flight ticket without having a room too, is it?" he asks Bukari directly, as the transporter move down to the service deck.

Bukari stand thoughtful for a moment "If she already has a cabin, it will do. Or if she has an invitation to stay at a cabin with someone else, it will do too. The Crew Office has to license the cabin for a guest, you know" he reassures. They continue though all the sections till the transporter get to the Oeuvre section where it moves up to first floor. It is a short ride, and the cabin door open to a narrow corridor next to the Maintenance Department. "Good luck" Bukari salute and leave Ray on his own.

The Maintenance Department looks more like a command bridge than a department office. Ray look surprised at the amount of control's and operators at work. A mid-age woman in uniform walk confidently up to Ray *"Hello Mr. Barton*, I can tell you we are very fortunate to have you aboard today" she greets as they shake hands, she has a decisive tone, and a firm hand. "Please come along, we are in the middle of a meeting making the first assessments" she insists.

Ray follow aside as he glances at some of the monitors they show data for trajectory navigation and engine control. "Assessment of what? If I may ask?" he hesitates as he looks at the woman, she wears an officers emblem and a name tag: Elisabeth Stand.

She stops and fix her sight at Ray "We have hit a Space Mine and are making assessment of the damage..." She exclaims and hold the door for Ray to enter the full packed conference room.

Elisabeth Stand take the word and introduce Ray to the assembly, in front of her is a table sign: Captain, she continues "This afternoon a Korean PL-5 class Space-mine impacted our ship, unfortunately it came in from the side those escaping our supercharged plasma shield. The PL-5's were all deactivated after the last great war and given the Sun as there final target. Where it comes from and how it got in our way we don't know. Somebody must have activated the Mine and given it our ship as a target. Hellman can you give us a damage report?"

Ray looks at Hellman's table sign: Maintenance Director. The tall man stand-up from his seat "The Mine exploded when it was next to our communication module-2 attached on the Shield. The laser communicator on the module have a malfunction and can't send or receive data. We send a crawler-drone out to look at it, and it is a mess, take a look at this:" The wall-screen show a short video-recording from the outer shield, he continues "as you can see the newly installed parabolic antenna got damaged too. Some silica tiles on the outer shield have cracks, and it worries me the most. We have three communication modules and can do without one. But the parabola was a part of the new gear installed for this mission, and we don't have a replacement yet. As I said, the cracks in the radiation shield is our main concern. We need to know if some tiles loosened and if it is possible to repair the damage ourselves. Or we have to return and get replacement tiles from the Moon? If a section of tiles loosens and drift off, a part of our habitat have no protection against cosmic radiation. Or unexpected events like solar flares and micro impacts" he explains and take his seat.

Elisabeth looks worried "*Thank you, Hellman.*" She continues after looking staunch at each person at the table "Returning to the Moon is complicated. We cannot just stop the ship and return because the loose elevator-cables need constant acceleration to keep them straight. If we suddenly stop the cables will hit us from behind. Besides, we have no engines at the front and need to turn the ship for the rear engines to reduce speed..." she hesitates.

Elisabeth looks down at the man sitting to her left with the sign: Navigation. "Sabine what are our options?"

The man sit thoughtful for a moment gazing at the wall in front of him then he turns his head and look directly at Elisabeth. "It leaves us with two options: We repair the shield and continue as planned. Or, let me explain, our 3 years journey to Jupiter use a Sinusoidal trajectory with gravity assist from Mars to give us a kick in the right direction. About midway to Mars the elevator platform is completely retrieved. We can then turn the ship and reduce speed enough for us to get into orbit of Mars, within 6 months from now. We will have to stay in Mars orbit for 7 months till the next favorable Mars-Earth trajectory, and we return to the Moon for repairs. Our next window for a new journey to Jupiter is when Earth and Mars align with Jupiter within 4 years from now. We will miss the next alignment do to travel and repair time." He looks around the table to see if everyone follows his explanation.

Elisabeth has not raised her eyes from Sabine "What a bad option, any other options?" she objects.

Sabine stretch "*No. That's it, Mam*" he answers positively.

Elisabeth shake her head "*Well Hellman that leave it all to you.* What does it take to repair the tiles on the shield? And in time" she insists and lean a bit over the table to emphasize the importance of the question.

Hellman stands-up again "First we will need to get someone out there and see if any of the tiles got loose or fractions of them got loose. And we need to figure out how to repair the one damaged. That is why I asked for Ray Barton to join our meeting" he makes a gesture at Ray.

Ray stiffens at the sudden attention, he holds his breath as all in the room look at him as if he knew all the answers to the problem.

Hellman continues "Ray, we know you did the Spacewalk curse three years ago, here on Daedalus. We have a team in our maintenance department with spacewalk skills they just lack the knowledge to do structural assessment..." he hesitates.

Hellman and the rest of the room stare at Ray.

Ray smooth his cloths as he feels his heart beat harder.

"**Ray!**" Elisabeth calls out loud.

'They want me to go out there' Ray think as he looks around at the assembly "Yes, and no. I haven't been outside since then..."

Hellman interrupts "We will send an experienced technician with you, he will pick you up at your cabin at 4 o'clock, thank you, Ray" he insists outright.

Elisabeth looks satisfied at Hellman then toughen-up "You need to com-plete the repair before the elevator platform recover" she demands and gaze around the table "So... we don't know if we stay or pass Mars. But, our scientific craft to Ceres will dispatch as scheduled." She hesitates and look down at her notes. "We will have the next meeting tomorrow as soon as Ray has a conclusion from his space-walk" she concludes and smiles at Ray.

Hellman is the first to leave the office and Ray follow swift behind.

"*Hi Nikki*, I just left the meeting" Ray nod toward Elisabeth as he walks for the door while talking on his pad "did you see the final celebration show?" he queries fervently.

Ray have reached the transporter when Nikki finally reply "I feel sleepy, please call back tomorrow. Good night Ray" and she hangs up.

Ray enter his cabin, still wondering if he said anything wrong to Nikki.

Next day, Hellman observes the wall-screen in the Maintenance Department, three astronauts hold on to a crawler-drone as it move on the shadow side of Daedalus's radiation shield.

Ray hold his breath for a moment "*Look at that!*" he shouts and gaze captivated at the astonishing view of the Moon, and Earth flowing in front of them. They seem the same size as if double planets. Looking into the vast space he feels as in a hyper-reality with vivid stars sparkling all around him.

The drone get to a brute stop at the communication module-2, and Ray continues to move forward, drifting ahead of the drone. He has forgotten to hook on the safety line and looks desperate at the female astronaut next to him. Anxiously he stretches his arm toward her as he drifts into space. She latches out after his hand in a reflex, her grip slips, and she leaps after his safety line and get a firm hold on it. They keep the eye contact as the line stretch and Ray bunch back-wards and get pulled back in. "*Thank you, Sara*" Ray gasp relieved and grab onto the handle on the shield and hook his safety line on.

The bruised impact area seems intact at first sight, beside from the antenna. Ray feels tense as he moves around the shield, examining the large tiles one by one. All his problems in the past days are wiped off his mind.

He pulls a color marker from his bag and mark the tiles that needs scanning, counting them 'eleven'. "Hellman, we are ready to do the x-ray can you confirm that the crawler have the film in place on the inner side of the shield?" he asks over the voice-comm and searches for Sara as he waits for Hellman's confirmation.

"Sara, hand me the x-ray scanner and activate the positioning emitter" Ray implore.

"The x-ray films are in place" Hellman confirms.

Ray begins the dragging work of scanning the eleven silicon-tiles. The task gets significant only to itself.

After a 4 hour space-walk Ray sit in the infirmary with his sleeve rolled up. Dr. O'Barley enter the consultant room *"Well, hello Ray, how are we today?"* he salutes with a genus smile opening his arms slightly in a welcome gesture.

Ray look surprised seeing the Doctor, in a short pause he studies the half balled man wearing a white kilt. The old fashion glasses with a small squared frame make him smile back *"Hello Doc, I heard you retired?"*

Dr. O'Barley look serous at Ray "I got three kits at university down home, Ray. You never retire with school kits" he giggles as they shake hands. He conti n u es "Have you ever seen a retired Doctor with three school kids?
" he chants with a large grin.

Ray laugh "I am sure I heard you retired."

"I heard you left for good and returned to Earth" the doctor respond as he inserts the needle in Ray's arm, slowly filling the vial. "Do you have the dosimeter with you?" he insists unstrapping the rubber band.

Ray reach into his pocket and hand the radiation meter to Dr. O'Barley. Through the half open door to the consultant room Ray see the man following him passing on the corridor 'What is that creep sneaking around here for?' he fumes as the Doc move in front of him getting his attention.

"You know the blood test and dosimeter measure the radiation damage to the chromosomes in your blood cells, right?" Dr. O'Barley explains with a laugh.

"*It is suicide*" Ray respond seriously.

"You have to die anyway" Dr. O'Barley respond timid, while sealing the bag with the blood test and dosimeter.

Ray jumps down from the stretcher "*Not me* Henrik Hoffman, about two weeks ago, was it suicide?" he asks directly.

Dr. O'Barley look surprised at Ray "What a coincidence that you ask about Hoffman" he replies closing the door to the corridor. As Dr. O'Barley close the door, Ray gets a second glimpse of the man peeking at them through the door crack 'The creep following around' Ray figures to himself.

Dr. O'Barley tilt his head pensive "A man from Earth in a old-fashioned coat asked me the same question yesterday?" he marvels.

Dr. O'Barley look straight at Ray "*Are you on a license?*" he pleads.

Ray shake his head "*No, I am not.*"

Dr. O'Barley still looking straight at Ray to see if he got any mendacious reaction. As Poker player he recognizes a 'hammer bluff' gone wrong "You are sure you are not on a license from a government, like the other earthling?" Dr. O'Barley ask again firmly.

Ray got a blank look on his face as he tries to figure-out what Doc refer to "*No, I assure you I work on my own*" he insists.

Dr. O'Barley type into his medical pad with a satisfied look. He lay the pad on the examination-bed next to Ray. "I have to attend a matter, will be back in a second." He walks to the door "A favor to you dad" he says with a nod toward the pad on the bed and leave Ray alone in the consultant room.

Ray stretch his arm and grab the pad, it has the autopsy file for Henrik Hoffman on the screen. He reads all the pages and lay the pad back onto the examination-bed. 'What a strange conclusion, *suicide?* How can they get that result? The man was stabbed 6 times and then strangulated with his own belt or visa-versa'. Dr. O'Barley interrupt his thinking with his rash entrance, leaving the door wide open.

"So fascinating diagnostic made by our security department. We are done with you for now Ray" Dr. O'Barley say laughing.

"Thank you Doc" Ray salute and leave the sickbay. He walks back to his cabin thoughtful… 'who killed Henrik Hoffman, someone with a motive…

someone onboard Daedalus, of course'.

Finishing the report of the shield damage, Ray lean back relaxed in the chair 'accomplished' he drowses.

Falling in Love

Later in the afternoon in the Maintenance Department, Ray arrives at the meeting just in time to take his seat before they begin. They have placed a sign at his seat: Ray Barton, Maintenance. He looks around the table, all assembled as before, plus to his surprise a familiar face: Kei Enatsu Director of Hotel Daedalus.

Elisabeth Stand take the first word "Good to see everyone timely. We will get right to the point, Hellman what do we know so far?" she gazes anticipating at Hellman.

Hellman takes his time to examine the paper in front of him. "We have sent a crawler-drone to look at the inside of the Radiation Shield, the polyethylene sheet need repairs. Mr. Barton have a copy of the video-recording and have the inside damage included in his report" He looks at Ray "Barton please continue."

Ray wipe of a little cold sweat and suppress the pulse beating "Thank you, Mr. Hellman. As you know I went on a space-walk on the outside of the Radiation Shield together with two service-men. You will get our report in your pad's after the meeting with all the latest data included" he feels parched and take a sip of water.

He taps on his pad and read for a few seconds. The wall-screen light up and show a still from the report. He continues "The Mine exploded when it hit the shield at communication module-2 and made irreparable damage to the two antennas on the module..." he hesitates.

Mr. Enatsu interrupt as he gets up and leave, pointing at his pad. Ray continue "The tiles have repelled most of the blast, the good news is that none of the tiles got loose from their place. As you probably know the tiles are made of twelve centimeters or half foot thick compressed silicon powder and only 5 have cracks that need repair. From the radiography pictures Hellman and I assess that we can repair them by laser welding. We can replace the polyethylene plastic sheets from the inside using the drones. The welded tiles will still block 99 percent of the radiation. Hellman has estimated it will take 10 days to repair each tile. That give us plenty of time as we have 3 months till the cables redraw completely" Ray conclude.

After the meeting Elisabeth Stand ask Ray to stay, she pulls him aside and offers him a job in the Maintenance Department starting next Monday.

Ray feel happy as he walks down the corridor calling first Wang, then Nikki, none of them answer, he leaves them a message. He takes the transporter to the Botanic Club, it's packed and everyone stands silent as they move smoothly with a few bumps when they change direction. 'How strange, Wang just get missing? While looking for a girl? Or staying with the girl and not at his cabin? It doesn't make sense. And Nikki didn't answer the call?' He looks at the floor of the transporter as if the answers had fallen out of his pocket.

Entering the biosphere bring a smile on his face. He stops a moment to breath the fresh air while contemplating the dense vegetation mostly of different fruit trees and bushes 'Life giving' he marbles.

Inside the half empty Club the bartender salute Ray with a nod. "Have you seen my friend?" Ray ask.

"The gray haired man? No, but a young woman asked for you just a while ago. She sits just over there" the bartender say with a hand gesture at the corner table.

Ray takes the glass the bartender have poured for him "put on my tap" he mumbles and walk over to the table. He recognizes the woman from the Departure Party, she's the same lady from the photo Dr. Sheehaus had showed him.

"How are your ankle recovering?" Ray asks as he stands next to Veronica, "Veronica Wieeloff, am I right?" Ray continue politely.

She nods her head as she looks up at Ray "Do you always sneak up from behind?" Veronica asks with a bright smile.

Ray sits down on the chair next to her as he looks fascinated at the beautiful woman. Veronica is dressed in a gleaming yellow blouse, and wear a long elegant dark-blue slice skirt. "I got a claim by you on the Apartment of Henrik Hoffman here on Daedalus. I did not expect to see you up here" Ray reply, he notices her smooth leg passing her skirt and look courtly away toward the bar.

Veronica turn Ray's head gently with her hand and look him into his eyes "I am here to write the story about our endeavor to Jupiter. It is for the Thai News" she ventures.

Ray look away "I see..." he hesitates and moves slightly on his seat.
She continues "I already feel comfortable with you. You are a friend of Mr. Wang?" she asks as she moves her hand down to Rays neck.

Ray feels his hair rise "What have Mr. Wang told you about me?" Ray asks, his chins and ears get warm as he studies her natural beauty and removes Veronica's hand from his neck. He senses a need to defend himself and move his chair opposite to her.

Veronica notice how Ray get more defensive, and knows she has to let him catch the game. "He came up with you to Daedalus, please tell Mr. Wang to stop looking for me. It means so much to me getting close to my uncle, I loved him so much! When can I see the Apartment?" a teardrop run from her eye she moves slightly forward as she wipes the tears gently of with a finger.

Ray smile sad as he tries to connect the loose ends "What about an astrologist Dr. Marc Sheehaus? He is looking for you too!"

Veronica look offended at him and press her hand at her breastbone "Marc Sheehaus, he is a mad scientist a drunk and hateful man worse than Kei Enatsu. No, no, no one is worse than Kei Enatsu it is impossible to be evil as Kei Enatsu" she replies with a slow shaking of her head.

Ray vaguely rub his chin "I think Mr. Wang is looking for you because of the claim on the Apartment. Um... But, how do you know Kei Enatsu? And how do you know me?" Ray asks uncertain, still trying to connect the loose ends, he feels distracted by a growing desire to hold her, to comfort her.

Veronica can see her emotional approach is bearing its fruits and go on "Here on Daedalus everyone talks kind about you. You are known to be just and helpful. I asked for you because I need help. I am so tired, can I get some sleep at your cabin? Just a few hours then I will go and find a place to stay, Sheehaus kicked me out, he drinks too much!" She let another teardrop fall. Ray hand her his handkerchief, their hands touch accidentally as she reaches for the handkerchief sending a tingling jolt up his arm.

She continues as she reaches out for his hand "If you help me, I would..." she smiles playful.

Ray clear his throat *"Um... You would do what?"* he quakes while leaning a bit backward.

Veronica smile innocent "Be ever grateful to you" she replies tightening her grip at his hand.

Ray look serious at her "Only if you tell me all about Henrik Hoffman", he empty his glass and stand-up.

Veronica lookup at Ray her eyes capture his, and he gets lost for a moment, like falling into a deep lake. As he helps pull her chair away she let her body fall gently against his, her smell capitulate him, and a warmness flood his chest, she turns and whispers into his ear "do anything..."

Ray fight the desire flushing through his veins. He put his hand gently around her wrist as he guides her outside the club.

They walk back to Ray's cabin without a word. As soon as they enter the cabin they fall into each others arms kissing passionately.

In the morning the Pad sounds, Ray rub his eyes and takes the call still half sleeping *"Um... yes"* he mutter groggily.

"Hello Ray can I come over?" Nikki asks with her soft voice.

Ray sits up in his bed as he looks at the beautiful curves of Veronica still sleeping next to him *"Uh... what? Nikki?,* how are you...? I am busy today, have to attend Mr. Wang's business, you know..." he rambles uneasily and slips out of the bed.

Veronica open one eye as she observes Ray walk naked into the living room. Her mind-assistant record everything she hears, and she asks it with a thought to playback what she missed while sleeping.

"I see" Nikki reply disappointed.

Ray sits down in the armchair as he continues "When I get a window I'll call you back. Take care" he hangs up and flex his arm '*Blast it!*' he agonizes.

Veronica enters the living room wearing only one of Ray's shirts. She wrap her arms around Ray's neck and give him a long passionate kiss "*I am starving* " she says with a smile and turnaround.

Ray takes a deep breath, he stares at Veronica's lingering walk to the kitchen bar. She makes tea and pull everything out of the refrigerator.

As they have their breakfast Ray wonder if he will get the envelope with the claim on the apartment in time for his meeting with Kei Enatsu.

Veronica bounce Ray on his leg "What are you thinking about?" she frets uncannily.

Ray search her for a clue "What do you know about Henrik Hoffman?" he asks puzzled.

Veronica reach uneven for her cup "*Nothing,* he is my uncle I never know him so well. He was a loving man I recall" she gives Ray her Innocent look and grab his hand, "when will I get the apartment? You know I need a place to stay!" She asks desperately.

Ray fight a desire to kiss her and stand up "*I have a issue to attend*" he says firmly as he turns and walk toward the door.

"*Please let me stay!*" she begs him.

Ray takes a firm look at her "*Alright,* keep the room-assistant turned off till I come back and don't call anyone" he says as he leaves the cabin.

Ray walks down the corridor toward Nikki's cabin as he calls her "*Hi Nikki,* I am at your cabin" he cheers and ring her doorbell.

After a pause "*How is the exotic girl?* It is a small town you know!" She nags upset.

Ray look at the cabin door then studies his shoes 'How to explain about Veronica?' he wonders while waiting for Nikki to open the door.

The door open and Nikki stand in the middle of the small entrance with a firm look waiting for an answer. Ray moves side wards past her into the cabin. He turns around with his arms crossed "Just business I have to do for Wang. She is the reason we came up here" he looks as honest as possible at Nikki.

Nikki flash red in her face "*Yes!* That is why you take her with you home late at night, how can you think I will jump on that story, Ray?" she blazes.

"Just business, Nikki" Ray walk over to the table studding the flowerpot while talking, "You know Ben from security? I need you to call him and ask if he can find the envelope I lost. Crew Office have it on their missing items file. You know, they monitor all calls from newcomers. I need the envelope as soon as possible. Today I will have to do without and improvise at my meeting with Kei Enatsu" he explains.

Nikki look tired at Ray "OK, I will call Ben, just need to name the envelope nothing else? How about the explosion and the space-walk are you going to tell me anything about that?" she objects.

"*Yes*, Ben will know what the envelope is all about" Ray affirms as he head for the door.

"Fine... that's great" Nikki lament as she sits down in her armchair "what about that chocolate-bar in your cabin?" she looks straight at Ray.

"She stays till I get the business done. It's only for a few days" Ray reply with a hand gesture as the door close between them.

The overcrowded transporter have a damp smell, the trip to the hotel section seems to take longer than normal. Ray wish he could walk, but they closed all ring-sections after the mine blast. Finally, getting out onto the wide corridor give the impression of quiet and breathing space. He walks leisurely enjoying the spacey sphere curving upward till the floor fade away behind the ceiling.

An impressive black dice-shaped office complex dominate the corridor, over the entrance doors large gold letters says: Saymora Corporation.

A bright young man approach him in the hall and ask "I see you come without appointment, can I help you in any way? *Mr. Barton.*"

Ray are not surprised that they scan him "I need to meet Mr. Kei Enatsu" he replies and take a seat in an armchair.

Ray studies the hall where he sits, all walls are made of black crystal, you can look through some of them, to the outside or into a conference room.

Suddenly a wall opens, and it turns out to be a sliding door. A squared man wearing security uniform walk over to Ray "Follow me Mr. Barton." They walk up a wide stair and at the end of the corridor enters an office with a discrete tag on the wall: Director.

A short man stand up behind his work desk as he salutes "*Mr. Barton*, I am honored to have a visit from our new *hero.*" With a gesture he invites Ray to sit down in front of his desk.

Ray takes a seat "I didn't get the chance to salute you at the meeting, you left suddenly" he half smile.

Mr. Enatsu observe Ray "...Yes I have many responsibilities, please get right to the point of coming here" he replies flat.

Ray stretch over in his chair as he holds back a cough, and continues "I want to ask if a friend of mine have visited you, Mr. Wang?"

"*Mr. Wang... ?*" Mr. Enatsu quaver thoughtful as he looks into the distance.

Ray feel Mr. Enatsu is playing him "I heard the two of you are interested in the same girl, *Veronica Wieeloff*" he observes Mr. Enatsu's face, the man is obviously surprised as he suppresses his anger.

At the door, the strong build security man stare at Ray like a predator. He moves in the chair to loosen the tenseness, and looks around at the paintings decorating the office. "A Piet Mondrian, *but a copy*" Ray shakes his head toward a painting of a tree.

The security man tight his hands and move a step forward, but Mr. Enatsu stop him with a hand gesture.

Mr. Enatsu can't hide his anger anymore "Your friend Mr. Wang has paid me a visit. He is still my guest as we have to consider his business offer" he cautions densely.

Ray maintain firm eye contact as he observes how Mr. Enatsu is losing his self-control "What kind of business offer?" he smirks aridly.

Mr. Enatsu look into his desk drawer as he continues "You mentioned a woman called, Veronica?" he asks as he pulls Ray's envelope onto the table and continue "an very expensive apartment for such a young *Lady*" Mr. Enatsu lean back in his chair with a satisfied face as he glances at the envelope "Do you have her birth certificate?" he asks triumphantly.

Ray stiffen, he stares incredulous at the envelope on Mr. Enatsu's desk. 'I forgot to ask Veronica for her birth certificate' he recalls and put on a confident smile. "*Yes of course I do*" he insists in a blond lie as he lean forward and reach out for his envelope. "I will be glad to show it to you next time we meet. If you don't mind I'll like to have this one back." Ray try to slide the envelope over to his side.

Mr. Enatsu grab the envelope and pull it away from the table with a knowing grin "*No, no*, Mr. Barton, not so hasty... you know we need to chat with the young Lady first. This case is *much* bigger than, *You*" he laughs loudly and pull in a deep breath as he observes Ray potently.

"*Well, I will be back soon...*" Ray insists as he stands-up and walk toward the door. Mr. Enatsu nod to the security man, the man move forward and give Ray two heavy blows in the stomach, he bends over and fall to the floor.

Mr. Enatsu get up from his chair and walk over to Ray laying down on the floor in pain.

"Eventually you don't understand *how important* it is that I talk to this... *Lady*. So please don't be silly. Just tell me where to find her!" he demands.

Ray struggles to get up "*I don't know where she is*" he gasps half breathed.

Mr. Enatsu look angry at Ray as the security man hold his arm "I will let you go, but first time you see her you call me... *Understood!* or I will dump you into space!"

The guard through Ray out of the office, he falls hard onto the corridor floor with a pained torso he pulls himself up and walks half bend down the stairs. The young man in the front hall pretend not to take notice of Ray.

Back at his cabin Ray find Veronica sleeping in an armchair. He goes around the chair studying her perfect figure with a strong sense of affection toward her. When he gets to the back of the chair he shakes her shoulder gently "Hi sleepy" she raises her head tired, "are you alright?" Ray ask kindly.

She nods her head and rub her eyes sleepy. "Do you *always* sneak up from behind, *Ray?*" she turns her head and look at him with a genuine smile.

"Not in general" Ray reply embarrassed and smile back.

Veronica sits up in the chair "While waiting for you here I feel *so safe*, very protected. Knowing it is your place" she says looking Ray direct into his eyes.

"*Safe from what?*" Ray ask tensely.

She makes a jump and sit on her knees in the chair "You and Wang visited

Mr. Enatsu at his office. That don't go unobserved... I am not missing. I'm here with you Ray" she says with her head inclined playful. Veronica stands up and walk toward Ray "please help me to get my uncle's apartment" she pleads.

Ray hold her head with both hands and give her a passionate kiss on the mouth, then hold her tight at a distance "Tell me more about Henrik Hoffman. He did not commit suicide, did he?"

Veronica pulls back from Ray and shake her head as she step back a couple of steps "*I cannot say!*" she walks further away pressing her hands together.

"**Why not?**" Ray asks loud.

"He was there when they killed him, he told me" Veronica reply nervous.

"Who is *he?*" Ray ask, "Dr. Sheehaus" she replies.

"And who are *they?*" Ray ask again.

"Mr. Enatsu and his men" she says relieved getting it out.

"Oh, Mr. Enatsu" Ray say with a thoughtful voice looking down at the floor "what was Sheehaus doing there, do you know?"

"Something to do with his astronomical observations, a signal of some kind, I don't know" she replies with an honest look.

"What a tail..." Ray say looking doubtfully at her.

"*It is true Ray!*" Veronica say and run across the room and through her arms around him "*it all true, terrible true*" she kisses him over and over.

Ray gets absorbed by her affection, feeling her body touching him.

Veronica receives a mind call, she gets distanced and say abruptly "*I need to go to the restroom*" as she pulls away from Ray and leave.

Ray stands a bit perplexed as he rubs his eyebrow.

In the restroom Veronica connects the call "You got the code, right?" a man ask.

She looks at her image in the bathroom mirror as they speak 'Yes, I got it a safe place!' She thinks.

The man clear his throat and continue "And where may that be?"

Veronica look herself in the eyes 'In my mind-memory.'

After a sipping sound he continues "Bring it to me, I need it for my client. We have to continue to the next stage, *and you need to get your business with*

Ray done" the man command and hangup.

She feels as if she has lost something, sadden by the fact Ray is just the means to the goal. She knows she has falling in love with him and decide to enjoy the moment.

She returns to the living room and throw her arm around Ray's neck "*I need you so much*" she says and kiss him passionately. "*Will you let me stay a little longer?*" she asks as she embraces him with all her charm.

Her smell and the feeling of her body seduces him completely. He let go to the passionate kissing.

Next morning the room-assistant sounds and announce it is time to get up as he has an appointment at the Maintenance Department. 'Oh yes' Ray remember they gave him a job 'it is the end of my freedom' he thinks and look at Veronica sleeping at his side. He gives her a kiss on her back and get out of bed. She keeps her eyes closed without moving and let him leave the cabin silently.

At the Maintenance Department Ray sit down at his desk, he can see Hoffman from where he sits and salute him with a hand g esture. He got a welcome message on his pad explaining all benefits as an employee, with free Canteen food, healthcare, and a crew cabin.

A new message pup-up on his pad: >Welcome to Saymora Corporation, we are happy to have you as a part of our team! Kei Enatsu, Director of Hotel Daedalus.< Ray gets a slight pain in his stomach and delete the message with a feeling of disgust, 'who is in charge on Daedalus? Captain Stand or Director Enatsu?' He decides to ask Nikki at lunch, if she shows up...

"*Ray! Sorry to interrupt you*" Hellman stand next to his table. Ray smiles and salute with a nod, Hellman continues "let me brief you on the repair progress. Today they pull power cables on the outside for the laser welding equipment. Direct from the power breaks on the radiation shield to the communication module-2, we install it as a permanent upgrade, you know..." Hellman look intense at Ray to see if he follows his explanation.

"Yes, yes, I know" Ray reply with a distant look. He recalls dad telling about when they moved the Nuclear fusion reactors from the Moon to the center of the Oeuvre section. They were installed at zero gravity, just behind the elevator. Dad used to say "When two comes together excess mass is converted to energy" and he laughed...

Hellman shift his balance a few times, then in a louder voice "**Right then**..." he now got all of Rays attentions, "why don't you go to the Port and see how they progress with the cabling."

At lunch Ray enter the packed Crew-Canteen he spot Nikki at the salad bar and walk straight up to her "*Hi Nikki*, you look cracking in that uniform!"

"*Oh, hello Ray...*" Nikki salute halfhearted and continue "I called Ben as you asked for, he said he would let you know if he finds anything."

"Well, that's good" Ray reply as if it didn't matter anymore.

They join table and Ray ask eagerly who are in charge on Daedalus the Captain or the Director.

Nikki looks a bit surprised by the question, but she just gets on explaining "Mr. Enatsu was President Director General of Daedalus till recently. They send Elisabeth Stand up here when the modification work began, she managed all the works changing the Space station into a Spaceship."

Ray lean forward "So Mr. Enatsu is number one on Daedalus, right?" Nikki smiles at Ray and continue "After the renovation she got promoted to Captian in charge of the entire ship. And Mr. Enatsu reduced his power to Director of the Hotel in the new section. But he still has a lot of influence as many stays loyal to him."

"*Wow*" Ray gasp 'he lost his power and turned into a bitter and angry man.'

Nikki takes a sip of her drink as she wonders why Ray got so amazed. She continues fascinated by Rays reaction "Captain Stand changed our organization a lot with new departments and old ones lost influence. Security was a powerful department before, now they mostly work at the hotel, and the Navigation department is brand new. A lot of new changes to the Energy department..." she is interrupted by Ray's pad calling.

Ray look unevenly at his pad, and gets up from his chair

"*Oh, excuse me Nikki, its work.*" He walks out on the corridor in a rush and connect with an elevated heartbeat "*Hi Darling.*"

"*Hi Ray*, I miss you so much! Please bring me some food, will you, its completely empty here. You told me not to order anything..." Veronica begs with her sweet voice.

Ray get back to Nikki and begin to eat his meal in a hurry and with his mouth full say "*Wang's business... you know...*"

Nikki looks at how he stuff himself "*Yeah*, chocolate bar for dessert, I guess!"

Ray finish his dish in a rush and get up still chewing his food waving at Nikki, as he leaves she just shakes her head at him.

He hurries to the transporter. At the Botanic Club, Ray walk directly over to the bartender who as soon as he sees Ray burst out "*I haven't seen the gray haired man, Ray!*"

Ray stand still and think for a moment. With a deep breath he rubs his hands down his jacket "I need a meal, as take away, do you still take hard coins?"

The bartender look searching at Ray "Sure Ray, you know metal money are illegal but for old times sake, what do you want to eat, Ray."

After a long wait he finally gets the food-bag "*I will pay next time*" Ray say as he rush for the exit.

Back at the cabin, Veronica wait in the entrance she throws herself into his arms as soon as the door open. "Yes, yes, please let me in" the warmth grow from her affection, he wrap her tight and kiss her gentle.

Ray pickup a small envelope from the work desk "*What is this?*" he asks.
Veronica grab the food bag "*Wow, deep-fried prawn's with chips*, where did you get them from?" She jumps into an armchair and eat directly from the bag.

Ray opens the envelope and pull out Veronica's birth certificate, he gazes at the wall "Thank you... I need to get back at work" he says and rush for the door. Veronica tries to say something, but with her mouth full Ray have left before she manages to speak.

He returns late to his desk at Maintenance, Hellman look speculative at him without saying anything. Ray just dig into some reading till the work-day ends.

After work Ray needs to get away 'Where do you go?' He thinks, and decide to visit the Star Lounge. He orders a Green Tea and find a table in the back, looking out at the waste empty space carry a feeling of unity with something bigger. Gradually more and more stars get visible as his eyes adjust to the darkness, even the low voices from the neighbor tables sound clearer. 'There's the Bull' he thinks as he recognizes the star Tauri in the horns of the constellation. The smell of bakery brings his thoughts back home. He used to get out on the porch at night, the night chill sharpened the senses as he watched the stars... at home with mom.

He hears a familiar sound and look toward the entrance. In a silhouette he sees the outline of a man with a neckerchief. The man stand still moving his head from side to side as if he tries to see into the dark Lounge, then the man leave.

Ray get upset 'Him again? Who does he work for?' A cold shiver run down his back.   'and Veronica, what am I going to tell her about the apartment? About them looking for her?'   he thinks and look deep into the dark space for an answer. 'I can tell her they revise her inheritance claim... till I get the papers back from Mr. Enatsu...'

Food Shortage

Ray oversees the welding work from his desk. They expect to finish the last tile of the shield within a week, after that he have to scan the welded tiles again.

After work, Ray decides to go find Nikki at the lab. An extra food bag for Veronica would come handy. As he walks through the air-locks to the Biological-section someone calls his name. He looks around, nobody there.

"*Ray, I am in here!*" the voice shouts. The sound come from a ventilation grill in the wall, he gets close and look through the mesh. His mouth fall open when he recognizes the face inside the small duct "*Wang! What are you doing in there?*" he yells surprised.

Wang rub his eyes "*Take the grill of, Ray!*", Ray turn two handles and pull the grill off, he gives Wang a hand helping him out of the duct.

They sit on the floor in the corridor looking at each other. "*Oh Wang!* What happened, *two months?*" Ray shake his head.

Wang rub his hands nervously "The deal went a little sourer, and they locked me up in a small washroom for I don't know how long. Then one day I hear a boy laughing and sees him inside the ventilation duct. I manage to get into the duct and crawled till I got stuck here" Wang replies. He gets pale and point at the air-lock slowly opening "*let's get out of here!*" Wang gets up in a hurry.

They run down the corridor to the biosphere. At the entrance Mr. Mark stand with a broad smile holding an electric-rod in his hand. From behind comes Ben waving his rod extravagantly from side to side. "*Alright*, you two seams to make a lot of trouble in the hotel-section. *Come with us*" Mr. Mark says and swing his rod in direction of the next air-lock.

He stops Wang, pointing the rod at his chest *"So, you are the famous Mr. Wang, yeah!"* Wang nod confirming to Mr. Mark who looks firmly at Wang *"You and me are going to have a little talk, you know!"*

At the Saymora office Ben push Ray and Wang down the stairs and into a small staff office. The door lock with a swift click, Ray searches the room to see if they can escape in any way, non.

He points his finger at Wang with anger *"Do you know what happened since we arrived, Wang? Your nerves fall apart, your loose control... and the only mistake I made is feeling sorry for you!"* Ray rolls up his sleeves, ready for a fight.

The piddling make Wang explode *"No need to feel sorry for me! Better feel sorry for yourself!"* Wang shout furiously.

"What are you working at Wang, a little blackmailing?" Ray yell back.

"If it wasn't for you, I had terminated the business by now" Wang shout, shaking his head as he looks the other way.

Ben come back and pull Ray with him across a small hall to another filthy office. He pushes Ray down to sit on a chair in the middle of the room. Ray looks back at the half open door, he can see Ben standing outside in the hall. The office is scarcely furnished just a work desk, and a couple of chairs, the walls have marks and bruises from furniture and alike.

After a long wait Mr. Mark and Ben enters, Ben stays behind Ray with a hand on his shoulder. Mr. Mark take a stand in front of Ray leaning against the desk with his hands tucked in his armpits and thumbs pointing up.

He stares intensely at Ray for a long time, as if he tries to pull the memory out of Rays head *"Where is the girl, Ray?"*

"What girl?" Ray reply swiftly.

Mr. Mark lean forward looking down at Ray "How fast you forget about Veronica Wieeloff! We need to talk to her, remember?" Mark grab Ray in the shirt *"Wang says you are his middleman. You are his shop boy, right?"*

Ray jumps up on his feet pushing Mark away *"No I am not!"* Ray yells at Mark in anger. Mark slap Ray in the face with a flat hand.

His chin burn in pain Ray move his fist swiftly back aiming at the face of Mr. Mark. Ben reacts fast and grab Rays arm and pull him back onto the chair.

Mark look satisfied *"Careful Ray!"* he continues with a cocky smile "we are losing our patient with you... *shop boy.* How smart of you getting that job with Captain Stand! Hiding behind her skirt aren't you?"

Ray got pain in his jawbones from the high tension, he tries to get up, but Ben pull him back down on the chair.

Mark burst into an extravagant laughter "We will get back to you... it will be last time, if you don't cooperate!"

He whispers something to Ben, then leave the room.

"Follow me Ray" Ben say in a flat voice. He guides Ray down the hall to an emergency exit door, and pulls the handle bar. With a light push he let Ray out to the narrow corridor on the service-deck.

The humidity from leaking pipes make Ray cross his arms and try not to breath '*Disgusting!* It smells like the pub backstreet at college' he recalls and look up at the low ceiling to find relieve.

"And Wang?" Ray ask.

"We let him go" Ben reply short.

Ray nod confirming, he fixes his eyes at Ben's "Ben, can you get me the envelope back?" Ray asks with a hand gesture.

Ben looks surprised, he says something unheard as thunder sounds from a cargo-transporter passing by in the tunnel next to them.

"*Kei Enatsu have it*" Ray say loud. With the light still flickering, Ben nods and lock the door with a brute sound.

Ray thinks about calling someone for help as he walks past various sections trying all the doors up to the next level. Non opens. 'It will be hard to explain how I ended up down here' he mulls. You need service access to open any door down here even the transporter are locked. A slow smile brightens his face seeing the sign over the door, >Emergency EXIT<. He closes his eyes pulling the door handle softly down... the door opens. '*Finely!*' He rejoices. Taking two steps at a time, he hurries up the staircase.

The doorbell recognizes Ray and after a short wait, the door opens.

"Hi Ray" Nikki salutes from the bathroom "the food-bag is in the fridge. Something happened today..."

"Like what?" Ray replies, he opens the fridge and look for the bag "what food have you today?"

Nikki enters the living room bare-footed wearing a large white towel wrapped around her body, and a yellow towel on her head as a turban drying her hair.

"*Wow Nikki*, you look amazing!" Ray say spontaneously.

Nikki blush embarrassed "Behave yourself, *Ray!*" As she walks past Ray her face turn into a grimace "*ugh...* you smell awful, how can you visit me like that?"

She hurries back to the bedroom and continue "Our alga culture are dying in one of the process tanks, and we don't know why!"

Ray look disappointed into the bag "only Meat limbs and no potato chips or bread?"

Nikki lose her patience "*You are not listening, Ray!*" in a sharp voice she continues from the bedroom "We had to reduce the vegetable production, there are no production leftover to bring with me home!"

Ray rub his chin for a moment 'I'll have to buy extra food', as he stands thinking Nikki enters the living room, now dressed in an all-in-one body dress.

She continues "*Now you understand*, you will have to buy the vegetables for Veronica. I cannot bring any till we recover to normal production."

Nikki looks disgusted at Ray "*uff what a smell*, get out of here" she pushes Ray out on the corridor.

Back at the cabin, Ray walk direct to the bedroom and change clothes.

In the living room Veronica sits in the armchair watching a movie "Hi Ray..." she sounds bored by the movie, "any news regarding my apartment?"

"No, I have asked for it again today..." Ray reply knowing she doesn't take a no for an answer, he closes the door and go wash.

Veronica look sad down on the empty sofa-table "*How* long do we have to wait, Ray? *Two* more months? *Or...*" she is interrupted by her mind-assistant announcing an incoming call "Yes" she thinks excited.

"Did you do it?" The man ask with a dense voice.

"Yes, but I don't know if it works. Too dark in there and not enough for all the tanks" she thinks as she lean over to see if the bathroom door is locked.

"It will work alright. Get your business with Ray done, *Now!*" he says upset.

"You know I need my payment, first thing first" Veronica thinks with a rush down her spine.

"They fixed the shield because you didn't do your part. *Just skin the cat and bring me that code!*" The man rage and disconnects.

Veronica look distant and cold when Ray come back and sits next to her. 'I need to get those papers back' he thinks. "There are only Meat limbs today" He hands her the food-bag, and continue "they have a problem of some sort with the food production tanks. I'll buy you some vegetables tomorrow" he kisses her on the chin.

She lean over to his side and give him a hug "Thanks Ray, *I'm so glad you care for me!*"

Next day in the office Hellman come over to Ray's table "We got a meeting, *right now*, something urgent have come up" he waves for Ray to follow him.

In the conference room, Nikki sits next to Elisabeth reading her pad, Ray salutes her waving his hand discretely, no sight of Mr. Enatsu... he lean back relaxed and look at Nikki 'why is she here?'

Elisabeth Stand explains in a few words the situation with the contaminated food tanks and introduce Nikki Navarro from the Biological Department.

Nikki looks confident at Ray and then glance over the assembly "Thank you, Captain Stand. Our molecular agriculture started to die in one of the process tanks two days ago. Yesterday the die-off had spread further, and today we have three alga culture tanks, and a meat culture tank dying."

She displays an info-graph of the spectrogram analysis on the wall-screen. Looking up she continue "We cannot say what course the dying of the cell cultures. Most likely an illness of some kind affecting the one-cell cultures, because we haven't found any toxic or chemicals in the bio-reactors. However, we know the illness have spread through the life-support system as the bacterial breakdown of waist have started to show reduced activity."

Elisabeth nods at Nikki then look unfocused over the table a couple of seconds "Mrs. Navarro, we need to know how this illness effect our food security. Not to forget our life-support system of fresh air and water. Please *spell out* our situation!" she says heavyhearted.

Nikki gets distant as she glances at her pad, fingering at one botton. Ray is worried she have lost it.

Finally she looks up and continues "We live in a closed-loop life-support system. All degradable waste are recycled into the food process including our air. It is a sustainable synthesis where one organism's waste is food for the other. If one part in the chain break the system stop working.

In short, to save the system we have isolated each cell culture to avoid further contamination. We have however to ration the food by half, till we recover production capacity... *if* we can maintain a healthy cell culture to recover from... Air and water *may be* regenerated in the biosphere, we work on it right now." Nikki looks at Elisabeth with a long firm look.

Elisabeth stay silent for a moment "This voyage is dreadful spell bound" she says aloud to herself. And continue with a deep breath "*Right everyone,* I'll release the frozen food from our emergency stock. It will give us a couple of weeks extra, after that we will have to reduce the rations further. From today, we will reduce the portions and maximum two meals per day, that's one meal every five hours. Only heavy workers gain an extra meal."

She looks a Nikki "You have two weeks to get food production back to normal." She looks around at all on the table "Or we will have to return to the Moon for food and bio-culture replacements."

The meeting drags on with talks about how to regulate if they fail to resume food production, and how to extend the food for the long return voyage to Earth.

They agree to reduce food to one meal a day within a week.

Late in the afternoon on there way home Nikki and Ray share transporter. Ray catch Nikki's eyes "How well you handled the meeting. Let's have a nightcap in the Canteen?" He keeps the eye contact.

Nikki smiles at Ray "*Another day, Ray.* I need to get some sleep, tomorrow is busy" she looks exhausted as she exits the transporter. Ray know she has a lot of responsibility finding whatever destroyed the food.

Back at the cabin, Ray enters and find Veronica standing in the living room waiting for him *"Hi Ray!"* She throws her arms around his neck, *"I got something for you!"*

A pleasant shiver run through Ray's body, he hug her tight.

Ray spot the envelope on the work desk *"How did it get here?"* he asks surprised.

Veronica pull back from him "Ben gave it to me..." she says innocent. Ray look baffled at her as he places the food-bag on the sofa table. He takes the envelope and pull the papers out, his eyes widen as he looks them through 'all the papers for the claim?'

He turns toward Veronica *"Ben was here?"* he shakes his head unsettlingly.

"I asked Ben to give us the papers back, and he was so helpful..." She explains and sit down in the armchair.

Ray still can't figure-out how she knew Ben *"Oh, you went to meet him?"*

Veronica looks into the food-bag with a disappointed face *"Well,* we meet in the casino first, and then he brought me the envelope, *you know..."*

"I know what?" Ray say upset, he feels betrayed behind his back.

Veronica's cheeks flush as she gives him her innocent look *"You know,* now you can present my case at the Crew Office, *isn't it true Ray!"*

Ray enters the bedroom without responding. Changing clothes he thinks about Veronica and Ben 'How can she know where and when to find Ben? How come, Ben just give the envelope to the girl they were looking for? She got the envelope in just one day, I tried in two months!' He sits in the bed with a heavy sight looking unfocused at the wall-screen, brokenhearted he falls a sleep.

Later Veronica slid into bed and hold on to Ray. She whispers into his ear "Thank you for helping me Ray, I will make it up to you, tonight" and she starts to kiss him gently.

At the office Hellman come over to Ray's desk "They have completed the welding of all five tile's. It's your turn tomorrow."

"Sounds great, I'll go to the docking and prepare the space-walk" Ray respond and leave the office right away. He takes the transporter direct to the Crew Office, the office clerk register Veronica's inheritance claim in a

moment.

"We got all the data here, just needed the birth certificate" the clerk explain. 'All this trouble for so little, Wang could have done it himself!' Ray thinks with a knot in his stomach.

The clerk send Ray a written justification for the claim to his pad "Your client will hear from us within a weeks time."

The pad sounds as he gets to the center of the Oeuvre-section "*Did they accept my inheritance claim?*" Veronica asks in a rush.

Ray sense her eager "Yes I think so, they will call you within a week or two."

"*I have to go, Ray!*" She says and hangup.

Ray look at the pad as he tightens the zipper on his jacket 'She sounded happy, now with the claim filed why hang up on me?' he fumes.

The empty Stall next to the air-lock echos from Rays steps as he jump-walk in the low gravity, he looks for a door... nothing. The bright ceiling light make the walls look frosty, he rubs his hands by reflex. Then stands still for a moment listening, he hears nothing but his own breath. Now a distant sound of a metal door guide the way to a side corridor.

At the equipment locker he finds Sara and her colleague on the bench preparing there space-suits. They just salutes and continue concentrated with there work. Ray senses a distant attitude and start to prepare his space-suit too. He studies Sara from the bench next to hers 'She looks much like Veronica, same height and hair color, more or less, but more muscular build. She's a pretty woman'. He thinks, the sound of footsteps catch his attention.

Hellman drops by "Hello everyone" he salutes with a smile. 'He seems happier than normal' Ray think.

Hellman continues "We got an extra job for tomorrow." He looks directly at Sara "Our department have fabricated a new parabolic antenna, it is crucial for our mission at Jupiter. You will install it at the same time Ray does the roentgen scan." He looks at the three "also you will get an extra food ration on hard work permission, you can pick it up in the Canteen" he cheers.

Finally, Ray get back and place the food-bag on the kitchen table "*I'm home!*" No answer and no sight of Veronica in the living room, he looks in the bedroom, and the bathroom 'She's not here? How strange, leaving without telling me anything?' His head gets heavy and sits down.

Ray calls her again, the pad gives him a *You have been disconnected*, message at every call he makes to her. 'She will come back soon' Ray thinks and turn on the wall-screen.

The sound of noisy music on the screen pull Ray out of his sleep. The clock say 5 past 1,

"I better get to bed" Ray say aloud to himself and walk to the bathroom 'Where did she go? Without food or a place to stay?'

The space-walk starts early in the morning, they are out on the shield holding on to the crawler-drone as it moves to the communication module-2. Ray looks for Earth as they move, but without luck it's overshadowed by the bright Sunlight. When the crawler stops Sara grab Ray's arm, he turns and show her his hook attached to the safety line. They keep the eye contact for a moment then their bright smiles turn into a heartfelt laughter.

"What are you laughing at?" Hellman asks over the voice-comm.

"*Nothing*, just recalling a happy moment. Is the film in place on the inner side?" Ray ask.

Hellman confirms and Ray begin scanning of the tiles. Sara and her colleague move the new antenna to the installation sight.

Sara watch how Ray work concentrated as he follows the scanner move progressively along every tile. She observes till he finishes, and calls him over the voice-comm "*Ray*, we need your help with the antenna..."

Hellman interrupts "You have to hurry the cosmic radiation have spiked, wrap it up and come back inside."

Ray scans the last tile and hurry packing his equipment on the crawler, then he moves over to Sara.

She points at the mounting bolts "You have to fasten them when we get the antenna into position."

Ray try to fasten one of the bolts, but he moves like a spin top, and the bolt stay.

Sara laugh at him "You need to hold on with the other hand, *ha, ha*."

"*Yeah, yeah, I know*" Ray say embarrassed. Cold sweat on his fore head form a drop that flow in front of his sight 'ignore it' he thinks and give it another try.

"*You have to get back in, NOW!*" Hellman sounds anxious.

Ray ignore him and concentrates on fasten the bolts. They hurry onto the crawler.

Back inside the Docking-port, Sara come over and give Ray a handshake "*Thank you, Ray, for helping me out!*", she turns and get back organizing her gear.

In the sickbay, Ray sits on the stretcher pulling his sleeve up as he waits for Dr. O'Barley. He looks fixed at the open door 'lets see if that creep come snooping around again'.

A nurse enter "*Hello*" she salutes a little nervous.

"Hello" Ray replies with a tentative smile, remembering her 'The foreman's daughter'.

She pauses in the doorway "Do you remember me, *Cathie?*" and takes a quick look over her shoulder.

"New Year's Eve 2100" Ray reply weighting her with a look. 'Still nice'.

She walks straight over and straps the rubber band around Ray's arm "*Right, I'm married, now*" She says and tug the needle into his vein.

"***Av...***" – ***Bang*** "I'm happy for you" Ray erupt as his leg pull back and hit the metal structure of the bench with a bang.

Cathie lean closer to Ray as she takes the blood test "So how come you are back up here?" she asks while looking at the sample glass.

Ray bit his lip gently and wonder if she can help him find Veronica "We work on a case for Veronica Wieeloff, do you know her?"

She lean away a bit "Who are *WE*, Ray?" She narrow her eyes as she looks him into his face "it wouldn't be Kai Enatsu, now would it?"

Ray shake his head, 'how could she think I'm part of anything with that man!' "*Now excuse me*, I have nothing to do with Mr. Enatsu, *Nothing!*" he rants aloud.

Cathie lean in on Ray and continue in a calm voice "She came to sickbay last evening with her clothes torn apart. In a kind of shock, full of fear. She would only tell me she had escaped Mr. Enatsu and that his men was after her."

She pulls the needle gently out, and place a bandage on Ray's arm.

He breathes out with a smile, relieved by her gentle hand "Do you know where she is now?" he asks as he hands her the dosimeter.

Cathie drop her shoulders and answer with a sad voice "A man tricked the night-watch into letting her leave with him."

Ray stand-up with a thoughtful mind "Thank you" he salutes her with a kiss on the cheek.

Out on the corridor, a man with a neckerchief just take the corner in front of him. *"Was it him again?"* he asks himself aloud and feel his own heartbeat pulsating in the breast.

Ray slender down to the biosphere, thinking with a distant gaze 'So Veronica had left on her own reason, and with whom?'

He sits down on a bench next to a dark green Orange tree, full of large oranges. The smell of leafs, and the damp cool air feels so refreshing 'For bitten fruit' he thinks reading the sign: Enterprise Property.

A bumblebee buzz by and the sight of a butterfly in the Orange tree lightens his heart 'I wonder who's soul you are?' He thinks while observing the butterfly moving up and down on its way into the next tree.

"How are you, Ray?" Nikki embrace him from behind hugging her cheek to his.

Ray smiles with a sense of relief *"Oh, hi Nikki."*

"I got a food-bag for you at home" she says as she sits down next to him on the bench.

Ray looks down on the floor *"Right."* 'What a mess' he thinks, and continue "I'm glad to see you here... are you... off?" he stutters with a lack of air.

Nikki look examining at Ray *"Are you alright?"*

Ray straightens up on the bench as he takes a deep breath "Yes, sure I'm fine." He looks at her "How are the food situation? Have you found out anything?"

Nikki still looks examining at Ray, and move a bit closer *"No,* we don't know how the illness came into the cell cultures. But we know it course a mutation of cells that kills them. So we are growing new cultures in a separate system."

Ray's tension fade, he places his hand on top of hers in a short gesture *"That is great,* so the problem is solved!"

Nikki points at all the surrounding plants "Not yet, the illness have spread to our Eco-system. We need a new cell culture, resistant to this disease before food production can get back to normal. Or we have to turn back to Earth" she smiles sad "once loose, the genie can't be put back into the bottle, you know!"

He looks up at a big orange fruit hanging next to them, and points at it.

Nikki knows what he is suggesting before he names it *"No Ray!* In just a few days and we have eaten all vegetation in the biosphere. Besides, it's not a balanced food."

Ray remembers the farms back home "We can grow a garden!" he suggests with a bright smile.

Nikki shake her head as she laughs at him "No, no, we are way too many people here for that. You know first man was a hunter-, gather- culture, and needed a lot of land and sea to live from. Then came agriculture, and we required less land. Next came aqua-culture to feed a hungry world, and now we use bio-culture to produce all the proteins we need. Our biosphere is a botanic ecosystem for organic recycling on Daedalus, not for the food."

Ray lay his arm around her shoulder and pull her in for a gentle hug "You are so smart Nikki!" They sit a long time on the bench watching the plants and bees. He remembers the times they spend together when he stayed with dad. She always asked him about Earth, how it was to walk in the wood? Or if he ever had seen a fish while swimming? Or hold a bird in his hand? He smiles and begin to laugh.

Nikki pull back as she keeps looking at Ray

"What are you laughing at?"

She stands up "I have to go back to work. You can pick up the bag in an hour, right?"

Ray rub his ear as he looks away "Well you know... Its better if... I frankly don't need it now."

Nikki smile playful at Ray as she places a hand at her hip *"Oh,* so you are out of company now, *well that explains it!"* She turns around and walk away without looking back.

"*Nikki!*" Ray calls without response, she has left down the track. A cold feeling gives him a slight shutter 'What a day. How can I explain her all this...'

The days are dull with desk work on halftime. He just go to and from work and see no one between work hours, even the food portions have gotten smaller with no snacks or fruits.

There's no sight of Veronica or Wang and no one answer his calls. Nikki is busy working and keep telling him to call back later.

Ray sits at his desk as so many other nights assembling a hover drone as a favor to Hellman. From time to time he asks the room-assistant if there are any new messages, knowing it would let him know at once if any message came in. 'I better take a walk before I die from boredom.' He gets his jacket and leave.

A tall strong bold man enter the transporter together with Ray 'Someone new around here' he thinks as they start moving. "Are you Ray Barton?" the man ask as he looks down at Ray.

"*Yes*, do I know you?" Ray asks.

"***Transporter to Sickbay urgent!***" The man command loud. They stop and start to move in the opposite direction.

Ray gasps by surprise "*What, are you ill?*" he looks up at the man who stand with his arms crossed looking down at Ray.

The transporter opens the door, and the tall man grab Ray and pull him out on the corridor where Mr. Mark wait "Hello Barton. How convenient, we meet again!"

Finding the Illness

The empty corridor outside Sickbay gives Ray a claustrophobic feeling, it seems so narrow. Mr. Mark and Ben stand in front of him and the tall man behind him still with a grip in his jacket. Ray's heart beat faster as he tries to find a way out, he turns around and slam his fist into the man's belly. The pain in his hand is as if he hit a piece of wood. The man stands unhurt with a grim smile on his face. The blow come swiftly and thrown Ray down to the floor in front of Mr. Mark.

"I knew you would come back to me" Mark says with a satisfied smile on his face. The stomach pain makes Ray dizzy, he licks his lip, it tastes of blood. Mark lean forward and look down at Ray "where were you at 1:97 this morning?" he asks in a dry voice.

Ray struggles to get back up on his feet "At home in my bed sleeping, where else should I be?" he looks mistrusting over his shoulder at the tall man who haven't moved since he got out of the transporter.

Mr. Mark continues harshly "*At the place where it happened*, that's where!"

Ray shake his head "I don't know what you talk about?", 'What was this all about? Wang again?' he thinks with a sensation that something is very wrong.

Mark look at Ben "You got it confirmed he was home all night, right?"

Ben check his pad "Yes the data from the room-assistant confirm it. He asked for new messages 6 times! Once at 1:89 this morning..."

Mark scratches the back of his head, then look at Ben "What the heck... Take him down and show him. We are done with him, *for now.*"

"Ray, let's go" Ben says with a hand gesture to enter the sickbay. Down at the morgue Ben salute Doctor O'Barley "We are here to see Veronica Wieeloff."

Dr. O'Barley look serious and sad at the same time "I am so sorry, she left an hour ago."

Ben's eyes pup out as he gets pale "*She left?*"

"Oh yes. She was ejected overboard on a dump-pot, into space... toward the Sun. You know, the usual ceremony and all that."

Ben's face get from pale to red in an instant as he looks puzzled at the Doctor "*But, we are here to identify her!* You cannot eject anybody without identification!"

Ray start to get the picture, Veronica had died, somehow? He cross his arms over his breast as he looks around at the sterile clinic. The cold white light reflect in the walls and annoy the sight not to mention the clinical smell of formaldehyde, giving him fatigue.

Dr. O'Barley look at Ben with a vague smile of disapproval as he continues "*But we did!* Mr. Mark gave us a sample of blood for DNA test. The rest of her was collected in bags and stored in the Pot till we got the test results confirmed from Earth. *The diseased was Miss Veronica Wieeloff!*"

"How did she die?" Ray ask quietly.

Ben looks down at the floor and then up at Ray "She died precisely at 1:97 this morning at the biological-section down on the service-deck. A service-worker heard a scream at the same time, and the cargo-transporter registered the impact at 1:9703"

Ray lean back a bit "How many screams did he hear?"

Ben looks surprised at Ray "The service-man? Just one."

Ray takes a deep breath and look at Dr. O'Barley "Did Mr. Mark give you a tissue sample? or a blood sample?"

O'Barley look at Ray's blood stained lip, then at the torn jacket "Well you see Ray, she was pushed into the transport-tube just in front of the cargo-transporter and ripped into bits and pieces. They had to sterilize the whole tube section to avoid a bacterial contamination. Mr. Mark scraped a sample off the tube wall before they started cleaning-up the place."

Ray keep looking seriously at O'Barley "And?"

O'Barley close his eyes for a moment "The sample was mostly blood, some hair, dust and paint. The blood had started to coagulate as one would expect."

Outside the morgue Ray confront Ben "How did Veronica get the envelope?" he jeers.

Ben grab Ray's arm with a foul smile "She was very persuasive." He laughs and pulls out his pad "I need your opinion on one thing more." Ben show Ray a news article.

>*Strange signal coming from the edge of our solar system*< Ray read on, >*An astronomer in Chile have detected a radio signal from deep space. They are working on decoding the message that kept repeating itself for a whole week.*<

"When and where was it published?" Ray ask, handing the pad back to Ben.

"Back in 99 in a scientific magazine" he replies as he put the pad back into his pocket and continues "later it was said to be gossip or an example of bad science and everybody forgot about it."

Ray look heavy at Ben "*Right*, and what did the message from space say?"

Ben smile "That's what we thought you would tell us!"

Ray shake his head "*Me? How should I know?* It's time for me to go."

As he walks out of sickbay Ben shouts from behind "**We need the codes, Ray!**"

Ray walks by the Canteen, but it's closed 'Of course it's late, and Nikki?' He calls her "Hi Nikki how are you doing?"

"I'm working late" she replies tired.

Ray stop walking "Well, you can come over and have a cup of tea with me, if you like?" he asks in a low voice.

After a short pause Nikki reply "*Yes that sound great*, just need to mop up first."

"*Great! See you then*" Ray says excited with a joyful laugh. They hang up and Ray haste to get home 'I need to shower, fast!' he thinks.

Down the crew-corridor he runs into Dr. Sheehaus. "*Mr. Barton you look terrible!*" Dr. Sheehaus say as he looks at Ray's blood stained face and jacket.

Ray run his hand through the hair closing his eyes 'That man is so ignoring, I have to calm down.' He looks straight at him and yell "**Beat it Sheehaus! I'm in a hurry.**" Ray keep walking down the corridor.

Dr. Sheehaus follow behind "I heard you and Mr. Wang got interrogated by Security, right? Did he tell them anything about Veronica?"

Ray throw his hands up in front of him "What did Wang tell about Veronica?" he shakes his head in disbelieve "*Better*, what would you tell them about Veronica?"

Dr. Sheehaus look disappointed at Ray "Mr. Barton, you know very well what I mean. If I don't find her I may not be around for long…" he replies submissive.

Ray lose his temper '*That imbecile, how can he be such a fool all the time?*' he grab Dr. Sheehaus and pull him close to his face and yell "***I'm getting tired of your silly games. I'll beat some answers out of you, do you understand?***" Ray shakes him and continues "you was the one inviting Veronica up on the station to stay in your cabin, wasn't it? But why? For the code? Now she is dead, go ask yourself" he flash.

Dr. Sheehaus wrestle himself lose from Ray and run down the corridor. Ray thinks for a moment about running after him, but Nikki will come over soon, he needs to wash up. He let Sheehaus getaway and rush home.

He enters the cabin and notice a cracking sound as he works through the entrance '*Strange.*' He looks down and see some sugar grains on the floor '*Odd, I didn't have tea this afternoon?*' He hurries and brush it up and tell the room-assistance to let Nikki in, if she arrives while he showers.

After the shower still no sign of Nikki, he makes tea, and pull himself a cup while waiting for her to arrive or call…

The room-assistance opens the door as soon as it recognizes Nikki "**Hi Ray**" she shouts happy.

Nikki freezes with her mouth and eyes wide open, seeing Rays blueish head lay on the sofa-table with his body bend over from the armchair.

She runs in and drag him to the floor by pushing her feet toward the chair. He has no pulse or aspiration "He has suffocated" she says aloud to herself. She starts breathing air into him and then begin pumping his heart counting and then breathing air into him again.

Nikki continues giving him life support. At the same time she force herself to sleep and enter a dream-state where she step out of the physical body. She sees herself there on her knees giving life support to Ray.

Out of her body she turns around looking "**Ray?**" she calls out, "**where are you?**" no sight of him.

She closes her eyes and command herself to go to him. At opening her eyes she stands next to him in a beautiful grass field.

The grass waves to and forth from a light breeze as an ocean on a calm day, a water stream run at one side next to them glittering in the bright light.

She takes a deep breath of the fresh air and smell the wonderful sense of wildflowers. It is so peaceful, the sky over the field radiate a warm light full of love and knowledge.

Ray talks to a man and haven't seen Nikki at his side.

"You are born with the skills to solve your problems in life" the man exclaim reassured, "just let go of your ego!"

Ray shake his head affirming "Yes Dad, it just seems so pointless at times…" he replies troubled and looks down.

"Son *look at me!* There are purpose to your life", his father look at him firmly "you have things to do. You have to create your possibilities and care for others and yourself. **Go back!**"

"Hi Ray, *please follow me*" Nikki smile at his father acknowledging.

"Hey Nikki, how great to see you, let's go and explorer the hills over there… come on!" Ray rejoice.

"*No! Ray come here, follow me*", Nikki command, and take a firm hold on Rays arm "close your eyes Ray and think of going back to your Cabin."

Nikki close her eyes and command herself and Ray to go to his cabin. When they open their eyes they stand in the cabin and see themselves there on the floor with Nikki still doing life support on Ray. He watches himself there on the floor and wonder how that happened.

"*Go back into your body, **NOW!**" Nikki command Ray, without hesitation he lay down and just fuse into himself.

Nikki does the same and awake from the dream-trance still pumping Rays heart. She blows fresh air into his lungs and feel with her fingers that he got his pulse back. She sits back and at the same time Ray takes a deep breath as he opens his eyes gasping for more air.

Nikki give him a big hug and just hold him tight "Thank you, Ray! *Thank you!*" she says as she hug him tight.

Ray tries to get up, but fall back "What was that Nikki? You just pulled me back from the dead, how did you do that?" he asks dumbfound.

She looks him in his eyes "You need oxygen to get your strength back. Take a deep breath and then exhale slowly till all the air are breathed out, continue like that, till I tell you to stop!"

Ray sits on the floor leaning against the armchair, breathing as Nikki told him 'That was the oddest I ever experienced, how on earth did she do that?' he thinks and begin to get better. He forces himself up into the armchair.

Nikki put his tea cup into a plastic bag "Did you have anything else than tea? And I told you to keep exhaling slowly letting *all* the used air out, *right!*"

Ray straightens up "No, just sweet tea as usual" the breathing technique gets ignoring. He feel uncomfortable and try to find a better position in the chair without luck.

"Aha, sugar" Nikki says and go to the kitchen, she finds the sugar and salt, and all foods, and drinks and place them in the plastic bag. "I will have it all analyzed tomorrow." She makes sure again that she got all food related stuff from the kitchen "You can breathe normal now. How do you feel?"

"A bit sore, after a tough day!" he replies with a grimace and move to a more comfortable posture as he wonders 'How did all this happen? I couldn't breathe, and then I don't remember... till I drifted outside the walls...'

Nikki notice how Ray tosses around in the chair "Whatever made you sick we will find out. From now on you only eat and drink in the Canteen, *understood?*"

Ray nod complying as he admires her for all she has done "*I am not going to sickbay!*" he says loud and firmly.

Nikki looks straight at Ray "And who said anything about going to sickbay?" She gazes straight at him for a while "but... you should go, you know!" She says jerky and walk toward the door with the plastic bags "I will call you from time to time, it's late I have to get some sleep."

Ray smile and rise the hand as a goodbye, but the pain make it half done, and the arm fall back down "*Av!*"

Nikki gets worried for a moment *"You are as stubborn as you are troublesome!"* She says shaking her head as she exits the door.

Ray pickup the pad calling "Yes Nikki, for the third time I'm fine! I'll go to bed now", he feels grateful for the call, and has to pull the words out *"Thank you for… for looking after me!"*

"You should! Or you would be in sickbay by now" Nikki reply in a content tone.

Ray catch her good mood, 'She must have good news', "What make you so happy suddenly?"

She laughs a bit "You getting ill gave me a great idea!" she says playful.

Ray clear his throat "Well, that sounds sarcastic. *I died!*"

"Don't get melodramatic you just said you was fine, did you not? I will tell you at lunch, *see you tomorrow, then?*" She salutes fast.

Ray look at the wall without knowing what to say *"Um… Yes! Good night."*

Next morning Ray walk relaxed to the office, he gets the good news from his night-shift colleague "Good night Ray! By the way, the elevator cables have pulled in, let's see if we stay or get back home" he salutes with a genuine laugh. Ray salute back with a gesture. 'Yeah, if we get into Mars orbit and return to Earth it's because we are starving, and if not, I stay for the journey to Jupiter…'

Hellman comes over to Ray's desk, he lean over close to Ray and in a low voice says "The Captain want you in her office at 3:75, on a confidential matter."

Ray sit back in his chair and look Hellman in the eyes 'The Captain's office?' He thinks, before he gets to ask, Hellman have turned with a half-shrug and walk back to his table.

Ray looks at Hellman from a distance wondering what its about, but the man talk with someone on his pad and don't show any sign of worry or joy. 'I just have to go to the meeting clueless…'

The secretary show Ray into Elisabeth's office. A small room with Elisabeth seated behind her desk and two chairs in front, behind her a wall-to-wall closet. Next to the table a large wall-screen, it's turned off. The only notable decoration is the classic table-lamp with a green glass chapeau.

Elisabeth salute Ray with a handshake over the empty table and show his chair with a gesture. She smiles and start to small talk "So Ray, you fit in well onboard?"

Ray get uncomfortable with the uncertainty of the matter and change position on his chair "Yes... Yes, thank you I'm fine."

She continues, still looking straight at Ray "This morning we fully retrieved the elevator cables."

"Yes I was told" Ray replies wondering where she is going with the conversation.

She continues "It was relieving. Now we got free maneuverability, much needed as..."

The secretary interrupt with a knock on the door as she walks in and present "Nikki Navarro."

Nikki salute politely as she takes her seat. Ray nod partial to her and move his hands into his lap 'What do Nikki has to do in this meeting? Something to do with Veronica's death? Or...'

His thoughts are interrupted by Elisabeth "Thank you for calling me Nikki, please tell me all you have found out so far."

Nikki lay her note-pad on the table, and turn it on. Elisabeth smiles tentative as she places her hand upon the pad "Sorry Nikki just give me a summary of your work."

Nikki turns the pad off and lean back relaxed "Well, yesterday I found Ray dead on the floor in his cabin. Immediately I did life-support on him, he shortly after gained consciousness. It appeared to me, he had been poisoned as his head was blue when I found him. So, I collected all food related items from his cabin and run some tests on them this morning."

Elisabeth looks at her then at Ray "Ray why didn't you go to sickbay yesterday?"

Ray point his finger at Nikki "She made me breath oxygen, and I got better quick!"

Elisabeth widen her eyes "Ohoo..."

Nikki comes Ray to the rescue "It is a breathing technique, he was in good shape when I left."

Elisabeth nod and make a hand gesture for Nikki to continue.

"The result of the tests show a drug mixed into the sugar bowl. The drug gave him a epileptic disorder that resulted in muscle spasm that again made it impossible for him to breath. After 2 to 3 minutes he was dead", Nikki explains as she looks at Ray and place her hand on his arm. "Luckily I found him in time to revive him." She smiles wakefully.

Ray get eye contact with Nikki and in a moment loose the sense of where he are. It's as if the time stop, and the surroundings do not exist.

Elisabeth get their attention with a loud "**Hmm**" she smiles and look a Ray "You are a lucky man!" Then at Nikki "You told me you had progress in your investigation of the sickness in the food production? You know our whole existence depend on getting the food production back to normal!" She looks firmly at Nikki who pull her hand back as she straightens up.

Nikki pauses for a moment as she looks down at the table then direct at Elisabeth "The same drug that poisoned Ray was used to suffocate the cell cultures. The drug inhibit cell division in our food reactors by an illness of prolific constriction, and the cell production stops."

Elisabeth raise her eyebrows as she lean forward "*So, we were assaulted again!*"

Ray listening attend to Nikki's explanation as he ponders on the tidings 'I was poisoned? By whom? Only Nikki have access to my cabin... and Veronica, but she is dead...'

Nikki takes a deep breath as she smiles "*I found a cure for the illness!*" Elisabeth jump forward and grab Nikki's arm "**You are my hero!**" she shouts, at the same time Ray burst excited "*Tell us Nikki, how did you find out?*"

Elisabeth calm herself immediately and sit back in her chair "Nikki, that is the best news I have had in a long time!"

Nikki lean back as she watches their happy smiles "Yes, I know it is fantastic! It occurred to me after Ray recovered so fast, that the food cell–culture would enhance cell division if I gave them more oxygen, *and they did!*"

Elisabeth closes her eyes for a moment then she looks focused at them both. "I will order Security to investigate who's behind poisoning our food and to tighten security in the biological-section. Meanwhile, don't mention anything about it. *Understood!*"

They nod as Ray fold his arms, 'they are not going to snoop around my cabin' he thinks.

Elisabeth turns to Nikki "How long time till we get full food production up and running again?"

Nikki wave pensive "We need to sterilize all process equipment and rebuild the bio culture. It may take weeks" she laments.

"Speed it up as much as you can" Elisabeth insist. She looks straight a Ray "Your colleague Sara is missing, did you know?"

Ray sit back and hold his breath a moment "*Missing?* How is she missing, at work?"

Elisabeth raise her eyebrows as she looks fixed at Ray "No, she is gone. I mean, she is nowhere to be found. If you can help please let Security know."

Ray gets a tight feeling in his stomach 'I just worked with her the other day...' He nods as they leave the office.

Nikki and Ray walk down to the biosphere, some kits are playing hide and seek, a boy hide behind the bench they are sitting on. Nikki smiles as she looks at the girl who finishing counting and start looking for the other kits hiding. Ray see how happy the playful kits make her. The girl ask Ray if there is anyone hiding behind them, he shakes his head and Nikki lean over as she grab his arm with a trilled laugh. Ray look at her 'She truly likes children' he thinks, they watch the children play for a while.

Nikki jumps up on her feet. Her cheeks glow, and she looks so happy "I have to go back to work, I'll call you later."

"*No, no, wait!*" Ray say loud and grab her arm pulling her gently back on the bench. "You need to tell me how you brought me back to life yesterday."

Ray notice how her eyes are sparkling as she gazes toward the bleary green of trees in front of them. "Mom taught me to step out of my body just before falling asleep, moving and communicating consciously in free spirit..."

Ray look surprised at her as he interrupts "So, you can walk around outside your body?"

Nikki lean slightly toward Ray, grinning "*Yeah*, I'll come hunt you at night."

Ray looks at Nikki in unbelief "*No, inherently Nikki.* I was dead, and you came and fetched me!"

"I know Ray, it is hard to accept. You can learn it too" Nikki say seriously and continue "I mostly use it to gain knowledge from God's wisdom, you will be amazed it's omniscient!"

She jumps up on her feet "I'll call you later" she says joyful as she walks down the trail. She bends and whispers something to the girl who's looking for her playmates.

Ray watch till she vanishes behind a curve 'She's an enigma!' he thinks.

A long shadow fall on the trail and then vanish back into the trees with the crushing sound of dry leafs. A cold rush on the spine makes Ray jump up 'Time to get back home'.

Ray throws the shoe off and turns on the Daedalus N ews. They show the trajectory to Jupiter, explaining how the close Mars flyby generate propulsion as a gravity assisted slingshot. 'So, we continue to Jupiter' he thinks and sit down in the armchair. The next news inlet talk about the Ceres mission. A probe will be released from Daedalus toward the asteroid Ceres soon after they have passed Mars. They add that the Sun will flip magnetic poles again do to the Dzhanibekov effect... "Zzzzz" Ray enter a deep sleep.

Arrival to Mars

The office buzz with activity this morning, preparing for the Mars flyby. Ray glances at Dr. Sheehaus sitting at Hellman's table 'What is that chump doing here?' Ray thinks as he tries to concentrate on his work. He keeps an eye on Hellman's desk 'They are planning something, a new observation project for Dr. Sheehaus? or revising an old one?'

Dr. Sheehaus get up, and they shake hands 'he leaves now' Ray things and walks over to a colleague where he can't be seen. "Are you going to watch the Mars flyby tonight?" he asks as he watches Dr. Sheehaus walk out of the office.

The man look puzzled at Ray. "Never mind" Ray say and walk back to his desk.

Hellman comes over to Ray's desk. He claps Ray on the back as he takes a sit on a spar chair next to him, placing his work pad on the desk.

Ray's pulse accelerate, he tries to find a comfortable posture. "Hello" he salutes with the prospect to finally know what Dr. Sheehaus was doing in the office.

Hellman taps on his pad "We need to release a probe soon, take a look" he slides his pad over to Ray.

Ray read the document, >Thrust Displacement of Ceres by Dr. Sheehaus< His eyes widen as he read *amazing...*', looking perplexed at Hellman now and then.

He lean in on Hellman "Are we actually going to do that?" he asks pointing at the pad.

Hellman shake his head affirmative "*Yep*, and you are going to manage the project" he replies with a big smile.

"*Hi Nikki*, Food are improving" Ray salute with a smile as he places his tray next to hers on the Canteen table.

"*Yes I can see that!*" Nikki replies with a laugh, looking at all the chips on his tray. She looks searching at Ray "I have reserved two seats at the Star Lounge, for tonight... Are you coming?"

Ray lean over "You know I will" he replies with a tentative smile "who should I go with, if not with you?"

"*Oh Ray*, you are so charming today, what happened?" Nikki asks teasing.

Ray nods as he takes a deep breath "I got a project to manage. But, not any project" Ray talk in a serious tone as he looks focused at Nikki "we are going to geoengineering Mars! Giving it an ocean and an atmosphere."

Nikki grab Ray's arm "*Geoengineering... That sounds great!*" It then sinks in, she continues in a soft voice "Geoengineering Mars, really? *Are you sure?*"

Ray stretch his legs discreetly "Yes, for sure."

Nikki narrow her eyes as she looks serious at Ray pointing a finger at him "I'll ask for verification on that one..." she stays thoughtful for a moment.

Ray eats his fried chip with a lot of appetite 'The chip taste better today' he thinks eating and absorbed by his own thoughts.

"*Hello Ray*" Nikki call politely.

Ray looks up, he knows he got carried away, and wipes his mouth genteel with his napkin "Did you get a window table?" he asks in a soothing tone.

Nikki pickup her tray "See you tonight at 7 O'clock."

He waves at her and wonder 'Did she get upset or did she just have to go?'

The pad sound, a note from the Crew Administration Office, they ask Ray to collect Veronica's Death certificate, and her inheritance papers. Ray breath deeply with a grimace 'Now I'm her custodian'. He decides to go get it straightaway.

The Crew Office clerk looks pail, and a bit sad as he hands the brown envelope over the counter. "Now, as her lawyer you accept to supervise the case" Ray nod and signs the receipt.

On his way out Ray look through the papers, he halt in the doorway, she didn't inherit the apartment. Instead, there was an order of payment from Mohann Inc. for acquiring the apartment. Ray look at the bill 'Too little for such a luxurious apartment?' Ray wonder, he slips the bill into his pocket. At home, he drops the envelope on the sofa-table and dress.

The crowded Star Lounge hum from people talking mixed with the soft background music.

Ray look searching into the dark Lounge a light moves between the tables from a waiter guiding a guest. The attendant at the entrance brighten up "Hello Ray. I got room at my table, if you like?"

Ray returns the bright smile "Hello Rose. A table for Miss Navarro, please."

She makes a sad face and finds their reservation on the list "Table 18, you will find it straight down on your right. *Ray*, do you need a guide?" she asks with a renewed smile, touching his hand.

Ray shivers a bit from her light touch. 'Yes you are lovely Rose' Gently he pulls his hand back "I will find my way. Thank you Rose."

The dimmed light makes it just feasible to skim the way between the groups of small tables. He finds table 18 empty, and glance at his pad 'Its 7:05 maybe she works late again...'

He looks up and there she stands like a flower glowing in the dark, standing out from all the rest "**Wow**, I mean *Hi!*"

Nikki looks dashing in a fancy blue shirt and metal-blue pants wide as a skirt. Her moon jewels sparkle in the dim light, he just stares at her.

"*Ray!*" She looks down and walk over to her chair.

Ray unfreeze, 'She looks fantastic tonight' he pulls the chair out for her.

A large plate center the small round table, topped with chocolate confetti, muffins and pecan pie. They sip their tea gazing out the windows without a word, Mars pose majestic with a cloudy haze at the pole. "*Wow Nikki look,* Mount Olympus" Ray point at the impressive volcano coming into sight as they start to slingshot past Mars. "It's the larges in the whole solar system!" he adds with a shaken voice glancing at Nikki.

He tries to imagine Mars with an ocean and green vegetation. 'The ocean will cover all the low land, valleys, and form lakes in the massive impact craters. Water vapor and gases from the collision will create an atmosphere. The summer and winter seasons will bring snow and rainfall forming rivers, giving life for grass and other vegetation'. He takes a deep breath as if he breathed the new martian atmosphere.

The packed Lounge get lid up in a gentle brown glow reflecting from Mars. Nikki laughs at Ray, he looks suntanned in the soft light, "It's the Tharsis Mountains, *there isn't it?*" she asks fascinated.

Ray nod eagerly "Yes, they will be covered in snow soon" he winks at Nikki with a big smile.

"Sure Ray, if you say so!" she looks back at the panorama, the Marineris Valley come into sight as Mars get more distanced.

A strong sunlight appear at the edge of the shield, the Lounge light up as if hit by a blazing headlight. The window shades close leaving them with the soft light from table-lamps.

Nikki lean over the table inclining her head a bit, "Tell me Ray, how are you going to turn Mars from red to green?" she asks in a muse tone, looking straight at Ray.

Ray stretches up in his chair and catch her inquiring eyes "We will move the asteroid Ceres inside the synchronous orbit of Mars, where they eventually will merge."

Nikki narrow her eyes, keeping the eye contact "*Why Ceres?*"

Ray moves to the edge of his chair and continue eagerly "Ceres is mostly water, well one quarter, anyway it's just what Mars need to form an ocean." He lean back with both hands on the table, "if all goes well you will see the impact on our way back."

"Sure Ray, why do you pin that story on me?" She replies with a teasing smile crossing her face.

Ray move gently back on the chair and look deep into her eyes "Lets walk back through the Park. I got hot chocolate if you like?"

Nikki pull her chair back and get up without a word, they wander hand in hand down the corridor to toward the Park.

The quiet walk with a lot of talk ends when Ray sees a shadow leave his cabin "***Did you see that!***" he shouts.

Ray run fast over to the cabin, the entrance door is forced open... He stands still for a moment listening as he looks into the dark entrance.

"What have happened?" Nikki asks as she catches up with Ray.

"Shh" Ray signals Nikki to stay quiet. He enters the cabin using the torch on the pad, the floor is littered with broken stuff. He makes his way across the room and switches on the main breaker, the light comes back on.

"*What a mess!*" Nikki says aloud. She stands just behind Ray, he leaps, surprised to have Nikki close at his back.

He turns upset "*Can't you be quiet for a moment*" he responds loud.

"Why? We are the only one here?" Nikki say and walk into the bedroom, "wow, even the bed is sliced open." She walks back into the living room where Ray picks up papers from the floor, everything are smashed or cut into pieces.

She pulls out her pad and call Security "I want to announce a break in at Cabin 1C237. Yes, thank you." Ray jumps up as he stares perplexed at Nikki.

"Did you just call Security?" Ray asks with a trembling voice.

"That's what you do Ray, when someone break in and smash your Cabin" Nikki reply looking incredulous back at Ray.

Nikki watches as Ray walks into the bathroom pulling his hand through his hair several times. She shakes her head and walk out on the corridor and wait.

Mr. Mark enter the living room "Hello Ray, look like you are in trouble again." Ray sits in the broken armchair and turn his head surprised by the sudden appearance of Mark.

Ben and Nikki enter behind as Mr. Mark pull a small notebook out of his pocket. "Ray, tell me your version of the story" Mark asks in an accusing tone as he looks around the room. "What did you do to make the place look like this?"

Ray stands-up and salute with a forced smile "Mr. Mark" then nod toward Ben behind him.

Mr. Mark fix his eyes at Ray's and tap the notebook at Ray's chest "Your name keep coming up! Your colleague Sara are missing and now this..." Mark looks around the messed up cabin "Ben, drain the assistance and seal the room" he boss.

"I got all the room-assistance's data here" Ben says and show his pad. He guides Nikki out to the corridor.

Mr. Mark follows with a hand on Ray's shoulder. "Find yourself a place to sleep, Ray. We seal this cabin as a crime scene" he says with a tight smile.

"And my things?" Ray ask upset while moving closer to Mark.

Nikki walks between Mark and Ray as she pulls him with her "Come on Ray lets go."

Nikki and Ray walk silent down the corridor. Ray looks back, relieved to see Mr. Mark and Ben disappear out of sight behind the ceiling. He wonder 'Who would vandalize his cabin and why? Did it have anything to do with Wang or Sheehaus? Wang vanished, again... Sheehaus made threats every time they meet...'

Nikki gets Ray's attention with a shoulder puff "We are here" she says and open her cabin door. "You can crouch on the couch" she throws a blanket onto the sofa with a slack expression.

Ray grab the blanket "Thanks" he replies in a low voice as he sits on the sofa and untie his shoes.

Nikki look observing at Ray then leave and close the door to her bedroom.

Next morning Ray wake up to the smell of breakfast. Nikki places a hot cup of tea in front of him "Hurry, we need to get going." She turns on the news on the wall-screen.

Ray stretch sleepy as he moves and doze on the sofa. The news reporter talks about the four probes that Daedalus will send to Ceres. The probes carry each a small nuclear bomb, when detonated they will change the asteroids orbit till it gently collides with Mars. The merge of Ceres with Mars will alter its climate by adding water and a denser atmosphere. It will take 10 years till the dust settles on Mars. Then they will mass seed plants on the land and plankton in the new ocean.

Ray jumps out of the sofa recalling his meeting 'I got the Ceres coordination meeting in half an hour'. He rush for the door.

"See you at the canteen" he shouts to Nikki from the doorway.

After the meeting, Ray bumps into Elisabeth Stand in the busy office hallway. "*Ray*, good I found you" she looks a bit stressed, "sorry about your cabin. We got you a temporal compartment on second floor. Bukari will get you arranged. You know Bukari, right?"

Ray nod awkward as he clutch the binder in front of him.

"See you tomorrow at the probe launch" she salutes and continue down the hall.

Entering the office Ray finds Bukari standing sentinel over his work desk. Bukari spot Ray as he enters "**Hello Ray!**" he salutes aloud. Half the office turn their heads and look at Bukari then at Ray.

Ray smile and walk more decisive to his desk, "Hi Bukari, great to see you too!" Ray salutes with a handshake.

He searches his pockets and to his surprise find something. He pulls a note out '*Aha*, Veronica's inheritance.' The address on the bill look strange >Mohann Inc., Suite A67, Hotel Daedalus< he read.

"Crew Administration got a new cabin for you" Bukari wave a access-code to get Ray's attention, "Have you been promoted?" he asks curiously.

"To what?" Ray asks with a laugh as he throws the note into the desk drawer, "let's go."

Bukari lead the way to Ray's new cabin.

As they walk Ray wonder where Suite A67 may be, "Do you know anything about the new apartments in the Hotel-section?" he asks.

Bukari seem perplexed by the question "You mean the new ring section?"

"Yes, I have seen a lot of crawler-drones working on the hotel-sections end wall" Ray confirms.

Bukari walk slower as he talks "Well as you know it is restricted area. But, I know someone from Service who make an extra on delivery's to the new section. Hush, hush, you know!"

"Of course" Ray nod confirming as he stops walking, "do you know the way into the new section?"

Bukari stops, looking back at Ray then continue walking "You just let me know when." He opens the door to the new cabin and hand the access-code to Ray "Here you go, I got you luggage as well."

"Good afternoon" He salutes and leave the same way down the corridor.

"*Wow, what a smasher*" Ray shout when he enters the combined kitchen and dining room he walks round the small table and into the living room. A dim light enters from the ceiling, he stares upward, the room got a skylight facing toward the center of the station where lights sparkle from the other cabins. He lean a bit to the side and can even see starlight.

In the bedroom stand a Service-wagon with his clothe and personal stuff. Ray wonder for a second how Bukari manage to get his things. Then he walks back to the living room, move the armchair to the spot from where he can see the starlight and fall into the comfortable chair. Watching the stars bring him back home at the porch with mom...

The pad calling bring Ray back from the slumber, "You missed out at lunch?" Nikki sounds gloomy, "everything alright?"

"I got a new cabin with a skylight" Ray reply cheerful and send her his location, he continues "come over, need your help with something..." Nikki hangs up.

Ray wonder what happened... The room-assistance inform that Nikki at the door.

"Wow, Ray! You got a Prescribed Unit" Nikki take a self-guided tour round the cabin, "and your belongings as well."

Ray can hear the sound of closet doors and drawers, he gets up and into the bedroom "*What are you doing?*" Nikki have organized all his clothe in a minute.

Ray lets the self-driving Service-wagon out, it moves fast down the corridor and into the transporter.

They sit in the sofa with a cup of hot chocolate, the wall-screen show the news, a trajectory graph animate the movement of the Ceres probes.

Nikki points at the screen "How did the meeting go?" she asks looking a Ray.

"Good, all things considered not much to do, they got everything planned and programmed. We just need to coordinate the probe release." Ray look into his cup as he holds it with both hands.

Nikki sense Ray's disappointment "Security is so ignoring" She catch Ray's eyes, "they control every entrance of people and goods to the biological-section."

Ray straightens up "More poisoned food?" he asks tense.

"No, no" Nikki shake her head, "Ben was there today asking me questions about yesterday, your cabin and all that you know." She reaches for his hand.

Ray gets an electric jag from her touches "Any news about who did it?"

"Ben just asked where we been and when we got back" Nikki hold Ray's hand tighter as she lean back and watch the skylight.

"*Um!*" Ray clear his throat, they sit silent for a moment as he wonders who messed up his cabin. "Do you know the new section, the one in construction?" he quizzes.

Nikki sits up straight "The new ring section?" she asks puzzled "only contract workers live there, it's a ghetto" she impugns.

Ray nod affirming "Have you ever been there?"

Nikki study Ray for a moment "Yeah, once" she turns and sit toward Ray, "we made a biodiversity study for the hanging garden at the new sections main square."

Ray nod affirming again "I need your help finding Suite A67... will you?"

"For what?" she asks with a weighted sigh toward the door.

"Looking for Mr. Wang" Ray get up and walk cross the room.

Nikki rub her brow "*But, it is sealed off?*"

"Bukari will get us in" Ray reply with a relaxed hand gesture.

Nikki stands-up reluctantly... "I'll let you know... we are busy at work" she kisses Ray on the chin, "see you tomorrow" she salutes with a quick smile and leave.

Early at the Maintenance Office. Ray and Sabine stand at the main command observing the wall-screen showing the Docking-port where three Space-probes stand on racks next to the launch rail.

Ray instructs the trolley to collect the last probe. A crawler drone grab the probe from the shelves at the center of the Port-module where it has been stored at zero gravity.

The trolley wait till the probe is secured on the rack and begin the slow transport up to the docking port on second floor. It unloads the rack in perfect line with the other three.

Sabine walks over and tell Elisabeth that all four probes are on the port deck.

Elisabeth race her hands in the air and gets her attention in the office. She straightens out her uniform "Good to see everyone on duty" she takes a look around the office as a salute.

"It is a big moment today as we take the first steps to a new human habitat in our solar system, the geoengineering of Mars. The Sun continues to brighten every day, bringing more warmth to the inner solar system, pushing its habitable zone outwards. At some point, the Earth will be too dry for the ecosystem to survive. We need to make new habitats in time and geoengineering is a long and slow endeavor. Today we will begin the works for a new world for the coming generations. Thanks to Dr. Sheehaus." She turns and applaud at Sheehaus, he looks distracted toward the exit.

Ray tells the crawler drones to move the four probes onto the launch rail. The rail stand vertical on the floor and extend up to a portal in the roof.

"We can remove the hardware locks" he command on the intercom.

Two service workers enter the airless dock in protective wear. They flow over to the probes and remove a metal pin from each space-probe.

"Check if the probes are locked onto the rail" Ray ask on the intercom, "and see if they roll freely."

The two workers wave back "Everything's good Ray." They work their way back and exit the port.

He looks at Sabine who confirm with a thumbs-up. Sabine nod to Elisabeth and start the launch sequence.

The large roof doors start to open above the docking-port.

On the wall-screen, the magnetic launch-rail is seen from the floor angle, it races majestic upward, pointing into a deep dark void of space.

One by one the probes get ejected from Daedalus, they fade away into the darkness on their four-month journey to Ceres.

Ray bunch on his feet, happy with a job well done. He looks back at Hellman who stand satisfied with his arms crossed at his chest, there is no sight of Dr. Sheehaus.

Arrival at Jupiter

Nikki wait at Ray's door. When he gets out of the transporter she turns and make an entrance with her hands out to the side as she bow. He smiles happy to see her *"What a surprise!"* he calls from a distance.

Ray study Nikki, she looks sensational. She turns for him to get a better look.

She wears a slip dress, the loose fabric tailor her body perfectly. The color standout, a deep purple-pearl with a golden shine and an elegant mid–heel shoe in black.

"What's the occasion?" Ray ask shrilled.

Nikki stands a moment with a dazed look "The Zodiacal cloud... You have seen the news?"

Ray nod "Yeah, the Linear tail..." he keeps looking at her stylized dress, "where did you get that? You made that one too?" Ray marvel.

Nikki shine "Yes I did" she replies timid.

Ray touches the fabric it's soft like silk but more like cotton in texture "Where do the textile come from? I have never seen anything like it!"

"I extracted the ivory from the mussel shells we grow in the food section. Then reassemble the matter into fabric in the atom–assembler." Nikki smile.

Ray look baffled at Nikki *"Right... So its basically hair..."* he opens the cabin door.

Nikki look annoyed at Ray as they enter the cabin.

They sit on the sofa in the dark room, sipping tea as they look out the skylight.

Space is packed with stars, now and then a light sparkle bright close-up.

Nikki studies what is visible from the skylight "See, the Gaura Escape Shuttle" she points at the craft. It's slim as a mango seed, attached to the opposite side of their ring-section.

A brighter light sparkles close-up. Ray catch Nikki's arm "**Look**" he burst out.

"Its beginning" Nikki whisper excited.

More and more light-bursts out-bright the starlight as an authentic firework.

"Wow! Its amazing" Ray sit up to get a better view, "how long time will it continue, you know?"

"The news this morning said it will take a month before we get through the dust cloud, but less intense" Nikki pull Ray back and lean to his side.

"One month... a long time to have the plasma shield turned on" Ray think aloud.

"Well it save us from the asteroid belt sandblasting us" Nikki allude. They sit silent watching the colorful light-bursts from all the small grains of sand disintegrating in the plasma shield. Some larger grains draw a line of light as they pass out of sight.

A reddish light flashes close to the window, disappearing into the center back of the ring-sections followed by a light quiver.

"**Wow!** *Did you see that*, a rock just passed right through the plasma" Ray explode as he jumps up, "the inner side of the ring-sections don't have protection for that..." his pad rings.

Ray grab his pad at first sound "*Yes! Hello Hellman.*"

"Go to Maintenance straightaway, *we got an issue!*" Hellman bid severely.

Ray gazes at Nikki "Um... I have to go, Hellman just called" he moans uncertain.

Nikki sit alone on the coach fingering her necklace. She turns on the wall-screen an emergency broadcast is developing, something about damage to the Storage in the Oeuvre-section.

She select to see the announcement from the beginning. >An meteoroid have penetrated the plasma-shield and hit the back wall of the storage-deck. The area is sealed off and all section airlocks closed.<

Nikki wonder how big damage it coursed and if Ray had to go outside again. She tries to get a comfortable posture then grab a blanket and lay down, and falls asleep exhausted.

The Maintenance office buzz of activity. "Take this assessment to Hellman." A colleague hand a pad to Ray just as he enters. He looks around for Hellman but no sight of him, "he's in the meeting, *hurry*" she hastens.

Elisabeth are talking when Ray enters the meeting, he takes his seat as quiet as possible.

"... and the options on my table tonight!" Elisabeth stop talking and look at Ray "Get your gear on, Kareem will be your wing man" she snap.

Ray stares incredulous at Elisabeth then at Hellman.

Hellman takes the pad out of Rays hand as Kareem present himself to Ray.

"I'll brief you on the way" Kareem keen and help Ray with the chair as he gets up.

Bukari wait for them outside the door "This way" he leads them next door. "You can change here" he points at the protective wear on the office tables.

Ray and Kareem start pulling on overalls, boots, gloves and helmet. Ray look serious at Kareem, he catches the look and starts explaining "We got hit by a meteoroid. It has coursed damage on the storage-deck, and we are loosing pressure and oxygen fast."

Ray nods as he straps the air-pack tight "Right, we just need to patch it" he mumbles.

Ray and Kareem wave at Bukari as they leave the office.

Bukari rub the back of his neck "*Good luck*" he quivers. He looks down and see the tool-bag, grab it, and run after them and hand it to Ray.

Kareem leads as they walk down the narrow corridor to the transporter at mid-section.

Ray pushes the botton on the transporter a couple of times with no effect "Let's take the stairs" Ray suggest, Kareem nod confirming.

Next to the transporter Kareem removes an exit cover and turn a handle. The hatch to the emergency ladder open with a pitch sound from the air rushing into the shaft.

Ray's heart beat harder, he lean forward into the opening looking up the dark manhole, his head lamps flash on the dusty walls. "The whole section above deck seem to be locked down" he says tense as he step onto the ladder inside the shaft.

"Yes, it has disconnected" Hellman confirms over the intercom. Kareem follows behind Ray. The gravity get lower and lower the higher they get.

Ray step on the ladder as normal and to his surprise flow fast upward. He stretch a hand over his head, "*Av*" he smash against the round hatch at the end of the shaft then bunch back at Kareem.

"***Careful Ray***" Kareem shout.

"*Sorry*" Ray rant. He grab onto the ladder and open the hatch the air streaming in drags him gently out of the emergency passage. He stares into the pitch-black storage-deck, the only visible is a dim gray reflection from the floor as far as the headlight reach.

Kareem looks at a floor plan on his pad "That way to the wall" he points the direction to their left.

They walk with difficulty in the low gravity. At the end Ray search the wall with his flashlight, pipes run along the wall some large and others smaller. "***There***" he points at a fracture in the wall with the light.

"*Yes, I see it*" Hellman shout excited on the intercom, "patch it as good as you can! I'll send a team in to weld it, later."

Ray search the tool-bag "Lets inject coherent polythene" he suggests and hand Kareem the cater-tool.

"Look at that red-brown stuff it has clogged the pipe" Kareem point at a broken pipe next to the hole in the wall.

"Hellman, we found the power leak!" Ray cheer.

"Patch the wall first" Hellman respond rapidly.

"What is it?" Kareem looks suspicious at the brown substance.

"It's leaking from the electrochemical power line, that's why there's no power in this section" Ray explain, "careful, it oozes if it melts."

Kareem works on injecting the polythene, "*BANG*" they get blown backward by wall debris, a meteoroid toss by next to Kareem's head.

"*Send a medic, we got hit!*" Ray cry out loud as he gets up and bunch off toward Kareem.

"*Air*" Kareem yells in pain pointing at the shoulder scar in his suit. Ray uses the cater-tool to seal the air leak in Kareem's protective suit.

"*Let's get you out*" Ray bid and help Kareem over to the emergency way. An aid man come to the help moving Kareem out of the Storage through the hatchway.

"Hellman" Ray call over intercom.

"Yes, I follow you on screen" Hellman answer.

"Kareem is on his way to sickbay, I'll patch the wall."

Ray walk back to the wall and begin to inject the sealant in the two holes. "The power tube need to be replaced...." He patches the tube within the bounds of his possibility. "*Done!* You can turn on the light" he grunts with a slow smile.

"Perfect! Wrap it up" Hellman exult and reactivates the power from the control at the Maintenance Office.

Ray collects his tools as the light comes back on, he walks unsteady over to the transporter, 'Are we over and done?' he thinks on his way down to first floor.

Back at his cabin Ray find Nikki sleeping on the sofa. He looks up at the skylight for a while only a few light-bursts lights up 'What a relief' he thinks and go straight to bed.

The smell of breakfast and the sound from the morning news awakes Ray. He walks into the kitchen where Nikki hand him a cup of tea.

They sit at the table talking about last night. Ray turn his head and looks into the distance in silence as he tugs the napkin.

He lean back and look past Nikki "Um, have you thought about helping me go to the new section?" he asks elusive.

Nikki stand-up "Haven't you had enough action for one day?" She removes the cups from the table and wash them at the sink, "we can go tonight ... I'll be off early" she enthuses.

Ray try to restrain his big smile, he hug Nikki from behind and kiss her on the chin. She turns around and get disappointed seeing Ray walking into the living room.

He pulls his pad out and makes a call "Hi Bukari, we will go to the new section tonight. Right then, see you at 8 o'clock" Ray disconnect, "let's go to work" he rush standing at the front door.

After work Ray stands outside the Botanic Club waiting, he looks at his pad, again, 8:18:79 'Where is everyone?' he thinks.

Ray step back by surprise, seeing Bukari coming out from the Club "Hello Ray, are you ready?" he salutes.

"We are waiting for Nikki" Ray emphasis as he claps Bukari's arm.

"She's at the ladies" Bukari nod toward the Club, "we just talked while waiting. What a charm!" he winks at Ray.

"You been inside all the time?" Ray burst out, "I meant to meet *at* the Club, not *in* the Club" he objects and turnaround.

Nikki exits the Club "*Hi Ray*" she chants with a smile, "are you two alright?" Nikki looks observing at Ray and Bukari.

"*Are we alright?*, yes of course" Ray reply uncertain, "lets go."

Bukari take the lead, they take the stairs down to the service-deck walk through the airlock into the hotel-section.

Nikki and Ray cover their faces to avert the bad smell.

Bukari continue down to the back wall "We are off surveillance down here" he hoots.

Passed the airlock Bukari stops "There" he points at an Emergency Exit, "there's no service-deck in the new section" he explains.

Ray hold his arm "You don't need to go" he says as he shakes his head, "I will call you when we get back, *okay!*"

"*Are you sure Ray?*" Bukari murmur, "I'll wait here. You need to come back the same way" he explains and look back at the airlock pointing at the sign >AIRLOCK 5<.

Ray walks down the narrow passageway with Nikki following behind, she turns and salutes "Thanks Bukari."

"Don't talk to the construction workers just say you work for Inspection" Bukari shout after them.

They walk direct from Service-deck into the new sections main square on its first floor.

Nikki run into the middle of the square. "*Look the hanging garden*" she cheers and spin around looking up at all the green vegetation growing in containers, hanging from the balconies.

"*This way*" she calls and walk eagerly down the wide corridor, Ray hurries to catch up on her. He smiles seeing their reflections in the empty storefront windows. The corridor is open all the way up through third floor with a line of skylights centering the ceiling.

A light reflection flash from a moving window on third floor.

Ray jumps to the side "Nikki come over here, *hurry!*" he whispers, "someone's up there" he points toward the apartment window.

Nikki looks up as she walks close to Ray "The one with balcony?" she gasps short breathed, "*look!*" a man cross above them on a small glass deck.

"There are people everywhere" Ray whisper back.

Nikki pulls Ray with her up a stairway "follow me" she says.

Ray follow her behind "*Are you sure?*" he flutters.

Nikki looks back at Ray "It was on second floor, wasn't it?" she persists, turn the corner and walk down the narrow corridor.

Ray look at the door signs >Suite A59<, then >Suite A61<

"Here it is!" she chants ahead of him, "It was Suite 67, *yes!*"

Ray catches up "Yes, yes" he smiles complying.

She lean against the door "How are you going to open the door?" she teases.

Ray grab the handle and open the door "Like this" he emphasizes, Nikki fall into Ray's arms as the door opens.

Nikki gets back on her feet "*How did you know it was open?*" she calls out as she walks through the hall into the living room.

"All apartments are open, the place is in construction!" he replies plain, "how can anyone live a place like this?" he gazes at all the mess.

Ray picks up a pullover sweater on the armchair "Mr. Wang didn't stay here Dr. Sheehaus did ..." He wonders where Wang might be and keep looking around.

Nikki walks over to Ray "What are we looking for?" she watches him searching the study desk.

"Some code of a kind" Ray allude as he searches a drawer. Among a bunch of papers he finds a note, "look, an 10,000 advance from Dr. Sheehaus to Wang *hmm?*" Ray scratch his back-head wondering, "Issued on 04-06-28" he reflects aloud.

Nikki study the note "That was the day you arrived" she confirms and take a look around the room. "If I was him I would hide it below the sofa-cushion."

She walks over and lift the cushion "*Yak, what a fusty smell*" she wrinkles her nose, "*look, an envelope*" she cheers, and grab the envelope showing it triumphantly to Ray.

Nikki gets Ray's full attention he drops the note on the table "*Open it*" he shouts excited.

"*Shee*" Nikki hush looking toward the hall, "someone is coming" she whispers.

Ray listen too "*Hurry*, this way" he whispers back.

They run up the stairs to the apartments second floor where they reach just in time to hide behind a bench on the landing.

The door slam "***Move it***" a voice boom.

Sheehaus are pushed into the living room "*I haven't got it*" he cries out.

The man with the red neckerchief follow behind pointing an electric-rod at Sheehaus "*Brogan thinks otherwise.*" He shock Sheehaus on his arm with the rod forcing him further into the room.

Ray looks behind his back to see if they can escape into one of the bedrooms, all doors are closed 'Too risky he will hear us' he thinks.

"Stay low" he whispers to Nikki. She nods affirming as she looks downstairs through a crack between a vase and the bench.

Sheehaus hold his arm in pain "*Brogan got it wrong!*" he wails.

"Brogan has never been wrong, never" the man fume. He walks slowly toward Sheehaus who step backwards, "you said you got it all figured out. Now, where is it?" the man continues.

Sheehaus are pail, looking around for a way out "I can give you money, hard currency!" he says shrilled.

"I only want what I was sent for" the man bit and walk closer toward Sheehaus raising the rod, threatening to hit him.

Sheehaus lean back at the window as he shakes his head fearfully *"No, no, don't do it"* he cries.

"For the last time give it to me!" the man shout and hit Sheehaus hard in the head with the rod. The window shatter, and he falls one floor down on the corridor below with a dump sound.

Nikki scream frighten, she stands up, pallid, not knowing what to do.

The man look up at the staircase landing with a cold glance full of anger turning into a grimace of hate as he walks over to the stairs *"You nosy bitch!"* he hisses.

Ray stands up rigid in front of Nikki. The man is surprised to see Ray there and get even more furious. He race the rod into the air and run up the stairs swinging the rod aggressively at Ray.

Ray jumps to the side, the rod hit the handrail with a fire of electric sparkles. The man race the rod for a new blow, **Pow,** Ray punch his fist in his face, sending him tumbling down the stairs, with Ray following behind.

The man gets up furious like a wounded animal pointing his rod at Ray.

"I got him!" Bukari shouts as he rush in swinging a large spanner. The man move swift and hit Bukari on his arm, and the spanner smash onto the floor. Bukari hold on to his arm in pain and walk a step back.

Ray takes up the spanner as it slide unto his feet, he waves it in front of him as he closes in on the man.

The man swing his rod at Ray with all his force, Ray blocks the blow with the spanner and electric sparkles fly around them. The spanner conduct the electric chock and stun Ray's arm. He drops the spanner as he bends forward in pain just in time to avoid being hit by a large vase coming hurling down. The vase hit the man in his face with a loud bang, he stumbles down onto the floor in a rain of splintered porcelain pieces. The electric-rod get hurled out of the broken windows onto the corridor below.

Ray look surprised up at Nikki on the stair landing, she throws the second vase down at the man on the floor. Ray jumps to the side as it splinters with thunder in front of him. He grab the spanner and move toward the man on the floor.

The man jump up and turn to the window, with a growl he jumps out the window and vanish down the corridor.

Nikki run down the stairs and hug Ray "Thank you, Ray" she gushes. "Good to see you Bukari" she gives him a hand and hold it tight a moment. *"Let's get out of here!"* she exclaims.

As they leave the apartment, on second floor the bedroom door handle turn, and the door opens a crack...

"The other way" Nikki gasp and pull Ray with her down the narrow corridor. "How did you find us?" Nikki ask Bukari.

Bukari look to the side "I just followed the sound" he contests flushing as he swing the spanner.

"Oh yeah, sure" Ray smile, and they all laugh.

After a detour they are back at the airlock "Let's go to the Club" Bukari suggests.

At the table in the Botanic Club Ray gaze at Nikki "And the envelope?" he asks and tilt toward her.

"Sure, I got it here" she pulls it out of her pocket, and iron the envelope on the table before opening it.

She pulls out a handful of papers "Calculations..." she nags and toss them back on the table.

Ray picks up the papers and read them careful "Calculations to decode an encryption of some kind *hmm*" he gazes into the room wondering what kind of encryption it might be, "The encryption code is missing..." Ray scans the papers with his pad and search the Net. He looks disappointed at the result *'Nothing!'* "And Sheehaus is dead!" Ray think aloud.

Nikki drop her shoulders *"All that for nothing"* she groans, "shouldn't we let Security know?"

Bukari nods at Nikki "I'll let a friend from Construction call Security" he pulls out his pad and texts.

"*Look*" Nikki point at the wall-screen in the club. An impressive image show the Western Trojan Asteroids, faraway Jupiter can be seen as a shining dot behind the rough boulders.

"The Scout Probe" Ray confirm, "*we are arriving at Jupiter!*" he chants happy.

Ray salute Nikki and Bukari, they raise their glasses "*Finally*" he cheers as if the voyage was over.

Ray's pad calls, he takes a glance at the screen >Hellman<. "Yes..." Ray answer vaguely.

Hellman clear his throat "We got a meeting tomorrow morning, Sheehaus is dead" he hastens.

"Sh.. Sheehaus is dead, really?" Ray stutter, and pushes his glass into the middle of the table.

"Yes, tomorrow we know more..." Hellman hesitate, "at the Captain's office at 4 o'clock."

"Right, thank you" Ray hangup and look at Nikki and Bukari, "they found Sheehaus" he gushes, "let's go."

Nikki and Ray walk through the park on their way home.

"Here, you take the papers" Ray hand the envelope to Nikki, she folds it into her pocket without a query.

At the Crew section Ray give Nikki a kiss on her chin as they part.

Nikki walks down the corridor, she turns "*Don't forget The Arrival Party in The Gala Salon*" she shouts after Ray.

Ray turns around "*The Arrival Party... you said?*" he looks away an instant "of course not, *see you!*" he cheers.

Ray arrive early at Elisabeth, the door is open to the front office.

The secretary salute Ray with a bright smile "You can go straight in" she says with a polite gesture.

The office is empty, he takes a seat as he looks around, nothing have changed the same green lamp on the desk.

Ray rub his hands together 'Any security issues?' he thinks and look down at his shoes, 'maybe I dropped something in the apartment, or someone saw us...?"

Elisabeth and Hellman walk into the office, talking about the coming entry into Jupiter's orbit.

Elisabeth close the door and takes her seat behind the desk "Hello Ray" she salutes with a friendly smile.

Hellman sits down next to Ray, on the way he gives Ray a clap on the shoulder.

Ray rub his pant-legs "Hello" he mutter, he notices Hellman sit relaxed in the chair. He closes his eyes for a moment and feel a release of inner tension.

Elisabeth tap her fingertips together as she begins "Well, Security found Dr. Sheehaus dead in the new apartment section, yesterday" she looks searching a Hellman and Ray. "From what we know, he fell out of his apartment window and died from the fall."

Hellman and Ray nod understanding, and she continues "The apartment is clean without a trace of the work he has been doing there for months..." she pauses for a moment still searching Hellman and Ray.

"Dr. Sheehaus was working on probing the signal coming from one of Jupiter's moons..." she empathizes reaching down at her attache case pulling out a portfolio. "It is a grave situation as he was the soul person knowing how to unlock the signal" she places the portfolio on the table.

Ray move gently to the side and read the title on the portfolio >THE JOVIAN SIGNAL<

Elisabeth looks at Hellman "Hellman and I have talked about letting you in on the case" she slides the folder over to Ray. "Read this" she invites.

As Ray read the documents, they sit quiet watching him. Ray looks up from reading the papers "So, we are looking for extraterrestrial life?"

Hellman nods at Ray "*Maybe?*" he deludes, "the signal seems to be man made, you see..." he hesitates.

"What is my part?" Ray asks direct looking at Hellman then at Elisabeth.
Elisabeth fix her eyes at Ray's "Fist there is a lot at stake, what you have heard and read her stay her, *understood!*" she urges.

Ray straitens up as he nods "*Of course*" he affirms.

Elisabeth continues "You will plan our expedition on Ganymede"

Ray gasps as he lean back on the chair "Pl.. Plan an expedition to Ganymede?" he stutters.

Elisabeth and Hellman smile confirming at Ray.

At night The Gala Salon is packed with people, at the stage a noisy band play oldies and the dance floor are waving and rolling to the music.

Ray enters the hallway and look for Nikki, a couple of ladies from work grab him from behind "*Come on Ray lets dance*" they tease him.

He spins around and wrests himself free "*Later girls*" he laughs.

Nikki stand watching, she walks over to him with a big smile "You got a lot of admires" she flirts and drag him with her onto the dance floor. They dance energetic to the beat.

The stars move in front of the panoramic window as Daedalus turns. Jupiter comes gliding in from the side till it fills the entire view, the dance floor freeze, and the music stops.

They stand full of stupefaction "**Wow**" the gathering stun. Everybody stares at Jupiter's vastness with a feeling of falling into its abyss of vibrant colors in shades of white, orange, brown and red.

The music kick in and the dance gets intense. Dancing into orbit.

Expedition on Ganymede

Ray sits in his armchair watching through the skylight, sipping his morning tea. They are at the furthest orbit approach and faint sunlight shine behind a dark Jupiter as the glow in the dust rings draw lines in the darkness of space.

'What a bizarre sight' he thinks observing the waning crescent Io 'The sweetheart dressed in pail yellow...' he recalls melancholic. Then looking back at Ganymede it reflects a vague sunlight from its light brownish color with a blue aurora surrounding below its poles. Ray get inspired from the sight of Ganymede and writes on his pad:

> Beautiful young boy disguised as an eagle, flying on the Jupiter sky.
> Dressed as a humble devout, yet aesthetic dancing above.
> Carrying the ice-blue crown of light, sparkling all the colors hue.
> Lighthouse of Jupiter's might, protector of lovers delight.

He sends the poem to Nikki, and see it's late. 'Today we will change orbit from Jupiter to Ganymede's rear side' Ray remember as he gets dressed in a hurry.

At work Ray reread the portfolio Elisabeth gave to him. He lean back in the chair gazing at the sealing, close his eyes and ponders over the file he read.

'They send a probe to Jupiter, just like Nikki said, and it found the radio signal coming from a source on the moon Ganymede. What kind of source? It says the radio signal got earth made signature, strange, no one have never landed on Ganymede.'

Hellman comes over to Ray's desk, he looks at Ray sitting inclined toward the sealing, Hellman gently moves a chair and sit next to him.

The resound from the chair bring Ray back from his woolgathering. He opens an eye and see Hellman at his side "Hello" Ray salute as he moves to a proper posture on his chair.

Hellman looks at the open file on the desk "What do you think?" he asks.

"I don't know?" Ray reply thoughtful, "who send a probe to land on Ganymede?" he asks and pull a document over to Hellman.

Hellman takes a deep breath as he glances at the paper "No one, that's the enigma... a probe was crashed into Ganymede back in 34 that's all" he argues and lean back. "Sheehaus said it was a encrypted signal with a human signature..." he pauses, "... or simulating one."

"You mean an alien replica of a human signal?" Ray question.

Hellman flap his hand dismissive "Maybe?"

They sit silent for a moment, glancing at the papers on the table.

Ray look at his pad for no reason "What human signature, did he say?"

"Yeah... Russian, an old soviet protocol, he said" Hellman catch eye contact, then shrug his shoulders "but USSR didn't have tech to land on a Jupiter moon, **too knotty**" He dismisses.

"So, the soviet spacecraft signal was encrypted, and you needed a code to read it, right?" Ray ask eagerly.

"*No*" Hellman lean back waving off the question, "not as far as I know, no one encrypted the radio at that time."

Ray looks down at the table "Then what kind of signal encryption?" he asks a bit strained.

"An old voice protocol with a digital encryption algorithm" Hellman glance up at the sealing, "we need to know the algorithm and its code to decrypt the signal..." he hesitates, "Sheehaus said he had both the algorithm and the code, but he left nothing at his study..."

"Serious!" Ray burst and look away. 'We found the algorithm at the apartment... and the code where could it be?' he ponders.

Hellman clear his throat and stand-up "We know the signal come from the

Apophis crater on the surface. You just need to go down there and dig the *thing* out of the snow!" he turns and walk back to his desk.

"*I need to go down there?*" Ray laments at Hellman's back.

He lean back in the chair gazing at the sealing again. 'If we get the code, we will know what it's all about without going down there, *Brogan?*'

Ray sits up 'Who is Brogan, did he have the code? Sheehaus and the man who killed him both named Brogan, and I read something too...' He fetches his pad and search the name and address, he gets one result on Daedalus:

> Thomas T. Brogan, Comm Id 3111#2
> Solicitor
> Grand Plaza Palace, Suite 204
> Daedalus

After work, Ray takes the transporter to the Hotel-section. He walks down the main corridor to the Saymora Administration, in front of it he stops and watches The Grand Plaza Palace Building.

'*What a monument!*' he quizzes. The facade is in New Renaissance style with all its ornaments.

He enters the building and stand in the large hall for a moment. A large lamp hangs majestic in the center of the second floor sealing all the way down to first floor.

Ray study the pendent as he takes the wide curving stairs up to second floor, two steps a time, he finds door 204 and ring the bell.

The door opens and to his surprise he stands in front of the man with the neckerchief.

The man is equal surprised seeing Ray, he jumps at Ray grab his neck strangling him, pulling him into the lobby.

Ray can't breathe, by reflex he punches the man in his stomach and get free, they both grasp for air a moment.

A blow in the side hurl Ray into the man, they both tumble onto the floor. Another blow hit Ray in the back he rolls to the side in pain and avoid the third blow from a golf iron. The swing hit the man's head next to Ray, a spurt of blood *splash* onto Ray's chin.

Brogan throws the iron on the floor and stumble back a step "**What have I done!**" he cries out covering his face with his hands.

Ray gets up supporting his back pain.

They stare at the man laying dead between them.

Brogan look pail "*Oh dear how could I?*" he moans, "I shall miss my Gadin."

Ray look upset at Brogan "*I will not*" he reproaches.

Brogan look up at Ray "Oh it is you... I thought it was a burglar" he agonies and tighten his housecoat.

"A burglar don't ring the doorbell before entering" Ray bark and step over the man on the floor, "you know me?" he questions.

"Your face popped up a couple of times..." Brogan confirms.

Ray wonder how his face popped up "*... Where did I pop up, exactly?*" he asks flickering a bit.

Brogan look directly at Ray "At our board meetings, mostly Mr. Enatsu and I" he says with conceit.

Ray narrow his eyes "What a pitiful waste of time... and why are your little roommate following me all the time?"

"*Now Mr. Barton*" Brogan rage in a pitch-tone, then gain self-control, "... we need to talk to your friend Mr. Wang, we know he has the information we need" he says severely.

A playful smile grow on Ray's face "May it by any chance be the *code* you are looking for?" he asks with a wide grin.

Brogan look tense at Ray "Yes, so he told you..." he hesitates, "... we know he brought it onboard, and he asks quite an amount for it!"

Ray stretch his back "No he did not tell me, *you just did!*" he objects and shrug his shoulders.

"*Don't get smart-ass with me*" he hisses. "*Um,* my client is among the most capable organizations on earth. We will get hand on this alien technology one way, or the other" he boss. Looking down at Gadin on the floor sprout his arrogance. "Reverse engineering their tech will give us a power leap beyond comprehension" he takes a deep breath as he forcefully overlooks Gadin's body.

Ray see he got Brogan talking hot "You knew Henrik Hoffman, right?" he suggests.

Brogan can't stop looking down at Gadin "The poor man got his investments wrong, and my client needed his loan repaid. Then he, sort of, became the mean to the goal" he responds moodily.

"You mean the *payment* for the *code?*" Ray embolden.

"You are sharp minded Mr. Barton" Brogan blurt, "if you will excuse me I'll have to call security to clean up the mess." He fetches his pad and select the call "Hello Mark ... yes, yes I heard that ... My dear Gadin had an accident, yes, he slept on the floor, and now he's dead ... right ... here in my hallway ... you will ... thank you" Brogan disconnects.

An arm jerks as Ray listened in to the call. "Well, I see you are busy golfing" he step closer to the doorway, "thanks for the chat" he salutes and hurry down the stairs.

Ray sits on the bench in the park when Nikki calls, he smiles at the pad.

"I am at your cabin, where are you?" Nikki object.

Ray takes a deep breath "Just dazing here in the park" he laughs light-hearted.

"*What?*" Nikki burst out, "you never daze!" she giggles.

Ray stand-up "5 minutes, and I'm there, okay?"

"Alright" she mumbles and disconnect.

Nikki waits at Ray's door, as he exits the transporter she waves a hand downwards "Where have you been all afternoon?" she smiles uncertain.

Ray smiles back as he enters the cabin with Nikki following behind.

"You got filth in your face?" She questions and point at Ray's chin.

"*Oh really?*" Ray goes wash it off in the kitchen and make them tea.

Moving the pot casually he turns over a cup, it ends on the floor with a crash. "Did you like my poem?" Ray asks as he clean up the mess he just made.

Nikki observe Ray discreetly "Yes, thank you" she nods, "where did you find it?" she sits down in the armchair and turns on the exterior panoramic view 'It is a bit like being home' she thinks watching the craters on Ganymede.

Ray stiffen "*I composed it!*" he gasps, "can't you tell?" he stares clueless at Nikki.

Nikki turn her sight at Ray "Honest*ly, you composed it?*" she hesitates, "but it's great"

Ray still stand rigid "*But it's great?*, thank you" he complains.

"**No, no,** *I love it*" Nikki jumps up "*Oh, you wrote me a poem*" she rush over and throw her arms around Ray's neck and kiss him.

The kissing and closeness of Nikki carry Ray away he feels like he has recovered something long time lost. He moves her over to the sofa.

Nikki leaps to the side "*Let's have tea*" she urges and go to the kitchen.

Ray watch her every movement and feel like he has rediscovered something valuable 'Wow, she's so beautiful, so lovely' he thinks and notice how she glows.

Nikki brings the tea and sit close to Ray, she lean against him and fall into his arms.

They kiss again...

In the morning Ray wake up lazily rubbing his eyes. He takes a look at Nikki still sleeping next to him 'How passionate you are girl. I love you' he thinks and feel his heart beating.

He kisses her head, the smell of her hair makes him smile and he slip out of bed.

Ray go preparing tea. "Good morning" Nikki smiles, hugging him tight.

They sit in the kitchen having breakfast with the morning news in the background.

Ray glances into the living room and feel worried "Today... we will lower the elevator down on Ganymede's surface" he clamors.

"Yeah, they said that" Nikki nod at the wall-screen as she reaches for a second toast, "that is great, isn't it?" she mumbles still eating.

Ray sip his tea "Yes I suppose so" he smiles at Nikki.

Nikki stiffen "*Look at that!*" she points at the wall-screen where she has changed to the doc-channel.

The Reporter talks about Ganymede's formation showing images from a drone gliding low over Ganymede's landscape of tarnished ice.

The drone passes a shining white valley molded by a meteor impact ages ago. The rim of sediments forms an ice-mountain, that the hover-drone struggle to clime.

Large cracked ice-sheets rise as walls at the sides reflecting a snowy blue light. Below the rim the landscape divide into canyons and plains. A grooved terrain in milk brown gloss with ice-crystals forming bright frosty dunes.

Nikki glances at Ray "*Wow*, look at that Ray" she giggles, "amazing isn't it?"

Ray rub his chin "*Um*, yes" he nods and think about going down there. Now it looks cold and hostile to him at first he was excited to go hiking in the snow. But Ganymede is not like climbing a mountain back home. Down there they need to walk in a spacesuit carrying oxygen.

Nikki turns up the sound, the Reporter continue "Ganymede is tidally locked, like Earth's Moon, meaning the same side of Ganymede always faces Jupiter. Making it possible to install the space-elevator as back home on the Moon."

Nikki straighten "*Just like home!*" she yelps joyful and reach out for Ray's hand.

Ray smile seeing Nikki so happy.

The documentary continues "Below Ganymede's ice-sheet is a vast ocean it has more water than all the water combined on Earth.

Ganymede has a tiny magnetic field, it reconnects constantly with Jupiter's stronger field creating an impressive blue aurora around the poles..."

Nikki stands-up as she asks the screen to turn off. "Time to go" she chants.

Ray take Nikki's hand as they walk down the corridor to work.

At the office, Ray encounters a febrile activity, he sits at his desk looking around. He spot Hellman at the engine control and Elisabeth and Sabine at the command board. An alarm sound in a gentle but loud voice repeating "Alert out of trajectory." At the main wall-screen an icon red-flash with orbit data rolling down the screen.

"Are we on automatic?" Elisabeth burst out.

"Yes, all the time" Sabine confirm, "*we are drifting out of stationary orbit*" he continues stunned.

"Ship - *Take her out*" Elisabeth command to the Ship-control.

The alarm stop as Daedalus gets back to Lagrange point 2.

Sabine gazes past the wall-screen and turn toward Elisabeth "Ganymede's Hill sphere is wobbling do to the tide pull from the moons Europa and Callisto." He jabs his finger at the orbit control "we need faster station-keeping."

Elisabeth looks toward Hellman, "Override with full plasma ejection" she command over the intercom. Hellman confirms with a nod.

"Ship - Bring her back down to our docking position" Elisabeth command.

A total silence fill the office, everyone are fixed at the wall-screen showing the trajectory data as they descend toward Ganymede.

Hellman wave at Ray to come over.

Ray strolls over to Hellman "Um... what is causing the drifting?" he asks shaking his head toward Elisabeth.

"*Yes*, we got trouble maintaining position, this is the third attempt" Hellman jeer at Ray and glance toward Elisabeth.

"Do... do to Ganymede's gravity pull?" Ray ask uncertain.

"*No*, maybe the change in the axial tilt, I don't know" Hellman respond as he looks fixed at the wall-screen.

The screen flash a green bar 'Locked' with the Ship-control announcing "Locked in possession."

The background on the wall-screen change from blue-gray to the external view, Ganymede appear bleak compared to the pouring Jupiter light shining next to it drowning out the stars.

Ganymede is patched with icy craters, they seem so vivid forming bright mountain rims standing out from the long dusk shades on the brunet plains.

"Wow that's it!" Ray rejoice enchanted by the sight.

Hellman responds with a hopeless smile.

Elisabeth turns toward the office, everybody cheers relieved, she looks at Hellman who return a thumb-up.

"Let's bring it down" Elisabeth command over the intercom.

Hellman nod confirming and call the crew at the port-module "Lower the elevator platform" he command.

With a laud "***irrrrr***" sound the cables begin slowly to lower the platform pulled by Ganymede's gravity.

"*Follow me*" Hellman snap sharp, and walk to his work desk.

Ray follows behind 'What's up with him today' he thinks and sit on the chair in front of the desk.

Hellman takes a deep breath "It takes twelve days for the platform to lower down to the surface" he looks intense at Ray. He continues "We use the breaks on the cables all the time, a lot of stress on the pulley-blocks too..." he rubs his chin, still searching Ray for any understanding.

"You are afraid of overheating?" Ray ask leaning a bit forward.

"I'm afraid of the whole thing!" Hellman burst out and lean back in the chair, "the elevator was designed as a stationary installation not as a crane."

Ray nod thoughtful "Right... Can the elevator function as a crane?" a feeling of uncertainty grow within.

Hellman looks down at the table "It's... We must lower the platform down so precisely that it come to a stop just above the surface, without crashing against the ground." He gets eye contact with Ray, "All depend on Elisabeth, only the ship engines can add the needed counter force to keep us up."

Ray freezes a tight smile "To keep us up? Um.. you say we may be pulled down?"

Hellman cross his arms tight "Well, once the platform is anchored at Ganymede. The Spaceship need to stay stationary above it, or we will be pulled down by the drag on the cables."

"But, so it was on the moon too, right?" Ray light up.

"L2 is a unstable orbit..." Hellman pause and continue serious, "You got a week to present the expedition plan, any progress?" he boss.

Ray narrow his eyes "The expedition plan? Yesterday you mentioned something about a Rover?" Ray observe Hellman, he looks disturbed 'Something he is not telling is nagging him' he thinks.

Hellman glances at the wall-screen then fixed at Ray "Elisabeth was informed by Ben from security that Mr. Mark, had told him of a plan to mutiny" he pauses. "Have you heard any rumors about that?" he lean closer to Ray.

Ray stiffen "Mutiny? Here on Daedalus?" he gasps shaking his head puzzled. Hellman nods quietly "Some construction workers from the new-section, apparently for the purpose of selling the ship to a corporation from Earth" he argues.

Ray sit gazing clueless at Hellman.

Hellman continues "Elisabeth told me to watch Kei Enatsu closely" he hesitates "let me know if you hear anything, and lips tight!"

Ray looks down at the table "And the Rover?" he asks quietly.

"Oh yes, I'll send the info to you, let me know when you have sketched a plan" he takes his pad and start reading something.

Ray sit watching him reading for a while, he feels routed out and without a word he returns to his desk.

Ray shake his head 'Mutiny?' he dismisses and change his thoughts to how the expedition may work out. 'We will lower the Rover with all aboard, once down on the surface we drive to the target'. He writes a note...

'At the target we stay two to three days, we need spacesuits, mountain gear and a selection of hand tools'. He makes a note.

'Then, we drive back to the Elevator and a safety factor of 2'. Note it down.

He glances at his list 'A total of 10 days, not bad'. He lean back on his chair with his hands behind the neck.

A mail pup on his pad from Hellman. Kareem is refitting the Moon Rover in the docking-port, and he sends one of his private memos with an equipment list.

Ray gets up and wave confirming at Hellman as he leaves the office for the Port stall.

The bright ceiling light makes the yellow painted Moon Rover look like an exhibition object. Ray walks leisurely round it as he fascinated studies the eight wheeled truck, it is strapped to a trolley platform at its four corners.

"Hello Ray!" Kareem cheers hanging out the cargo door of the Rover.

Ray burst into a bright smile "Hello Kareem, can you give me a ride?" he jokes with a laugh.

Kareem stretch his hand out and help Ray up the door-ramp "I believe Bukari got license to drive this thing" he enthuses, "let me take you around."

He pass a low door into the cockpit "This old Moon truck is a self-sufficient camper" he looks back at Ray. "From the cockpit you control everything, driving, communication, life-support, hatches, roof-cam you name it, even the radioisotope unit" he points at the switches.

Ray takes the driver's seat "How much oxygen does it carry?" he accidentally pokes a switch a light flash with a strange sound coming from the back. He flip it off as fast as he turned it on. "*Sorry*" Ray look out the side window.

Kareem moves around behind Ray "Hmm... The Rover takes twelve people for four or five days" he explains, and lean over to see, which switch Ray activated "the waste dump" he mumbles to himself.

Ray look back at Kareem "I was thinking taking four people down with the Rover, on a ten-day expedition."

Kareem nod "We will bring the Rover down first, it is quite heavy, loaded with equipment and food. Thereafter, the expedition team take the elevator down."

Ray gets up from the driver's seat "Good, load it for four persons on a two-week Expedition" he pledges and shake hand with Kareem as he leaves.

In the morning Hellman wave at Ray to come over to his desk. 'He looks pleased today' Ray thinks fetch his pad and walk over and take a seat in front of him.

Hellman race his hand as he answers an incoming call. "Yes, yes we will be ready, right, see you at 300" he keeps eye contact with Ray the whole conversation.

'It's Elisabeth' Ray think and keep the eye contact with Hellman.

"The elevator platform are almost down at the surface" Hellman says and lean in on Ray, "tomorrow we will discuss your Expedition Plan. If it gets through, which I think it will, we will bring down the Moon Rover to Ganymede."

Back from the meeting Hellman walks over to Ray's desk and pad him on his shoulder. "Splendid work" he encourages and take a seat next to Ray,

"Elisabeth loved your Expedition Planning…" he paused "just, she insists Sabine to be part of your team."

Ray jerk his head back awestruck "But he has no EVA training, *I need skills!*"

Hellman turn his chair "Listen Ray, Sabine have a lot of skills. He is a very bright man you will need him to troubleshoot when you get to the sight of the signal. Who knows what you find? Besides, Sabine stay in the Rover all the time!" he says with sympathy.

Ray look at his pad on the table "Well yes he's canny, I know" he begs off.

Hellman turns on a wide grin "*Settled!*" and stands up, "They will load the Rover onto the elevator this afternoon" he comments and return to his desk.

Through the window in the airlock door Ray watch the two crawler-drones move the Rover onto the elevator in zero gravity.

He stares past the window till it bluer 'How do I tell Nikki that I'm going down on Ganymede?' He laments, and gets distracted 'Strange, It's as if I saw people inside the Rover?' he shakes his head in unbelief.

He stays watching until the elevator close its doors and start its descend. 'No, it must have been an illusion' he concludes.

He walks all the way on second floor down to the Botanic Club. The bartender smile happy to see Ray "*The gray haired man was here the other day, Ray!*" he stresses.

A tentative smile build on Ray's face "*When exactly?*" he gasps.

The bartender look at the glass he's polishing. "A couple of days ago, he had a young lady with him" he replies rapidly with a grin as he pulls Ray a drink.

The door at Nikki's cabin open as it recognizes Ray "Hi Nikki, I got a takeaway for us." He embraces her and they kiss passionate.

Nikki takes the bag "Aha, you have been at the crew bar again, I told you not to buy food there, its so expensive." She looks into the bag curiously "uhmm it smells good, fried chicken limbs. What's the honor?" she giggles and look searching at Ray.

Ray smile joyful to see Nikki so happy, but feels the tension grow and take a step back. "Um, we go down on Ganymede tomorrow." He runs his hand through the hair observing Nikki.

Nikki drops the bag on the sofa table *"Are you going down on Ganymede without telling me?"* she shudders.

Ray look surprised at her, as he tries to find a response "Well no, we are talking about it now, right?" he flaps his hands out to the side and change subject, "We will need the papers we found in the new section, Dr. Sheehaus's encryption algorithm."

Nikki gazes toward the sealing with a deep breath before she draws the envelope from beneath the sofa table. "Here take it", she hands the envelope to Ray and goes to the kitchen.

Ray hesitate then walk over and give Nikki a hug "We are going down with the Moon Rover, I will be back within a week."

Nikki hug him back "I'll wait for you" she whispers sad.

At night a side-way shaking followed by a creepy metallic sound *"**iiirrrr**"* pull Ray and Nikki out of there sleep.

Nikki jumps up in the bed *"**What was that?**"* she cries out and grab Ray's arm.

The shaking continue but less intense.

Ray and Nikki get an Alarm on their pad simultaneously. Ray searches for his pad on the floor >EMERGENCY ALARM, join your quarter< he read it out aloud.

Nikki looks perplexed at the wall-screen where the same alarm popup "**An emergency!**" she quivers.

Ray leaps out of bed and dress fast. "**Get dressed**" he yells at Nikki. She jumps into her clothe, next to nothing they run down the corridor.

People run dedicated in both directions on the corridor. Some dressed in first response outfit wearing oxygen pack and masks other wearing spacesuits carrying their helmets.

At the office they see Elisabeth and Hellman running to the Command Board, and people come pouring in ad-lib and take their seats.

"What is it?" Elisabeth rage.

Hellman reads the elevators drive log, "An high electric current is flowing from the stratosphere down the elevator-cables to the lower atmosphere. It has fried the elevators heat elements that keep the gear and breaks warm. Coursing the main shaft to brittle from the low temperature" he looks up at Elisabeth. *"The elevator is in a free fall!"* he exclaims, holding tight to the handrail.

The elevators emergency breaks kick-in every second, making Daedalus shiver. Suddenly the Breaks hook into the cables and bring the elevator's fall to a sudden stop. The forceful stop pull Daedalus down on a collision course toward Ganymede.

Elisabeth gets thrown to the floor, she grips onto the handrail and pull herself up.

The alarm repeats "Alert out of trajectory, Alert out of trajectory, ..."

*"**Ship – Take us out**"* Elisabeth yell to the Ship-control.

The alarm continues.

She looks desperate at Hellman then at Ray "Ray go to the elevator-port and blow the elevators explosive bolts, **NOW!**" she turns and waves at Kareem "**Follow Ray**" she yells.

Ray and Kareem run down to the port and enter the weightless Port module, past the entrance they gaze for any emergency indications. Kareem receives a pad call, "Yes, right. Yes I see it now."

Ray wonder why Hellman call Kareem and not him. "What?" he asks as Kareem disconnect the call.

Kareem set off to the back wall "Over here" he calls back.

A large handle behind a glass panel is marked >Elevator Safety Disconnect<

"That's it?" Ray ask. Kareem nod confirming.

Ray knocks the glass out and pulls the handle without hesitation.

BOOOM - Daedalus shake from the explosions. Part of the suspension section of the elevator wrest itself lose from the ship and fall toward Ganymede's surface.

Daedalus start to accelerate upward free from the weight of the elevator cables and with all engines on full thrust. Kareem and Ray fall toward the wall from the sudden shift in gravity pull.

"Let's get out of here" Ray shout, they crawl toward the exit in the low acceleration gravity.

123

The Crash Site

Kareem and Ray enter the office everything seems quiet. Ray looks around perplexed "Where is everybody?" he asks the first one he meet.

The woman smile at Ray "At the meeting, they will transmit universal any moment" she replies pointing at the wall-screen and hurry on.

At Ray's desk, Nikki jumps up and hug Ray as soon as she sees him "You saved us" she sniffs and kiss him. She looks a Kareem "Thank you, Kareem, if it wasn't for you..." she sniffs again.

The wall-screen brighten up with Elisabeth seated in her office wearing her uniform upright, a couple of seconds pass.

Silence conger every corner of the ship as everyone stare at the screens.

Elisabeth speaks in a formal tone "Dear fellow crew and guests, as Captain on Spaceship Interplanetary Explorer Daedalus. I have an important announcement to make. We have just saved ourselves from shipwreck on Ganymede, in doing so, we lost our space-elevator and equipment stored onboard it. We will move to the moon Callisto after an initial damage evaluation. At Callisto the radiation from Jupiter is low enough for external maintenance. The ship will stay on high alert, and you will be informed as our situation develop. Thank you for everyone's contribution to our recovery."

Hellman and Sabine returns to the office, they walk direct over to Ray's desk where Ray, Nikki and Kareem discuss what to do next.

Hellman interrupts their conversation "Great work lads!" he looks affirming at Ray and Kareem, then at Nikki "Nikki, you took the Emergency diploma, right?" he asks as he studies her firmly.

Nikki feels intimidated by his gaze, she hesitates and glance at Ray "Yes, but I haven't any assigned post" she eludes.

Hellman bright up "Oh, but you do" he smiles and continue "you are assigned to fly the Relief Shuttle, *right?*" he booms and move closer to Nikki.

Nikki leaning on to Ray wonder what Hellman imply "Yes, I took virtual flying lessens as specialty at the Emergency course, and?" Hellman catch eye contact with Ray "Nikki, you passed with degree of excellence, the best on Daedalus, that's why" he cheers with a grin.

Ray look surprised at Nikki and give her a gentle hug.

Hellman get serious "We need you to fly to the back side of the shield and take a look at the damage. This close to Jupiter the radiation is too great for a space walk" he hesitates looking firm a Nikki "*You need to go now!*"

Hellman and Sabine stand watching Ray, Nikki and Kareem leaving the office. Hellman look surprised at Sabine "What are you waiting for, you are a pilot too" he gestures at Sabine to go with them "**get moving**" He booms.

Sabine run down the corridor and catch the transporter door as it's about to shut.

Nikki pushes the button signed >Emergency<, and the transporter takes them up past second floor into the Relief Shuttle and open the door inside the passenger compartment.

The low gravity make walking awkward, Nikki and Sabine moves determined down the idle between rows of vertical seats.

Ray pause and adapt his eyes to the dim red light, he studies the interior of the Shuttle. The passenger compartment is a large ovoid room with the air lock at one side, and the cockpit door at the other of the ovate shortest distant. The compartment is filled with seats suspended upright, 'They look like standing stretchers, there's room for a lot of people' he thinks.

Kareem locks the external door to the transport-tube. "The crew strap-in standing, it gives room for more people" he explains as he pass Ray, he ties himself to a stretcher.

Ray continues down the idle and enters the cockpit. Nikki and Sabine sit in the only two pilot seats "Very comfortable in here" he greets.

Nikki smiles at Ray "Strap yourself in" she nods with a bright grin toward Kareem behind them.

The Shuttle detach from Daedalus with a little judder. Nikki steers the Shuttle away from the docking.

Ray stays in the cockpit doorway watching the inner-ring of Daedalus with lights sparkling from all the small skylight windows. It seems as if the habitat-rings rotate faster as they move closer to the center. He holds on to a handle and float weightless as he studies the Star-lounge windows. They look smaller from outside than he recalls, and the new-section have a faint ring of light from the corridor skylights centering the ceiling.

The Shuttle moves out of the habitat-ring sections. Ray get absorbed by the sight of the vast dark space. 'Dad had told him that the Lifeboat had never been flown and that nobody knew if it actually worked... *well here we are!*' he concludes. As they turn he gets overwhelmed by the sight of Jupiter they glide along Daedalus's metallic blue-gray radiation shield. Straight in front of them is Ganymede covered in bright gray and brownish colors. Jupiter posture huge with a chromatic orange at the left with the moon Europa shining like a silver pearl between.

They reach the end of the shield, the ionized cloud from the huge engines light up with a thin turquoise hue.

Nikki look back at Ray "We better make distance to the engines and get a view from the side" she asserts mindfully.

"Can you give me a video link?" Hellman ask iffy over the intercom.

Ray move closer to the window making a video with his pad, "Hellman, you see this..." he films the back side of the shield. "A piece of the elevator cable are still attached" he snap upset, "look, some tiles have been ripped off too."

"Right, the cable seem to be attached to what is left of the suspension" Hellman respond dry. "We will meet with Elisabeth when you get back in, over and out." He disconnects.

Ray lean over Nikki's seat "Take us all the way round the engines and then bring us back home" he urges. He films the backside of the shield as they circle around it. 'What a disaster, even the elevator suspension was torn off, and the surrounding tiles'.

Ray keep filming Nikki as she steers the Shuttle back to the docking-port. Nikki shakes her head flattered "Come on Ray give me a break" she coo.

Back at Daedalus they walk direct to the conference room. Hellman stands at the door absorbed by his pad, he step one step back without looking up, making room for them to enter.

Ray find his name-tag next to Nikki seated at his right.

Elisabeth enters and begin the meeting straightaway "I can confirm that we got the elevator suspension damaged, we continue under coercion with reduced speed to Callisto. Hellman, give us your damage report" she bid.

Hellman fumbles with his pad "Our team took this video today." He cast the video on the wall-screen, "As you can see many tiles are missing near the elevator section. Sad to say it is impossible to replace them as the damage is too extensive. Therefor the Port module will be sealed off due to high radiation..."

Elisabeth interrupt "And what's left of the elevator?" she asks weary.

Hellman turns off the video as it show Nikki in a closeup p ic. He continues "The elevator suspension need further inspection, we will see how to disconnect the cable stub when we reach Callisto."

Elisabeth looks firm at Hellman "We need that suspension disconnected before our return trip, *get the work done!*" she barks.

Hellman cross his arms defiant, "*Yep!*" he groans with a shrug of his shoulders.

Elisabeth takes a sip of water and turns to Nikki "You piloted the Relief Shuttle?" she asks sharp and meet her eyes.

Nikki break eye contact and glances at Ray "*Yees?*" she drags her answer.

Elisabeth looks up at all around the table "The Relief Shuttle was designed by the mining company for emergency flight from the Moon with reentry to the Earth. Ganymede's escape velocity is a bit more than the Moon back on Earth", she takes a deep breath. "What I want to say is that the Relief Shuttle can take us down to Ganymede and back up to Daedalus."

She looks direct at Nikki with a proud expression.

Nikki lean back in her chair and covers her mouth "*No way?*" she gasps.

Elisabeth looks seriously around the table "Last night Mr. Mark was detained in his cabin for plans of mutiny. He claimed the whole thing was a scam. But, in his office was found a list with names of officers, crew and workers labeled *faithful*" she pauses and look at each person. "None of your names was on that list" she smiles confirming and leave the room.

Ray lean in on Nikki "I never liked that ghoul" he whispers.

In the morning Ray and Nikki takes the transporter into the Relief Shuttle. Bukari work busy strapping down provision. "Good morning" he grab Nikki's arm "You know, the Lifeboat have never flown, who knows if it works?" he clamors.

Nikki smile back "It worked alright yesterday, *don't worry*" she smiles back at Bukari and enter the cockpit.

Ray see Sabine at the back rearranging stretchers as horizontal beds. "You don't like to sleep standing?" he jokes.

Sabine laugh "It reminds me too much of work", they both laugh heartfelt.

Ray stall, and pulls a folded envelope out of his inner pocket "Sabine, I got something you need to help me with..." he takes a seat on a bed and with a gesture invite Sabine to sit down in front.

He glances at Kareem who work at the entrance as he opens the envelope. "I got the encryption algorithm for the signal, we need to find the code" he hands it to Sabine.

Sabine take his time and read through the papers. He shakes his head in disbelieve "Dr. Sheehaus's cryptography research of the signal, how did you get hand on that?"

Ray feel emphatic and scratch his neck "Well it... came into my hands... sort of" he mumbles and point at the papers.

Sabine smiles comprehensive and stand-up. "With a little of luck I find something significant, and can tie some significance to it" he declares and stuff the envelope into his pocket.

Ray turns on a wide grin "Sure you will" he cheers and pull himself up, Bukari calls him from the air-lock.

"*Ray*, I got new climbing gear for you" Bukari lifts a leash into the air, "I've storage the last provision, have a safe trip!" he stresses and leave with the transporter.

Nikki looks back at the air-lock then at Ray and Kareem. They stand strapped in next to the open cockpit door, she got a sense of eagerness to get it over with.

Sabine enter the cockpit and close the door behind him "All clear" he affirms as he tightens the safety belts.

Nikki close her eyes a moment and breath out calmly "Ready for the takeoff" she confirms over the intercom.

"You are clear to go" Hellman repeat decisive.

In the passenger compartment the light dim into red. Ray feels the judder as the Shuttle detach from Daedalus, he gets a sensation of disorientation as gravity begins to twist to the side. Then comes the weightlessness, and he floats loosely in his seat, Ray examines Kareem, he got his eyes closed and seams to be sleeping.

Ray closes his eyes too. The calmness seams endless, no sounds, the intercom is silent, he let the daydreaming takeover. 'Back home he would sit in the veranda rocking gently on the chair as the reddish sunlight warmed his face. Now and then he would open his eyes slightly to see the sun slowly settled behind the trees, as a soft breeze cooled his face...'

He gets distracted from the feeling of acceleration pulling him slightly back into his seat. Ray and Kareem look at each other "We are entering Ganymede's gravity field" Ray mutter.

Kareem hold fast at the suspension "*It is getting stronger*" he cries out, as a vibration begin to shake the Shuttle.

Ray gets pushed harder into his seat, he sees the empty stretchers shake viciously as they tilt backwards from the acceleration.

An alarm sounds from the cockpit "**Add thrust**" Nikki yell over the intercom, "***You are descending too fast, get...***" Sabine rage back, the communication brake up into static noise.

Ray look bewailed at the closed cockpit door then at Kareem as a second alarm adds to the first one.

The noise from the alarms and the shaking continue, it seems to drag on forever.

Then the acceleration begins to ease gradually, '*Finally!*' Ray rejoice, shortly after the shaking ends, Kareem look relieved and give Ray a handshake.

When the alarms stop Nikki giggles on the intercom "Turn the seat belt sign off."

"*Yes mam*" Sabine laughs alleviated.

"Well done" Hellman cheer on the intercom, "you are at the emission sight in less than 10 minutes."

Ray and Kareem strap themselves free and enter the cockpit. The first sight meeting them is the smiles of Nikki and Sabine, from the cockpit windows the landscape of Ganymede surpass below.

Ray stands in the low gravity holding on to Nikki's seat. 'Wow, Ice mountains they are brighter than seen from space'. He contemplates the mosaic of ice rafts and steep grooves in the surface. At places cut by impact craters forming deep valleys circled by high mountain rims of ice and rocks. 'Are there snow or just ice down there?' Ray wonders as the glacial terrain pass faster, the closer they get to the surface.

Ray see something scattered down on the ground "*Look over there*" he calls and point at an object on the ground, "a crash site?" he marvels.

Nikki takes the Shuttle down close to the ground and hover over the site. "Some kind of probe the size of a moon rover" she affirms.

The engine trust creates a plum of dust and vapor from the ground.

Ray's eyes sparkle of excitement "*Take us down*" he rants and moves closer to the window, trying to see through the dense fug. "Let's go take a look" he insists and look a Kareem.

"**You are not at the coordinate yet**" Hellman boom over the intercom.

"We need to see if the object is related to the signal" Sabine affirm with a glance at Ray and Kareem.

"*Alright*, but make it quick, the radiation is high down there" Hellman pledge uncertain.

Ray, Nikki and Kareem stand in the transporter on their way down they wear spacesuits and life-support packs all in light tangerine color. Ray carry his ice axe and a large rope.

Kareem raise his eyebrows "Ray, we are just outing onshore" he slap Ray on his shoulder with a laugh.

Nikki half smiles "You may need it too... who knows" she mutter. The door opens to the outside, Nikki is the first to step out on the frozen surface of Ganymede.

She stands gazing at Jupiter hanging still in the east, the glowing amber dominate the tiny bright flame from the sun.

Nikki takes her first steps, the low gravity make it hard to walk. She nearly stumbles raising a haze of fine dust and ice-crystals that blow away in the light breeze. She hardly lifts her feet when stepping forward and draw a cloud of haze behind her.

Kareem walks with ease setting off in large jumps. "Just like home on the moon" he cheers and make a large jump. The tool bag he carries get in his own way, he falls and glide down a low-angled slope of polished ice "**Ooh**" he cries.

"*Wow*, be careful Kareem. The ice is slippy and watch out for the rocks" Ray boss and flits his gaze from Kareem to Nikki. 'What a kindergarten' he thinks and take the lead toward the crash site.

Nikki follows behind and get the phase, taking small firm steps she advance and reach up beside Ray, followed by Kareem.

The wrecked is scattered over a large area. Centered by some kind of metal cylinder smashed flat by the impact into the steel-hard ice surface.

They walk around among all the scrap covered with a mix of ice crystals and fine sand powder. Nikki dusts a box like piece "*look at this!*" she gasps and look for Ray "Over here I found a strange engraving?" she waves at him to come over.

Ray and Kareem join Nikki to see what she found a piece of metal reflects in her helmet.

"Stay still for moment Ray, I try to see through your head-cam" Sabine inquire over the intercom. "*It's the vault plate from the Clipper probe!*" he cheers.

Nikki carefully studies the engraved signs "It's like a star radiating wave-forms..." she contemplates, "*Ray, screw it off for me, will you? Please!*" she queries softly.

"What will you do with that old piece of junk?" Ray hush and look away. Some movement at the Shuttle catch his attention, he gazes at the Shuttle while trying to make up his mind if he saw something or not. He looks back at Nikki and Kareem, but they are busy unscrewing the vault plate. "*Um, a radiating star?*" he hesitates.

Nikki's eyes glow "Wow, look at that" she shows the back side of the plate to Ray and Kareem.

Ray look at the plate then glance back at the Shuttle "*Aha, circuit instructions?*" tailing off the sentence uncertain. "Let's get back to the Shuttle" he insists edgy.

Nikki are absorbed reading the text "Its a poem..." she coo softly.

With a roaring sound the Shuttle take off, it levitates for a second then accelerate at low altitude and vanish behind a cloud of ice and dust.

Ray, Nikki and Kareem stare incredulous at the frosty cloud, tardily the haze settle, and they see the Shuttle faint into the iffy horizon.

Kareem watch his bio-meter and Nikki flap her arms out in disbelieve "**What?**" she yells. They look at each other, then gaze toward the horizon.

Ray walks a bit away touching his helmet as if he hears better "*Sabine do you here me?*" he calls over the intercom, "*Hellman are you there? Anyone?*" he shakes his head and turn to Nikki and Kareem.

Ray pushes the navigation botton on his bio-meter, then make a quick decision "**Lets walk!**" he command, catching eye contact with Kareem they start walking steadfast.

Nikki follows behind holding on to the engraved vault plate "*Why? Where are we going?*" she asks sharp and shakes her head, "what am I doing here on this dreadful place" she mumbles.

Ray look back at Nikki "We are going to the Apophis crater, the Shuttle flew in that direction" he argues and keep the pace.

The terrain gets ruff with steeper uneven slopes of rocks and ice. Nikki drop further behind, sometimes she has to rest with a hand on the ice to maintain balance, and the plate she carries doesn't make it easier. "**Ray!**" she cries over the intercom, posing a hand on to a large rock.

Ray turn and see how far behind Nikki are. "*Kareem*, wait for a minute" he calls and walk back to Nikki.

He finds the mid-point of the rope and clip it to Nikki's cincture. "Kareem help me out, tie this rope-end to your cincture." Then he clips the other end to himself and strap the vault plate onto his back.

They move steady with tension on the rope. Nikki follows with short easy jumps pulled forward by the rope. "This is great Ray" she cheers gratefully "we are there soon, *right?*" she questions.

Ray move forward with firm steps "Yes... within one day if we can avoid the ravines" he cautions and hesitates a bit. "The sun sets in three days, and the night is too cold for our suit-heating to cope."

"You are a true cheerleader, Ray" Kareem jeer from behind and trow the tool bag off to the side.

A ice-cleft cross in front of them, Ray stops and lean forward peeking over the rim, he shakes his head with a short breath. The ice walls erect deep down into a faint bottom 'no way to cross over' he thinks. He makes a turn and walk along the groove of plain ice and pushed up rocks.

The walking gets easier along the ice edge, Nikki walk faster, and the rope loosen between them. "**Ahhh**" Kareem yell followed by a large sound of rocks and ice falling, the rope stretch and pull Nikki down **"Ray Heeelp"** She glides backward on her back and with a severe force she hit a rock. Her helmet and backpack save her from the heavy blow as she continues being pulled down by the rope.

Ray watches as in slow motion how Nikki glides toward the edge of the rim. He awake by his own reflex, slamming the axe into the ice as an anchor, he throws himself to the ground holding on to the axe.

The rope pull Nikki further back till she gets stuck between two large rocks and get to a brute stop.

Ray fasten his rope to the ice-axe and creep step by step toward Nikki with a firm grip on the rope. There is no sight of Kareem and Nikki lay motionless close to the edge.

He reaches Nikki and place his feet against the rocks "**Nikki?, Kareem?**" Ray calls as he holds the rope firm.

Nikki tries to move but are stuck between the rocks "*Oh my back*" she complains, she looks at Ray "Kareem is pulling me down" she exclaims distressed.

"I can't get a hold on the rope, can you pull me up?" Kareem plead hurt, he hangs facing head down the crevasse cliff.

"*Hold on Kareem*" Ray gasp and pulls the rope till Nikki get free from the rocks. He tightens the leash and clip her free "*Nikki*, clip yourself on to the rope behind me and crawl up to the axe" he exact sharp.

Bruised, Nikki creep back to the anchor of the axe, she sits and check her bio-meter, all seem to be fine.

Ray holds the rope tight as he looks back at Nikki "Are you alright?" he asks.

Nikki smiles "Seems so" she quivers.

Ray plant a foot against a rock embedded in the ice. "Nikki, tighten the leash at the axe whenever it's slack" he direct and begin to pull Kareem up.

Kareem showing his head over the cliff grab the rope and pulls himself back over the rim. He turns with the sound of a lot of hurt and sit next to Ray.

"You look alright to me" Ray smiles watching his own reflection in Kareem's helmet.

Kareem makes the effort to punch Ray on the shoulder, but his arm hurts, and it ends up in an anguish gush.

Ray stands up "We have to get moving" he boss firmly "and keep the leash tight" he tosses commanding. They walk along the edge for a long time, finally, a crater rim forms a natural bridge over the groove. At the other side they reach a plain of rocky dirt and walk steady in the same direction as the Shuttle vanished.

After a dragging walk Ray stops "Look" he gushes and points toward the horizon.

"*The Shuttle*" Nikki cheers as she stands next to Ray.

Kareem comes along "Let's get onboard" he rejoices and take the lead "*hurry!*" He unsnaps the rope and move fast with large hops unto the Shuttle.

The Apophis Crater

Ray and Nikki reach the Shuttle, they stare at the Shuttle laying inclined with the front partially buried in the ground, and the elevator entrance pulled down.

Ray gazes in disbelieve at the Shuttle. 'Someone must have left the vessel' he thinks, "A ruff landing..." he hesitates "...and we are just halfway to the signal sight?" he says quizzed.

Nikki stand and wonder what have happened for the Shuttle to land like this when Kareem return from circling the Shuttle. He race his hands in despair "Its all locked" he mutter feebly at Nikki *"How do we get in?"* he quivers on.

Nikki walks over to the elevator tube, open a hatch on the side and turn a handle *"Voilà"* she smiles, and the elevator door opens.

Kareem, Nikki and Ray enters the elevator, as it moves up into the Shuttle fresh air pulls into the cabin with a whistling sound, once up, the door opens.

Ray glances into the dim reddish light in the compartment, a stripe of sunlight torch through the open cockpit door.

"It looks empty to me" Ray exclaim as he stays in the elevator doorway adapting his sight to the dim light.

Nikki push her way past Ray, she detaches her helmet and run to the cockpit **"Sabine?"** she calls in vain, the Shuttle is empty.

Ray and Kareem following behind "It's all shutdown!" Ray exclaims.

Nikki take seat at the controls and searches the flight logbook. *"He crashed?"* she gasps looking past the cockpit window.

"Why?" Kareem asks looking over Nikki's shoulder at the control screen reading the log data "a power failure..." he stares incredulous at Ray.

"A power failure?" Ray repeat looking around in the cockpit. 'No sign of fighting or damage to the controls' he thinks and walk back to the passenger compartment 'nothing, everything as we left it?'

Nikki switches the emergency communication system on, without luck, she flip the switch a couple of times "The em-comm is dead as well as the voice-comm…" she takes a deep breath "We are without communication" she groans with her head down.

"Can you fix it?" Ray ask eagerly.

"Can I fix the intercom?" Nikki repeat thoughtful, she taps into the command section, "lets try to isolate the power tank" she looks back at Kareem.

Kareem leaves and searches the wall of the passenger compartment till he finds a hatch signed >Power Bank<. He enters halfway into the Power hold.

Ray places the engraved vault plate next to Nikki and follow Kareem.

"*Got it*" Kareem rejoice from inside the hold. He pulls out and sits back on the floor looking up at Ray. "The electric charge in three of the tanks are zero. There is some power left in the fourth tank isolated for life support, everything seems to be alright here…" he pauses and tilt his head wondering "We run out of power, let's check the breaker's too." Kareem walks to the opposite end of the compartment.

"*Nikki*" Ray call as he walks back to the cockpit "*It just ran out of power*" he blazes.

"*I hear you*" Nikki jeer back at Ray.

"Restart the reactor!" Ray boss.

Nikki looks up at Ray "The Shuttle don't have a reactor, *Ray*, it's just a return Shuttle" she nags and turn back taping the controls.

Ray takes a seat next to Nikki, he rubs the back of his neck and wonders how the Shuttle can fly without any power source.

Nikki lean back in her seat in a sagging posture "The communication protocol have been deleted, why would Sabine do something like that?" she asks with a long low sight past Ray.

They sit quiet for a while watching the rocky plain outside. The landscape seems unchangeable at a distance but in contrast in front of the Shuttle a light soundless breeze moves ice-crystals and dust low on the ground.

'The wind always come from the west' Ray conclude from the small dunes of dust on the east side of the scattered rocks.

Nikki reaches out and take Rays hand, she looks Ray in his eyes without a word.

"How dos this thing work, do you know?" Ray asks flat.

Nikki smiles sad "I learned to fly it, not to repair it" she quenches. Then brighten up as she continues "The Shuttle get electric charged from Daedalus before the takeoff. We draw energy direct from the main power line till the field is established, it only takes a few minutes."

Ray lean closer to Nikki "Just enough electricity to keep the ion-drive running for a while... Right?" he smiles agreeable.

Nikki tilt her head "This isn't an old fashion Cargo Pod" she smiles comprehensive at Ray and continue "It uses a Magneto-hydrodynamic thruster!"

Ray nod confirming 'What?' he tries to maintain his understanding expression as he ponders what kind of engine use hydrodynamics. Then he notices the look on Nikki's face and feel embarrassed, and race his shoulders in excuse.

Nikki turns on a playful grin as she studies Ray "The technology was developed on the Moon, but never tested outside the lap... I just know the basic principles to fly the Shuttle" she lean in on Ray as she continues.

"A cluster of charged particles rotate in the cavity there" she points out the window at the front edge of the Shuttle. "They generate a magnetic field that bend inward till it snap at the intense rotation. The magnetic reconnect convert a part of the field energy into kinetic energy. This new matter is repelled in a focused thrust" she notes seriously.

Ray squeeze his eyebrows "How can the magnetic field generate and extracts work from nowhere?" he asks thoughtful.

Nikki waves to the side "By rotating the charged particles the magnetic field lines wrap around themselves in a vortex motion till they snap over and over in cyclic pulses. Generating more kinetic energy thous self containing the magnetic field. Basically the field erases its own memory on a quantum level." Nikki look fixed at Ray to see if he follows her explication. "The excess of particle energy is forced into the magnetic vortex, and ejecting as a concentrated beam... Well, and when within an atmosphere the air is charged by the plasmoids and used as propellant" Nikki ends with a flush across her cheeks.

Ray sit silent for a while "Well, that was impressive Nikki. I must say you know your stuff" he rubs the back of his neck again trying to get a grip of her explanation. Then he looks back at Nikki "Can you start it up?"

Nikki fold her arms across her chest and look surprised at Ray "**I just told you.** The Shuttle get precharge before launch" she objects and leave the cockpit.

Ray gazes out the cockpit windows "Right then, at least we got shelter..." he clamors to himself as his gaze melts away by his thoughts. 'If we hike to Apophis we may find Sabine and even find out what the signal is all about... Had Sabine gone rout?' He tries to envision the moment just before the Shuttle took off. 'Did I see something or not?...'

Kareem pup his head into the cockpit "Come over, we have arranged a food ration for you" he cheers.

Ray look searching at Kareem "How's your arm?"

Kareem touch his shoulder "It's fine" he smiles "lets eat."

After a silent meal they all three sit satisfied on their beds. Ray catch Kareem eyes "Get ready to leave in half an hour. We are going to the signal sight" he command firm and turns at Nikki, "Nikki, you stay here and protect the Shuttle. And, don't let Sabine in without us..."

Nikki stands-up interrupting Ray "*You are so paranoid*" she rages and flaps her hand dismissive "I don't stay here alone, *period*" she leaves furious to the cockpit.

Kareem shake his head as he speaks "You are too tough on Nikki, Ray" he stares seriously at Ray.

Ray look hard at Kareem "*Who* left us behind and *Who* disabled all communications?"

Ray stands-up "*Sabine did!*" he spread his arms out leaning a bit back.

He continues harsh "We need to protect the Shuttle it's key to our survival.

Nikki has to stay behind and guard our back" he insists.

Kareem nods at Ray "I will talk to her" he turns tense and walk to the cockpit.

Ray glances toward the cockpit from time to time as he straps supplies onto a bed. Kareem returns from the cockpit with a serious face, then at a sudden "Let's go" he gushes and swings his helmet triumphing.

Ray turns a large grin on "Let's go hiking" he rejoices and race his climbing gear high.

Nikki watches from the cockpit door "*What a couple of puppets you are!*" she chants and turn back to her seat working at the command board.

Outside on the plain Ray turn and gaze longing at the cockpit window he can't see Nikki but wave at her any way. "See you soon" he salutes without response. He feels bitter the way they left, so few words, he wished he had told her how much he loved her.

"She can't receive voice-comm inside the Shuttle. *Come on*, let's move" Kareem implore and pull the improvised sled out of Ray's hand. He struggles to walk pulling the sled, it bumps up and down on the rocky plain.

"Let's take a corner each" Ray suggest and grab one corner of the bed. The walking got easier, they look at each other and smiles.

Ray look appreciated at the icy landscape as they walk. He has missed hiking for a long time, and feel a desire to take the helmet and gloves off to feel and smell the air. But he knows if he does he will freeze rock solid in an instant.

A mountain in the horizon grow lager and higher as they walk toward it. Ray get worried about its size. He points at the mountain "We have to take a route around it" they pause walking and look at the huge mountain rim in front of them.

Ray studies the navigation route on his bio-meter to the Apophis crater at the coordinate 8°13'S, 84°5'E. "The location of the signal is *on the other side* of the mountain, inside the crater formation" he grunts.

Kareem takes a seat on the sled sipping water from his straw "How about a shortcut between the two peaks on the rim, *there*" he points the direction.

Ray study the slope calmly "It looks steep to me" he ponders. "If we approach from the south crossing north we may get up between the peaks" he points the track in the air.

They click on the rope and start walking at a quick pace. The scree get steeper with an unstable mix of ice litter and loose rocks. Kareem pulls the sled and falls behind tightening the rope, Ray tugs at the rope, annoyed by the dragging speed.

"**Yeah, yeah**" Kareem yell "why don't you take the sled for a change" he rambles.

Ray waits for a moment and stretch the rope lose. As he begins to walk up the steep scree the rope drags through the rubble, loose ice and rock start rolling down at Kareem. "**Careful Ray**" he shouts and fall in the gravel.

Ray stop Kareem from sliding down holding the rope tight. "*You have to stay at the side, not straight below me*" he criticizes and coil the rope back in helping Kareem up at his side.

The climbing get more complex as they get closer to the notch with teetering boulders blocking the sled. The breeze have turned into a fierce wind blowing fine ice and dust up hill, Ray and Kareem drag the makeshift sled over the rocks at their best.

The aura flashes with static discharges thundering over head, as ice crystals sharp as iron chips sand blast them from behind. Ray hide behind a large rock "Let's shelter here" he urges and studies his bio-meter. 'Its taking too much time' he thinks and look for a shortcut on the navigator.

Kareem squeezes in behind the rock "The storm will be over soon, Right?" he appends with an awkward hug at Rays shoulder.

"It has to, we are running out of time" Ray affirms, shielding from the blistering storm.

Kareem stand calm watching the aura storm as he sips his straw till its empty "I'm out of water" he cast a glance at the supplies.

Ray nod "Lets celebrate with soup when we reach the summit" he smiles and unpack a water bag and hand it to Kareem.

Ray glances up into the waving aura, it has begun to lighten. "Let's go" he takes off before Kareem get the new water bag plucked in "we need to gain time" Ray beams optimistic.

The climbing above is easier with short bulges of rocks, they advance with a good rhythm and reach the acme of the notch, ragged from the climb. Ray and Kareem stand dumbfounded watching the grand view high above the smooth crater basin with the awful Jupiter shining a yellow hue on the horizon. A handful of stars sprinkle overhead.

"*Wow*, look at that bright white blanket, down there" Ray cheers and gaze over the rim. 'Steep and sleek' he thinks, but the view erase his worries. He feels trilled as always when conquering a summit.

Kareem shake his head in awe "*Yeah*, it's beautiful" he gushes and hold his arms out to embrace the view.

Ray unpacks a container from the sled. "Let's celebrate with a protein soup" he smiles and offer Kareem to pick one of the two food bags "Mushroom or asparagus flavor?"

They sit quiet on the sled sipping their soup. Ray contemplates the crater rim, the low sunlight cast a shadow down into the basin on the other side of the crater. He searches for any alteration or structure out of the normal.

"**Look**" Kareem stand-up excited and points down toward the left side of the basin "*There's something orange colored moving down there at that small crater*" he cries out.

Ray stands-up too "There's more than one?" he hesitates and look at Kareem searching for an answer. "**Let's go**" he charges and feels his pulse beat harder 'Now its it' he thinks and set off dragging the sled.

Kareem follow Ray down the rubble-pile of ice and rock they pick up the pace partly walking, partly sliding down on the loose gravel. At the base they turn left and walk fast toward the two silhouettes.

"Can you see what it is?" Kareem asks with a forced breathing.

"**Kareem it's you?**" Sabine rejoice on the intercom.

Ray looks at Kareem as they keep walking, he connects from broad transmission to direct transmission. "Switch the comm direct to me" he boss.

Kareem looks dazed at Ray and spread his hands out as a question.

Ray stop walking "*Switch it over*" he command sharply.

Kareem select Ray on the intercom "Sabine sound happy to me?" he replies dazzled.

Ray point in direction at Sabine "We don't know *why* he took off and *who* he is with..." he rush and pause "Let me talk to him, right?" his smile freeze as he waits for Kareem's answer.

Kareem wavers a bit as if he struggles to give in "Right" he mutter.

Ray walks a couple of steps to the side and switch his intercom to general "Hello Sabine how are you?" he asks politely.

"*Hi Ray!*" Sabine cheers.

Ray feel relaxed by Sabine's friendly voice "You went off? Tell me what happened?" he quests.

"You are a true mortal, **Ray!**" Veronica break into the conversation.

Ray shuffle back a step 'Veronica? *How...* She is dead!' he ponders.

"I didn't expect you to make it out here" Veronica continue sinister "have you lost your breath my dear?" she laughs.

Ray feel sick and lack his breath, an overwhelming feeling of anger flush into his veins.

Kareem look dumbfounded at Ray "Are you alright?" He switches the intercom back to broad transmission "**Ray?**"

Ray starts to run toward Sabine and Veronica, he ditches the sled and take up speed.

Veronica watch Ray advancing fast at them. She laughs nervously and look back at the hover-drone. She jumps over to Sabine and wrest a piece of equipment out of his hands, throw it into the storage box on the drone and take off.

The drone accelerate fast and move up the crater slope in an angle.

Ray reach Sabine and bend forward as he catches his breath. He check the oxygen on his bio-meter, then watch Veronica flying off the rim in a hazardous jump, vanishing out of sight.

He turns toward Sabine who try to get up but fall back on the ground. Ray kneels at his side "You are hurt? What happened?" he charges.

Sabine clasp Ray's forearm "*Thank you Ray!*" he gushes and continue "She came suddenly from behind and knocked me out, just like that" he laments.

Ray lean back and search Sabine "Didn't you hear her enter the Shuttle?" he objects.

Sabine look up at Kareem who have come dragging the sled.

"What is that thing?" Kareem points at the crashed wrecked next to Sabine.

Sabine smile at Kareem "It's an old Soviet Lander" he jests and point at the marking on the side of the wreck >CCCP Mapc-7<. He makes a grimace and hold on to his arm.

"What's wrong with your arm?" Kareem asks worried.
Sabine move to a better position, leaning against the wrecked "Its broken, I think... at the crash" he glances down at his arm.

Kareem looks indigent at Ray. Ray nod and begin to unpack the sled. They move Sabine onto the now improvised stretcher and strap him tight.

Ray look keen down at Sabine "How about some soup?" he smiles and plug a protein bag into Sabine's Spacesuit.

"She knocked you out and then what?" Ray continues.

Sabine sip his meal "Next, I woke up as we was crashing. The Shuttle went nose diving and hit the ground throwing me out of the chair" he wavers and glances after Kareem.

Ray looks with unease in the direction where Veronica left 'How did she come down to Ganymede, and even bring a hover-drone with her?' he check his bio-meter again.

Sabine observes Ray thoughtful "She wanted the control box from the lander..., but I only got the radio emitter disconnected... from there" he points at an open panel on the side of the Lander.

Ray brightens up and turn to Kareem "Kareem, we need to dismount the controls" he points at the shipwrecked lander.

Kareem, happy to see Ray in a better mood give him the thumbs-up and drive his head into the Lander and begin clearing out a crunchy fabric covering everything.

Ray pickup a piece of the crispy stuff "What is this stuff? Anyone knows?" he studies the light gray substance, it pulverizes easy in his hands as he save a sample for Nikki in a bag.

Kareem pulls his head out of the hatch "It's kind-off fluffy deep inside, when it freezes it get crunchy, maybe its insulation of some kind?"

Sabine try to say something and flap his hand expelling a grunt in pain with sweat gleaming on his face.

Ray examine Sabine's bio-meter 'Too low blood pressure, he seems to sleep now' he thinks and takes a seat next to Sabine leaning against the lander.

"Kareem, we need to rest and then head back as soon as possible." He tries to rub his face and knows he can't, with a dozy glance at Jupiter high in the distanced sky, he glides into a deep sleep.

Dreaming, Ray sees himself standing naked on the frosty ice of Ganymede, he takes a deep breath, the air smells dry and fresh. Just next to the crashed Lander is a pond of water sparkling in the dim light from Jupiter now settling low in the horizon. He looks further to the side and see Io shining as a giant sliver dot. The whole place looks as conceive from somewhere else and then again he knows he is there together with Sabine and Kareem. He looks around, but they are gone, and he knows it doesn't matter now, everything transcend peace and quiet. The brilliant pond of water draw his attention, the water seems to be warm with a low haze hanging above it.

He feels an irresistible desire to swim in the hot water tub. He let himself glide down into the cozy pool, *oh it's so good*, the hot water is just right a bit salty, but nice.

Swimming around in circles the landscape seem gray and dull. He looks down into the magic water and dive below. The ice walls stand steep radiating a beautiful light emitted from within. He observes the different colors reflecting from the smooth surface, a mixture of opaline-green, -blue and -white. 'Wow, this is fantastic and no difficulty to breath', he giggles with a wildly feeling of entering a drenched utopia. He dives further down with a comfortable feeling and swim down the center of the shaft adding speed.

The walls change shape as he gets further down the icy shaft. They turn from the smooth surface to a pattern of triangular crystals twinkling and moving even more beautiful than before.

Further down a deep steady humming fill the background as a relaxing mantra. The volume is just hearable and add to the comfortable feeling overwhelming him. The descend seem forever till the shaft open into a massive ocean with an ice ceiling tugging down any sense of movement.

Ray follows the sound of the steady beating, pulling him down till he lost orientation and just follow the sound down and further down. Faintly at first, he sees the sea bed... 'Wow, its all over' he laughs.

The sea bed is covered in a fluffy pinkish coral like substance, stretching as long as he can perceive. He feels vivid full of life never have he seen or even imagined anything so strange and beautiful.

He reaches out his hand and strike gently above the gist of coral, it subtracts as if it senses his touch and Ray feel a flush of happiness.

He hears a sound from afar "*Raaay*", and a force pull him away, like passing a transparent sheet of reality. Ray returns to the harshness of life next to Sabine.

"*Ray, wake up.* We have to get going." Kareem is shaking Ray's shoulder harder.

A Way Home

Coming out of the profound sleep, Ray stretch and feel heavy. He looks to his side and see Sabine observing him. "Hi there, are you better?" Ray asks him genuine.

Sabine smile with a grimace "Sure..., I feel an odd delusion..." he replies achingly.

The first thing on Ray's mind is an urgent need to contact Daedalus. *'But how?'* he thinks and search Sabine's face "Can we use the Lander sending a signal to Daedalus?" he queer with a nod toward the wrecked.

Sabine gasp jerking the head back "Send a message using the Lander?" he laughs revived "not now, the woman took off with the transmitter module" he laments.

Ray moves to get up *"Find a way"* he boss seriously.

Sabine flap his hand dismissive followed by a grunt in pain.

Ray look at his Bio-meter again 'Too much radiation' he laments and walk over to Kareem "We need to get going" he stresses and tap at his wrest.

Kareem empty's the tool bag and packs the hard-drive he scraped from the lander. He tosses it onto Sabine on the stretcher "Hold on to it with your life, it's all we came for..." he agonizes as they lift the stretcher and set off.

Ray lead them the same way up the crater-rim as they came. Carrying Sabine is tough, and they slip from time to time on the loose ground. The relaxed rope, up-slope, save Kareem more than once from gliding back down.

At last, they reach the acme of the notch and just continue down the rocky slope on the other side without talking. Knowing the route down hill make Ray feel his courage getting back, and his muscles loosen up. 'This is good, we'll get to the Shuttle fast' he thinks letting the brightest star in the sky leading them home.

"**Look the Shuttle**" Ray yell happy and tug the stretcher to make Kareem speed up, he feels hot and wish he could take the spacesuit off, it nags. 'How was Nikki doing, was she in the cockpit watching them now?'

Kareem stop walking, Ray let the stretcher down annoyed and turnaround "*What now?*" he barks changing his stance with a jump.

Kareem points at the hover-drone outside the Shuttle "*She is here!*" he gasps.

Ray turn and look at the Shuttle "**Nikki!**" he cries seeing the drone next to the Shuttle. Furious he set off running to the entrance of the Shuttle.

Kareem unstrap Sabine and follow behind as good as he can supporting Sabine.

Ray wrenches the handle that opens the elevator door and see Kareem and Sabine coming close behind. He decides to wait at them 'If that bitch have done anything to Nikki I'll kill her!' he fumes.

Sabine come humping along with Kareem "*You can walk?*" Ray flashes at Sabine as they all enter the elevator.

The elevator door opens, Ray glances into the dim compartment only a crack of light enters from the cockpit.

He signal to be quiet and point at the closed cockpit door. They undress from the onerous spacesuits '*uff what a stench*' he laments.

Sabine hump onto a bed still holding on to the tool-bag.

"They are in the Cockpit" Ray whisper eagerly to Kareem, he nods prodding Ray to move forward, they tiptoe to the cockpit door.

Ray pulls the door open, and they rush inside.

Nikki turn her head happy to see Ray, she turns her eyes and look at a gray haired man sitting next to her in the second pilot seat.

Ray stare incredulous at the back head of a familiar face "**Wang?**"

Mr. Wang turnaround "Hello Ray, we was watching how eagerly you came running back to us." He nods toward the cockpit window and continues "Nikki agreed to let me in. Instead of letting me die out there on that frozen and radioactive desert" he smiles pitiful at Nikki.

Nikki stands-up sicken and look down at Wang *"You tricked me!"* she cries out and bunches into his seat as she leaves the cockpit.

Ray takes the seat next to Wang "Sorry, you two took me by surprise riding the Rover, did it hurt?" he inquires rudely.

Wang bend and touch his leg "Yeah, when the elevator smashed against the ground, it did hurt!" he laments pallidly and sit back "the Rover wheels busted and took most of the impact" he sends Ray a long painful look.

Ray jerk his head in dismay 'How dare he play me like that' his eyes turn flinty "Do you want me to petty you?" he snaps harsh and lean closer to Wang, "what are you and Veronica unto, felony?" he charges grossly.

Wang laugh "We got what we came for, now you just have to give us a ride home" he glances at the controls with a nod.

Ray look surprised at the flight control. The charged particle field flash at 16% field-strength.

Wang smile confidently "She is smart, that moon-girl of yours. She has worked on starting this thing up since you left" he lean back in his seat folding the hands behind his neck.

Ray look puzzled at Wang 'If the Rover was intact the radio onboard may work...' he wonders and glance out the window. He turns and cross his arms on the chest "So you and Veronica went through all this just for that piece of equipment she ran off with?" he disdains.

Wang turn-on his all-knowing grin "Well, reverse engineer alien technology is no small thing. Who ever buy the equipment will create the next game-changing technology, we have quite a few interested players" he said self-assured.

Ray smile playful back at Wang 'He thinks they got a piece of alien technology, so where are Veronica?' he wonder, "Right, you are all after the big price. You almost did outsmart the corrupt power group on Daedalus. Thomas T. Brogan the corrupt lawyer, Kei Enatsu the corrupt hotel manager and not to forget Mr. Mark the corrupt security officer. But you have to hide on Daedalus all the way back, if we get off this frozen planet, have you thought about that?" Ray relaxes and lean back with a slow confirming nod.

Wang look firmly at Ray "Don't you worry, we got it all figured out" he rants and point at the control panel. "Now its 17%" he smiles satisfied and pull his pad out of the pocket signaling privacy for a call.

Ray leaves the cockpit, but stay next to the door to listen-in on Wang's call. "Hello Sweet Cat, you did get the equipment?" Wang asks.

There's a static fizzle "*whiiirrr*" he looks surprised at the pad. "Do you hear me?" he asks again.

"*whiiii...* Yes *iiirrr*...out. Where are you?" Veronica respond barely audible.

"At the Shuttle, come over here we will fly back any minute" Wang urges.

"But Ray will kill *iirr*" she complains.

"No, no, I will take care of him you just hold on to me Sweet Cat" Wang hangs up.

Ray feels uncertain knowing Veronica is coming onboard. He looks around and sees Kareem holding Sabine as Nikki is bandaging a splint onto his arm. "Now you are in good hands" Ray cheers as he mingles in.

Nikki places a belt as sling "You stay quiet, *you hear*" she smiles and help him to sit in the bed.

She grab Kareem's arm as he is about to leave "We need to cycle the power tanks. To squish-out all the juice we can get" she laughs as they wend off talking how to get it done.

Ray takes a seat on the bed next to Sabine "Have you thought about the code breaking?" Ray rush alert.

Sabine brightens-up "I did read the papers you gave me, before that mad woman attacked me" he agonizes repulsively.

Ray shake his head vigorously "She is coming back onboard. She and Wang tried to steal the equipment from the crash site, and they think its alien tech" he waves the idea off with a nervous laugh. "But why and how did an old probe start to send a signal?" he asks himself aloud as he looks toward the entrance.

Ray scratch the back of his head "What do you think about the code?" he asks again.

Sabine takes a thoughtful pause "The signal contains a system where each tried letter is assigned a unique value. This value is then expressed as a trinomial. The digits of which sum to the selected value of the letter" he explains as he watches Ray to see if he follows.

Ray slowly nod pensive. Sabine continues eagerly "First eliminate the impossible values. Then in the remaining can be found the distinctive patterns of the stereotype, and all keys are known. With the keys you can decipher the message" he smiles satisfied.

Ray raise his eyebrow "*Great!* What does it say?" he cheers.

Sabine look surprised at Ray "*I don't know!* First we have to decipher it all" he looks around "we need a lot of computer power" he puzzles.

Ray stands-up "See what you can do with your pad, and *lips tight*, don't let that snake trick you again" he smiles satisfied and look for Nikki.

Ray spot the two of them halfway inside the power hold "Hi Nikki, you need to let Kareem rest a bit, his overdo." He sees they got the power line rewired.

Nikki pulls out of the hold, with a jump she is on her feet.

"What are you working at?" Ray ask curious as he wonders how to tell her about Veronica.

Nikki smile bright "Getting the particle field up and running" she chants happy.

Ray sways a bit "*Hmmm Well*, you said it was precharged?" he objects.

Nikki incline her head "I recalled a nanny show I watched as a child with a boy rolling a wheel by kicking it with a stick" she charms.

Ray touch Nikki's shoulder "Look at that, a child game make you restart a plasma-field, really?" he laughs disbelievingly.

Nikki takes a step back and cross her arms "*Don't fool about what I do!*" She cries and wages Ray's stiffen posture "We rewired the energy from life-support to the main tank. The field grows stronger little by little by adding the energy in small kicks of high current. With enough field-strength the Shuttle can reach the lickety-split speed required to get us free from Ganymede's gravity and into low orbit. *Got it!*" she snaps impatiently.

Ray clear his throat "And how much is *enough field-strength?*" he asks vaguely.

Nikki smooth her uniform as she probes for an answer "*I don't know!*" She turns around.

Ray grab her arm "*Nikki wait!*" she stops throwing her head back with a

"*What?*"

Ray nipple his ear in a tic "Veronica is coming onboard, she's the one kidnapping the Shuttle not Sabine" he exclaims softly.

Nikki moves uneasily "Yes I know, Sabine told me she almost killed him" she takes a deep breath, "and she is coming onboard?" she gasps looking at Ray for an answer.

Ray look away "Well, if we don't let her in its murder, right?"

Nikki gazes past Ray pensive "If she does not make it in time it's not! In an hour or so we have recharged the field with all the power left, and we have to take off" she replies sharply and leave for the cockpit.

Ray feels heavy minded '*Wow*, I need to take a nap' he exhausts and go to his bed laying down. He closes his eyes and falls into a deep sleep.

Once again dreaming, he sees himself standing naked on the frosty ice of Ganymede. He breathes the fresh air and look around. On the left is the Shuttle and in front of him another pond of warm water with a cozy haze inviting him to slip in.

He glides down into the pleasant pool of water and next find himself deep down at the bottom of the ocean. This time he feels conscious knowing he is dreaming, also, he knows that he can wake up anytime he wants.

The scenery is different from last. There is a big wholesome structure in front of him, it seems like a huge machine of some kind. He can feel the steady humming vibrating through the water. The thing looks organic as a snail shell, just enormous with a smooth light marble color. High as a tower-block and wide as long as the eye can perceive, huge!

Ray contemplates the massive straight wall, at places it is almost transparent, and he can see something moving inside, like a flow of light or energy. 'What is that?' he wonders.

"It's my shield" a kind voice manifest to him in his mind.

Ray looks around, but there is no one just the huge machine in front of him and the pink coral covering the rest of the sea bed. "What are you afraid of?" he thinks and feel a response of pleasant amusement.

"The light from our mother" the voice manifest.

Ray feel it is a half-witted dream and want to wake up. He pulls himself out of the dream and opens his eyes with a sensation that the dream was real. Only a few minutes have past, and he feels rested and clear in his mind with an urgent desire to call Daedalus.

Ray walks over to Sabine's bed "Hi there how are you doing?" he cheers.

Sabine look surprised at Ray as only a few minutes have past since he left "Yes, yes I'm working on it, can't you see?" he lifts the pad in the air.

Ray smile awkward "*Great! Hmm,* have you given it a thought how to send a message to Daedalus?" he queer with a nod toward the Pad in Sabine's hand.

Sabine smile incredulous "Sending a message using the Pad?" he laughs "you know the Pad can't transmit that far" he objects and get back to his work.

Ray feels disappointed "*Think about a way*" he grumbles and look around for Nikki. He only spot Kareem at the back, busy strapping loose luggage.

Nikki sits in the cockpit at the flight controls, switching the load botton manually from time to time charging the field in small kicks. She looks up with a relieved smile when Ray enter, sending him a glance toward the second pilot seat.

Squished between Wang, seated in the chair and the wall stand Veronica leaning on to Wang as an insecure girl adhere to her father. Gazing with sullen red eyes at Ray.

Seeing Veronica, Ray thrust his hands into his pockets. '*Her*, she must have slipped in as I slept' he vexes and bend close to Nikki's ear "How is it going?" he whispers.

Nikki smiles and point at the display, now at 34% field strength. "We need the field to be as strong as it can get..." she whispers back as she wipes a running nose. She turns on a sad face "*Look*" and points at the almost empty power indicator.

Ray feels as if Veronica's peevish gazing penetrate his body. He takes a deep breath as he stands up folding his arms across his chest. 'This is too annoying, what to do with that woman' he fumes shaking his head, avoiding looking her way.

"*What's wrong, feeling peaked mountain-man?*" Veronica scoffs jealously with a repulsive laughter.

Wang grab her arm "Now you calm down, *you hear*" he rants and turn at Ray "*Why don't you mind your own business and leave the girl alone!*" he thunders biased.

Nikki points toward the door "If you two don't like it here you can leave, **NOW**" she yells commanding at Wang and Veronica.

Veronica get distanced and race a hand for silence "Yes?" she says with an unfocused gaze.

Wang lean toward Nikki and Ray "She receives a voice call in her mind" he rush in a quiet voice and point at his head.

Nikki and Ray look surprised at each other "Did you know?" Nikki whisper and point at her head.

Ray shake his head dismissive 'So, she had that implant all the time…' he wonders and try to find a comfortable stand.

Nikki incline to Ray "They say people get crazy from these implants" she whispers pejoratively with a slow nod toward Veronica.

Ray pull his ear as he nods softly 'Was Veronica going crazy? Or was she mean bottom down?' he wonders observing her.

Wang waits for Veronica to get clear focused "Who was it?" he asks as soon as she looks down at the floor.

She looks up at Wang with tears in her eyes "I'm loosing my best friend" she sniffs, then she burst into tears.

Nikki rub her eyelid as she looks at Ray "Now she's a real crackpot" she mumbles softly with a wide grin.

Wang brace her with his arm "Now that's not true, I'm right her for you, *always!*" he comforts her, till she gets herself together and stop crying.

"Not you, *stupid*" Veronica object "my mind–assistant!" she smiles at Wang and hold his hand. "The radiation, out there, make holes in the memory–crystal" she sniffs holding back her tears "and, I can hardly understand what it is saying" she sniffs-in a running nose.

Wang looks worried "Yes I see, who called? Did you hear that?" he questioned eagerly.

"It was Brogan" she replies with a half smile "*Brogan called you?*" Wang is surprised "how did he know to call you?" he looks clueless at her.

Veronica lower her eyes "Well, I meet him one day, *you know*" she smiles innocent.

"*I know what?*" Wang ask upset "you was supposed to stay low, *right?*" he argues distressed as he lean back.

"What did Brogan want?" Ray interrupt dryly.

Wang nod confirming "**Yes**, *what did he say?*" he booms alert.

Veronica looks toward the cockpit door "Well, he said that the Saymora Corporation had gone bankrupt. And something about the investment in Daedalus have been too big a gamble for the company..." she pauses with a fading smile as Wang interrupts.

"He calls you just to tell you a company are bankrupt?" Wang disrupt brute.

Veronica looks agitated as she tries to think "*No*, Brogan told me that Kai Enatsu and Security have taken control of Daedalus. He said that Kai Enatsu is captain now. He wants us to bring the exotic equipment before they take off back to the Moon" she sniffs and lean onto Wang hugging him with a small alleviated smile.

Ray feels his heart beating harder, and a tenuous headache rag his concentration 'Mutiny on Daedalus! What have happened to Elisabeth and Hellman?' he puzzles as he sees Nikki talking to him "Did you say anything?" he asks baffled.

Nikki sit pail gazing out the window, she punches the switch again racing the field a digit to 41%

Ray lean closer to Nikki "We need to find Elisabeth when we get up there" he whispers in her ear.

Nikki flinch back "They are not going to take away my home!" she whispers harshly with a firm look at Ray. She kicks the switch hard, and it ticks to 42%

She turns to Wang and Veronica "**You two shrug off!**" she blazes with a rusty voice, then looking at Ray "*Ray*, tell Sabine to take his pilot seat, it's time to go!"

Ray find Kareem sleeping he shakes his shoulder lightly "Wake up we will take off any minute" he stresses with a smile. Kareem nod affirmative as he stretch and sit at the edge of his bed. He shakes his head "I dream so heedful…” Ray waves at him to follow.

They walk over to Sabine, who sit in his bed working on his Pad. He looks up, pleased to get some company.

“Hi, we need to talk” Ray salute and continue “Kai Enatsu and Security have made mutiny on Daedalus. We need to take the ship back as soon as we get onboard.”

Kareem and Sabine look surprised at each other.

“How do you know?” Sabine queries with a dazed look at Ray.

Ray aim at the cockpit door “Veronica have a cybernetic implant, they called her just a minute ago” he points out.

Sabine study Ray closely “She receives the call inside her brain. How do you know she’s telling the truth?” he asks with a firm look.

Ray feels certain Veronica told the truth, he returns a hesitated nod at Sabine “Right, let’s wait and see” he replies reluctantly.

Kareem intervenes the conversation “We take off in a minute, let me help you to the cockpit” he reaches out a hand to Sabine.

“I can manage” Sabine smiles and stand up with Kareem’s help.

Wang and Veronica have cleared the cockpit and Sabine strap-in next to Nikki. He skim over the controls with a tight smile “Um… We only got 2% power left, giving us 6 hours life support and 45% field strength, do you think we can lift off with that?” he questions observing.

Nikki shake her head softly “*I don’t know!*” she laments sorely.

Polar Night

Ray and Kareem strap-in next to Wang and Veronica they all watch the cockpit past the open door.

Nikki takes a calm breath "All clear?" she asks over the intercom "We are ready" Ray confirms.

Nikki glances at Sabine who assert with a silent nod, she takes the Shuttle up and hovers close to the ground "***Kick it!***" she yells. Sabine punch the handle to full thrust, a plum of dust and vapor raise from the ground engulfing the Shuttle.

They start to accelerate gently taking them out of the dust cloud, and climb faster and faster into space with a light vibration. A vivid blue aurora glow in Ganymede's horizon with the sun shining brilliant in the dark sky. Nikki looks happy at Sabine as the weightlessness ease their ascend.

Ray get absorbed by the brink of space, with Ganymede at their back the stars sparkles in the dark competing unfairly with the radiance of Jupiter.

An alarm break the silence "***We lost the field!***" Sabine call out.

Nikki thrust the field switch draining the last power, with no result. Another alarm adds to the first and all lighting shutoff "Our life support have kicked-out" Sabine say dry with a grave look on his face.

Nikki look pained out the cockpit window as the alarms silence "We are lost" she coo to herself.

They glide silently through space steadily adding velocity as the Shuttle begin to descend back to Ganymede.

Ray feels the acceleration pulling him slightly back into his seat '*That's it!*' he acknowledges. He looks at Kareem "We are falling back" he mutter doubtfully as the vibration begin to shake the Shuttle ceaselessly.

The shaking gets more violent and Ray can't hear what Kareem try to tell him. He sees Kareem gasping as his face turn ash-white with his sight fixed at the cockpit window. Ray follows his sight, a mountain-rim is coming rushing against them. Ray feels his hair lifting, he grab the seat-frame and squish his eyes tight, embracing for impact.

The Shuttle skirt the surface of the crater-rim sending them on a horizontal glide over the flat plain. The impact hurl Ray hard into his seat blowing his breath out.

They crash onto the ice-plain sliding breakneck on the frosty-dross, plowing up ice and stones till the Shuttle comes to a sudden stand.

As the mist of soiled ice settles around the Shuttle, the sunlight gradually returns and Ray can see Kareem looking back at him.

"*Dam it!*" Wang blasts furiously.

Nikki appears in the doorway to check if everyone is alright. She runs over to Ray and throw her arms around his neck "I'm so sorry Ray" she clamors "*what shall we do now?*" she cries and burst into tears.

Ray comfort Nikki padding her back "We will find a way" he assures calmly. He looks out the window at the bereaved icy plain. 'By Gods help' he laments with a heavy heart.

Veronica strap herself free and jump over to Wang shaking her fist at him. "*How are you going to* fix *this old imbecile,* **hee**" she rages baring her teeth. She walks over to the entrance searching for her bag in the dark.

Wang pounds the seat to the side and follow her "What are you doing?" he sneers grabbing her arm.

Nikki presses her chin at Ray's "I told you, she has lost her mind" she whispers as she observes Veronica and Wang wrestling.

Ray looks at them discussing who's to blame "It's too dark to see anything down there" he reflects.

Nikki pull herself away from Ray "*The life support system!*" she shouts breathless. She looks at Kareem's empty seat then toward the cockpit. "We have to get the life-support back on" she murmurs and leave Ray for the cockpit.

Ray feels dizzy and overwhelmed by a strong need to call Daedalus 'But how?' he wonders with a struggle to stay awake. As he closes his eyes he enters the familiar conscious dream again. He sees the Shuttle crash-landed on the icy patch with a deep ravine cutting though the plain in front of them. Way behind he can skim some metallic structure standing out in the monotonous landscape.

Looking down at his feet he sees himself moving down to the bottom of the ocean where the pink coral cover the extent of the bedrock.

The constant hum hale a sense of elation. 'Why am I here?' Ray wonders. "Because I called you" the familiar voice manifest to him in his mind.

Ray listen hard but only feel the vibrating hum 'You called me, why?' he thinks queerly and perceive a sense of delight.

"To in-bright you" the voice instill candidly. Ray feel puzzled as the voice continues "I come from afar and was sleeping all the way till I was taken into orbit by our new mother who give me the light of life. I have lived with many different suns and have memory as long back as time exist."

Ray looks around at the coral on the sea bed and get a sensation of confirmation 'You are the pink stuff growing allover?' he questions somehow knowing it is so.

"What you perceive is me" the voice confirm "when you make one persuasion, I make billions of alignments. You seem so slow to me, but you are the only one I have ever known beside myself" the voice beams blissful.

Ray feel loved and try to imagine what the voice look like but perceive nothing, besides a wired mess of strings 'How can you talk to me?' he thinks.

"I perceive your minds wavelengths and copied your way of communicating. We can talk because some activity in your neural brain network develops at the quantum level connecting with our divine multidimensional universe. A double reality where your thoughts manifest as both a radiant in the divine and an entity in your mind."

Ray struggle to grab the essence of what he hears 'How do this thing know I'm here?' he wonders still shrouded in gratitude.

"When you perceive a wide wavelength from infrasonic to gamma waves, pixel it on a planetary level the perception get billions of times grater than your hearing and sight combined. Even more than your mind can grasp" the voice revel.

Ray feels a streaming flow of love overwhelming his senses as a mental climax expand his mind. He loses his consciousness and deluge in a timeless ecstasy.

Ray regains consciousness hearing Nikki calling his name and shaking his shoulder "Ray come on, *wake up*" she urges hasty.

He gazes dozy at Nikki "I got these weird dreams, you know?" he mutters sleepy.

Nikki bunch a foot at Ray's bed sending a shutter up the frame "It is not time for sleeping now." She glances toward the entrance "Your two friends have left outside. And frankly we need to figure a way out of here fast" she gasps sharply.

Ray stretches "Um... Yeah" he mumbles and gaze around, Kareem is at the power tanks recharging their life-support packs "Are we leaving?" he asks with a slack expression.

Nikki tear Ray's safety lock and unstrap him from his bed. "***Move it***" she yells and walk defiantly over to Kareem helping him with the spacesuits.

Ray find Sabine seated in the cockpit "We're kind of stuck!" he laments and take the seat next to Sabine.

Sabine jerks surprised in his seat as Ray enters, he sits silent watching Wang and Veronica outside on the frosty plain. They seem to keep arguing as they walk toward the ravine where they stop at the edge.

Wang rip a bag out of Veronica's hands, and she tries to pull it back without luck. They stand arguing for while, *Puff...* Veronica push Wang hard

in his chest with both hands. Wang steps a step back to gain balance from the sudden thrust the ground give in at the edge of the cliff. He grab out at Veronica in panic, but she jumps back just in time to avoid him. Wang waves his arms around trying to fall forward, he drops the bag too late and vanishes into the ravine.

"***WOW*** *Did you see that?*" Ray shout and lean closer to the window half standing.

Nikki and Kareem come running to the cockpit "*What happened?*" they call out in dual.

"*She pushed him into the chasm!*" Sabine cries bewailed pointing out the window where Veronica walks along the ravine, alone.

Kareem looks out at the deep ravine crossing just in front of them "Where is she going?" he questions shaking his head dismissive, he turns around and walks back to his work, recycling the power tanks.

Ray look for a structure of some kind 'Strange? I saw a metal construction in the horizon, didn't I?' he ponders and remember it was in his dream. He taps into the navigator on his pad and nod confirming. 'The metal structure I saw is the elevator platform' he thinks satisfied.

"*Nikki look*" Ray point at his pad "the Rover is just ahead of us" he rejoices "Veronica is going back to the Rover" he smiles.

Nikki looks perplexed at Ray "I told you she is loathsome! She just killed your friend..." she clear her dry throat "and you seem...."

Ray interrupts "**No**, *no*, not her the Rover, it got a working life support system, supplies for two-weeks, and a *radio!*" he smiles brighter "here, the Shuttle is without power and nothing works" he vexes spreading his arms wide.

Nikki rub her chin with a flickering gaze between Sabine and Ray "Kareem got the power back... for a while... Sabine you are not fit for walking, and we don't know what's left of the Rover. Besides Ray, you got half the radiation allowed, if only..."

Ray interrupts again "Kareem and I go, you and Sabine stay, it's our only option left, all right?" he hesitates "We have to find the Rover before sunset... It will get freezing cold..." Ray gush desperate with a glaze at the window.

Nikki nod gently and leave the cockpit with an elusive glance over her shoulder.

Ray feel guilty leaving her on the Shuttle again. 'At least she got Sabine' he laments and recalls Wang throwing the bag as he felt into the ravine. He clear his throat "Sabine, do you have the bag with the hard-drive?" he asks troubled.

Sabine kick softly at a bag besides his feet "Sure I do!" he smiles vague.

Out on the plain Ray waves at Nikki and Sabine in the Shuttle.

"I'm sure they are watching" Kareem consoles, waving a salute at the Shuttle too.

At the cliff Ray anchor the axe in the ice and fastens the r ope. "Keep the rope tight, I'm going to look for Wang" he hands Kareem the rope and lean forward as he glances over the edge. Ray feels faint seeing Wang lay placid deep down in the ravine. He shakes his head "No way he survived that deep a fall" he laments and move quickly back onto the plain.

He looks at the Sun in the horizon standing closer to the prevailing edge of Jupiter "*Lets move on*" Ray hurry keenly.

They follow Veronica's footsteps along the ravine "It looks like she was running" Kareem marvel slowing his pace.

"Hmm... yeah" Ray respond pensive 'she must be devastated or raving mad...?' he worries, with a flash he recalls her pushing Wang into the abyss. He stops at a natural depression "She crossed over to the other side here" he points at the bridge formed by the cliffs fallen in on its sides.

Kareem hesitates, and look at his navigator "Seems to be in the right direction." He follows Ray down the slope and up on the other side onto a flat plateau. Not faraway is the elevator platform standing as a dysphoric steel tower nailed down into the icy ground. "It looks intact, can you see the elevator-cabin?" he questions observing.

Ray look searching down on the ground "*Yes.. Come on*, she walked this way" he rush and trace her footsteps to the left of the tower. They come across the large elevator cables shattered on the ground.

They follow the cables as the Sun pass behind Jupiter turning the long shadows on the ground into disfigured dark taints. The walking get harder as they drag their feet in an effort not to stumble on a colorless boulder. Finally, the cables lead them to the elevator cabin. The cabin lay creaked open like a nutshell with the Rover still strapped to the trolley platform with a couple of busted tires.

Kareem walk eagerly over to the Rover "The air-lock only take one at a time" he explains stepping up the latter pulling the door open.

Ray watch Kareem inside the air-lock as he turns slowly till only the red painted sign >LOCKED< is visible. The waiting seems endless till the air-lock turn back empty. As he waits, he wonders what Kareem may find inside the Rover and if Nikki and Sabine will have enough power to keep filtrating the air in the Shuttle.

Ray's first glimpse into the Rover show Kareem undressing his spacesuit. As the air-lock turnaround completely he notes trash littered allover the floor, it smells bad, and he feels sour in his throat. Veronica sit curled up in a corner with her helmet and gloves tossed to a side 'She has gone mad alright' he repents.

Ray find Kareem in the cockpit glaring out at the total darkness "What are you looking for?" he asks queerly.

"We just made it in time…" Kareem respond thoughtful "the temperature is plumbing fast. It is too cold for us to make it back" he mutter and tap at the indicator on the controls.

Ray nod understanding as he studies the control switches "And the Rover, can it drive?"

Kareem brightens up "The Rover is fine, besides the wheels…" he turns on the headlights and study the terrain ahead of them "if we avoid the rocks… maybe? We can try!" he cheers.

Ray freezes a bright smile "Lets call Daedalus first. The radio works, right?" he hesitates.

Kareem clear his throat and taps into the radio application, Daedalus popup on the screen "Who do we call?" he scrolls down the large list of contacts.

"Not the main channel" Ray think aloud and look pensive at Kareem "Lets call Elisabeth" he chants with a glow of excitement.

Kareem select Elisabeth and lean back in his seat. Nothing just silence and they get a disconnected message in return.

"*Um… Hellman?*" Kareem suggests and tap his name. Again a disconnected message is displayed on the screen.

Ray looks out the window at the shadows cast by the scattered rocks. At the right he can see a part of the elevator cabin laying disfigured on the ground. 'What have happened to Elisabeth and Hellman?' he puzzles 'And Bukari?' He turns quickly toward Kareem "Is Bukari listed?" he lean over and look for his name as Kareem scrolls up the list.

Kareem makes the call as soon as he finds his name. "Yes..." Bukari appear perplexed on the screen, then his mouth fall open. "*Ray, Kareem,* how are you?" he rejoices with a suppressed voice. He looks over his shoulder nervously "I call you back in a minute" he mutter and hang up abruptly.

"**Yeah**" Ray exult with a large grin and give Kareem a high five.

"**Ha Ha Ha,** do you really think it will help to call Daedalus? *We are all dead anyhow!*" Veronica yells from the back and throw an empty can down the floor.

Kareem lean closer to Ray "What shall we do with her? She is self-destructive. Who knows if she tries to kill one of us?" he whispers with a darting gaze at Veronica.

Veronica makes a face and throw more trash at Kareem.

The incoming call shift Kareem's attention away from Veronica. He jerks around and take the call.

Bukari stand looking down the gangway, behind him is a wall mounted with tubes and cables. "Hi Bukari, you are online now" Ray try to get his attention.

Bukari smile tense "Hello Ray, I'm not sure if I heard someone coming... I'm using the emergency jigger..." he pauses and looks away again "we are waiting for your chaps to come back helping us to organize the resistance" he wails.

Ray scratch his jaw looking at Kareem 'So there was a mutiny' he concludes and look back at the camera. "*Well Bukari,* we are working on that" he insinuates with a grimace.

"**Ha, Ha, Ha**" Veronica laugh foully from the back.

Kareem lean closer to the camera "We tried to call Elisabeth and Hellman?" he pleads hazily.

Bukari look downward with a thoughtful gaze "You see... All officials are shut up in their cabins... We bring them food, that's it" he agonizes. After another look down the aisle he continues "they paid the 16 construction workers at the new-section to join security. Anyone who resists are locked up" he laments.

Ray shifts in his seat with a distance gaze "Can you get down here anyhow?" he asks vaguely.

Bukari look stunned "*With an eject capsule?*" he quivers "It can fall anywhere!" he scratch the back of his head troubled.

Ray shakes his head heavyhearted "*No, no,* forget that." He suppresses a feeling of despair and gain self-control "Any departure plans for Daedalus, do you know?" he asks as sincerely as possible.

Bukari looks observantly past the screen "*No...*" he hesitates with an intended smile as he changes subject.   "They even opened the main gates to the new-section and named it Ming City" he agonizes removing a tear from his chin.

Ray read Bukari's face and smile comprehensive "Right, we will call you back, *Okay?*" he gasps wavering as he looks out the window.

"*Anytime!*" Bukari utters and disconnect.

Ray observes the disfigured landscape outside 'What was calling Daedalus all about?' he wonder and close his eyes with a feeling of delusion.

"You're all deadbeats" Veronica yawn dully, laying on the floor she turns toward the wall.

Kareem cast a digressive glance at Ray "I'm going outside to untie the Rover, *you stay!*" he taps at his bio-meter as he leaves the cockpit "It's better than doing nothing, *right!*" he fetches his spacesuit and begin to dress.

Ray sit gazing outside as he sees Kareem walk around the Rover to unstrap on the other side. He fights a sleepy feeling '*Not now!*' he fumes and feels an embracing sensation reliving his sleepiness. He tries to envision a way to return to Daedalus, but nothing appears. "Ask God" he perceives in his mind, he shakes his head dismissive and look back at Veronica sleeping on the floor.

'Odd?' he thinks mystified by his own thoughts as he observes the air-lock turning slowly facing the inside.

"It's freezing outside" Kareem greet returning to his seat, he claps his hands to restore circulation.

Ray smiles at Kareem "*Lets go!*" he cheers excited.

Kareem pulls the handle into drive position, the Rover start to move slowly and tilts forward off the trolley platform, onto the ground. He drives cautious avoiding even every insignificant stone on their way.

Ray gets bored from watching Kareem's easy driving. 'At least he drives better than he hikes' he thinks and begin to daydream about taking Nikki back home on Earth. A hot sunny day on the beach...

How are Nikki doing at the Shuttle? He wonders with a feeling of fear arising within, 'Without power this polar night will turn the Shuttle into an airless fridge' he worries. Ray kick at the wall panel in front of him with a **Bang** "**Can't you drive faster?**" he burst out.

Kareem jumps in his seat "*What?*" he gasps bewildered with a gaze bouncing between Ray and the terrain in the headlights.

"**Shut up Ray**" Veronica yell from the back as she punches her helmet further away.

Kareem stops the Rover and look hard at Ray "What's wrong with you? *Earnestly!*" he challenges.

Ray looks beyond the headlights into the pitch-black night.
"They are
freezing to death, we need to get back to the Shuttle today, *not tomorrow!*" he argues.

Kareem takes a deep breath.
"If you pay a little attention, we are almost there" he points at the navigator and proceed driving steadily ahead.

An incoming call echos penetrating. Seeing it's Nikki, Ray feel nervous 'A distress call' he fears and connect "Are you alright?" he frets.

Nikki giggle "We are fine... I can see your headlights" she rejoices and continue "the power went out, and... We are coming over to you" she exclaims with a heavy breathing from walking.
Ray feel relieved and gaze searching out the window. A flashlight is swinging in the distance "*I see you*" he cheers "don't get too close to the cliff" he urges.

Kareem stops at the edge of the flat plateau. "We have to stay on this side of the cross-over" he laments and turn on the roof-cam zooming in on Nikki and Sabine passing over the ravine.

Sabine is the first to exit the air-lock "Wow it's cold outside" he salutes. Ray help him undress the spacesuit as he looks for Nikki to appear from the air-lock.

She enters sluggish and cast a look around. "*Uff*" she covers her face from the bad smell "it's crowded in here" she sobs with a gaunt appearance and hands Sabine his bag. She undresses her suit at the side bench.

Going Home

Ray help Nikki onto a makeshift bed as he gazes down into her red-eyed face "Now you need to get some rest" he comforts gently and straighten her blanket.

Nikki holds onto Ray's hand "Thank you, Ray" she coo and close her eyes still holding on to him.

Ray sits at her side with an overwhelming feeling of uncertainty. "We will be home soon" he encourages vaguely and remembers the voice he perceived. "I got odd dreams with a voice talking to me. It's as if I am awake, like we are talking right now" he confides dubious.

Nikki open her eyes and look into his "And what does it tell you?" she asks intrigued.

Ray shifts on the bed finding a comfortable position as he clear his throat "Well, it says it wants to in-bright me..." he pauses "and that I need to ask God for help?" he explains with a tight smile.

Nikki brightens-up "Who is talking to you, is it your father?" she marvels.

Ray shake his head softly "No, no... *Um*, it's a thing living down in the ocean below us..." he hesitates "in my dream I was swimming down a gateway hole with dimly lit ice curving around me till I made it into another realm below the ice" he emphasizes.

Nikki nod positive "Yes, I had a dream too where I was swimming in the ocean below. But I only heard a constant humming sound" she inclines her head and look past Ray.

Ray lean in and catch Nikki's eyes "The hum is made by a machine powering the magnetic shield on Ganymede. *I saw the generator,* it circles the whole planet!" he rush eagerly.

Nikki stare pensive with a distant face.

Ray study her as he wonders how to place the question "You said God's wisdom is omniscient! Right?" he asks wakefully.

Nikki returns a comprehensive smile... Ray continues before she gets a chance to answer "How do I gain knowledge from God?" he hastes.

She takes a deep breath as she looks up at the ceiling "You can only know what God allow you to know or understand. God is not an Oracle of fortune" she asserts.

Ray sway back, 'How can she ignore the mess we are in?' he mulls touched "*Well*, we have only fortune left!" he laments holding out a hand "*So*, I need you to help me with this one" he stresses severely.

Nikki pushes herself up in the bed and sit slumped against the pillow. She cast a toiled look at Ray "You go to bed with a question in your mind. When you wake up at night you recall your question." She studies Ray to see if he follows her and continue "As soon as you fall asleep the second time. You stand up within your dream and go find Gods wisdom. Whom you ask for a solution to your question... and in the morning you got your answer" she encourages with a strained face.

"That's how" she reassures and crawl back into bed.

Ray sit quiet gazing through Nikki. He wonders how to stand-up while sleeping and if he can find a way getting them back up to Daedalus. "How do I stand up while sleeping?" he asks and look down at Nikki now sleeping.

He walks over and study Veronica sleeping on the floor, she too looks sick, he views her bio-meter 'The radiation is within limits...' he scratch his head 'What is going on?' he wonders and gaze around the narrow compartment with a nuisance feeling in his stomach.

Back in the cockpit Ray seats next to Kareem "All three in bed sleeping" he smiles bittersweet. He catches Kareem's eyes "Any ideas what to do next?" he asks blunt.

Kareem looks away "No" he breathes heavily.

They stare out the window at the snowy ground in silence, after a while "Why are the headlights still on?" Ray asks puzzled.

"Because I like it that way" Kareem respond flagrantly gazing out the window.

A growing stomach pain distract Ray from Kareem's sour temper. 'If we only had flown directly to the Apophis crater... we would be back at Daedalus by now... or, would we?' he speculates dazed, he moves to get comfortable in the seat and closes his eyes dozing.

Ray wakes up and look around, the headlights are turned off only a faint control light illuminate the contour of the front screen. He gazes into the back of the shaded compartment, it's quiet too. He turns to get back into sleep and remembers what Nikki explained 'recall your question and stand up within your dream. *I need to know how to get us back aboard Daedalus'* he thinks with a wholehearted desire.

Ray observe how he gradually slide back into sleep, then a metallic sound in his head catch his attention, and he listen-in to his interior sensations. Without thinking, he just stands-up and look down with a blurred sight at his body seated in the co-drivers chair. He finds his way with his hands against a wall. Slowly his sight get better, and he recognizes the corridor to his cabin "Wow! I'm on Daedalus" he voices to himself.

He gazes back and forth the corridor, he is alone, '*Oh, God cannot be up here?*' he agonizes and continue down the corridor.

"Command yourself there" a voice advice in his head. He recognizes the pleasing sensation from yesterday's dream and feel so aware.

Ray closes his eyes and command himself to go to the wisdom of God. Instantly his skin feels cool and damp, he breathes in the fresh moiety air with a tang of wet rocks, it makes him smile.

He opens his eyes and looks around and find himself engulfed by a lily-white mist. He can sense the imposing rocky scree around him. 'I'm on a mountain hill' he pictures as he observes the ash-gray gravel on the ground.

The fog hem in an unnatural quiet he listens in to catch any sound. Nothing just his own breathing, he listens harder and recognizes the sound of a distant stream trickling down the craggy slope. He feels lighthearted with a desire to reach the summit and begin walking.

Ray listens to the rattle of loss scree displacing as he walks the narrow path uphill. The sound of someone following his pace persist, he stops and listen 'nothing' he puzzles and continue walking. He listens harder, it sounds like someone walking faster to catch up with him. As the sound get closer he turns around on the spot and stand face to face with a creature... "**What**" Ray gasp.

"Can I help you?" the creature ask.

Ray study the creature, a naked man with twisted horns, hairy tail and legs *of a goat, 'a faun?'* he doubts and step a step back "What are you?" he asks.

"You know" The creature smile acknowledging and step closer to Ray "Where are you going? I can show you the way" it persists with a foul smile and turn to the sound of a young woman singing a seducing lyric streaming from the murky twilight.

Ray race his head with an irresistible desire to see who's singing.

The creature contemplate Ray's reaction "Lilith invite you to dance with her" it entices with its tongue hanging out of the mouth lustful.

Ray feel disgusted "**Go away!**" he shouts and grab a stone on the ground threatening to stone the creature.

The faun laugh nervously as it step backward "*Ha, ha, ha*, you will get lost in these woods..." it responds and vanish into the fog.

Ray step around searching for the creature, trying to look past the dense fog. He stands quiet for a moment, listening again 'nothing, the singing have stopped, *it's gone*' he feels relieved for a moment then uncertain why he is here 'What am I doing on this mountain?' he wonders searching his mind 'Oh yes, *I am dreaming!*'

He remembers Nikki laying sick in the Rover... and Sabine... 'I need to get us home, back up to Daedalus' he recalls and walk decisive up the stony path.

The fog fade into a thin mist, and he can see the summit. Ray walk faster with his eyes fixed at the path. A light shine brighter in the night sky as he gets closer to the summit.

Within the mist a huge translucent globe of light shine nitid high in front of him. Ray walk as close as he can up to the shining globe. He stands breathless looking up at the huge sphere of light "How do we get back aboard Daedalus?" he supplicates.

He feels swept away by joy and blissfulness.

Ray feel dry mouthed, a pain in his back force him to change posture in the chair. He opens his eyes and see the faint light from the controls, 'I'm in the Rover' he concludes and look at Kareem who's sleeping. A sentiment of enlightenment fill his mind, surprised, he sucks in a quick breath and glance at Kareem "***Wow, I can't believe it!***" he burst out.

Ray grab Kareem's arm and shake him awake "*Kareem, Kareem,* wake up, I got it!, I got it!" he laughs happy.

Kareem look sleepy in disbelieve at Ray "What now?" he asks dozy.

"We are going home!" Ray keep laughing as he shakes Kareem's hand.

Sabine turn on a small wall light at his bed "*What is all the fuss about?*" he protests leaning out of his bed.

Nikki and Veronica sit up too, all are looking at Ray for an answer.

"We are going home!" Ray repeat happy.

Sabine pull his legs out of the bed and sit up "Can you be a little more specific?" he grunts impatient.

Ray stands-up still smiling "We will recharge the Shuttle and fly back to Daedalus" he cheers.

The excitement on Nikki's face faint "We did try *just that,* **Ray**" she jeers and pull herself back to bed.

Ray keep smiling "Yes, that's why we know it will work! Just this time we make a full charge before the takeoff, *you see*" he explains joyfully.

"*How?*" Kareem asks doubtful as he turns on the main cabin light.

Ray point at the controls "With the Rover! It got an isotopic power plant that works for years, Right?" he looks straight at Kareem.

Kareem nods with a big smile.

Sabine stand up "**It can work!**" he rejoices and leap a few steps forward.

Nikki run over and embrace Ray kissing him joyful.

Even Veronica look happy for a moment then she walks over to Sabine "What happened to you?" she asks uncertain as she reaches out to help him back to his bed.

Sabine turn away "You should know *that*" he rants at her and jump back onto the bed on his own. He sits down with a stiff gaze avoiding looking at Veronica. "**Kareem**" he calls "let's talk what needs to be done" he waves a hand for him to come over.

Veronica lay down on Nikki's bed ignoring she still wears the spacesuit. She searches Sabine frequently with a faint gaze trying to recall what had happened to him.

Ray see Veronica sleeping in the bed and take Nikki into the cockpit.

"Thank you, Ray" she smiles weak, seated in the cockpit chair "I feel so ragged. You need to know how to fly the Shuttle" she exhales sagely and begin to explain the maneuvering of the Shuttle to Ray.

Ray listen attend to Nikki with admiration till an anxious feeling wrest away his concentration. 'She needs to get to sickbay as soon as we get up there' he laments with a blank look.

"**Are you listening?**" Nikki hark back Ray's attention. Ray's feet shuffle in reflex "*Yes*, you said Sabine need to do the docking, *right!*" he hesitates and run his hand through the hair.

Nikki takes a shallow breath "You will do fine" she smiles and lean back for a nap.

Kareem excuses himself as he lean in and turn the generator switch from Automatic to Manual ON. "We need to charge the Rover before we dismount the power generator" he explains cheerful and slap Ray on his shoulder.

Ray see Nikki sleeping and follow Kareem to the back of the Rover "How big is it?" he asks as he gazes into the engine compartment.

"The reactor is the size of a crawler-drone, more or less" Kareem reply confident.

Ray look surprised at Kareem "That big!" he gasps "How do we get it out of the Rover then?" he gazes at the air-lock.

Kareem shake his head "Not that way, through the cargo door" he nods at the opposite of the cabin as he begins unscrewing a pump section.

Ray look at the cargo door 'That mean the cabin will be air-less' he reason. He begin collecting the trash scattered on the floor and dump it in the disposal container. 'What is this?' he pulls out a bulge of clothe from the container. '*The signal transmitter*' he marvels, incense rise from the bulge and Ray feels a pain in his eyes and nose and struggle to breathe. "***Aha***" his hands burns. He throws the lump on the floor and run over to the sanitary-unit to wash his hands.

Kareem rushes over and hand Ray a cleaning wipe "What happened to you?" he asks worried "it smells of ammonia, are you alright?" He examines Ray's face "You look okay, and your hands too" he reaffirms relieved.

Ray tosses the lump with his foot "It's soaked with that stuff" he snap and scrap it into an empty food container. He shows the sealed pack to Kareem "It's the Transmitter Veronica nabbed at the Apophis crater" he gushes.

Kareem takes the packaged and stash it together with the hard-drive in Sabine's bag "Now it ours!" he smiles satisfied and get back working in the engine compartment.

Ray wonder where the ammonia may come from 'Was it added to the fabric or did it come from the crater?' he can't find any connection and decide to talk with Sabine about it.

"*Hi Sabine*" Ray shake Sabine awake and sit next to him on the bedside. "We found the transmitter Veronica took at the Apophis crater" he smiles with a wink toward the bag below the bed.

Sabine nod sleepy.

Ray bite his lip as he continues "I got burned from some ammonia substance on the transmitter, do you have any idea where it may come from?" he questions uncertain.

Sabine pull himself up in the bed "I found some on my gloves too back at the Shuttle, when we returned from the crater..." he hesitates "it maybe ammonia hydroxide" he concludes.

Ray lean closer to Sabine "So, it comes from the crater, do you agree?" he asks nodding.

Sabine nod back "Yes, there might be ammonia hydroxide in the sub-sea, it's possible" he assumes.

Ray smile content "And the transmitter, can you install it on the Shuttle?" he encourages.

Sabine laugh "No, no, it's too old and may be damaged too..." he pauses thoughtful "better if we download the radio application from the Rover and install it on the Shuttle" he smiles confident.

"Right, do that!" Ray replies with a snap of his fingers and leave for the cockpit.

Sabine swat at the air "*Sure*" he echt stock.

Nikki smiles seeing Ray entering the cockpit "I have copied the reactor applications for the Shuttle" she points torpid at her pad.

"Aren't you marvelous" Ray cheers kissing her on the chin. He sits for a moment studding Nikki, she looks sluggish and pail.

Nikki zip tight her overall "Stop pity me" she coo wanly.

Ray moves closer to the window "Alright" he muses gazing outside into the blackness. Looking up he recognizes the dolphin constellation sending a feeling through him that they are on their way home.

"Sabine found ammonium on his spacesuit, did you know?" he asks looking at his hands.

Nikki catch Ray's eyes "I did smell a pungent odor..." she pauses "outside ammonium freeze-dry to a salt crystal. But, if we bring it inside on our boots it gets aqueous and gaseous, intoxicating us... *We need to filter it out*" she quivers with a pained gaze at Ray.

Ray slides the ventilation at maximum and check the CO_2 meter. 'The CO level is low, so the carbon filter must be working' he concludes. "It may take hours till we get all the ammonium filtered out" he laments.

Nikki gazes into the cabin "That's why it hurts breathing, I need the emergency respirator" she urges and move to stand-up.

"*Let me!*" Ray rush out of his seat "you breathed ammonium contaminated air longer than any of us" he complains bitterly. Hurrying to the emergency closet and return with the respirator kit for Nikki.

Kareem enters the cockpit behind Ray "What with her?" he questions studding Nikki wearing the inhalator mask.

Ray cross his arms tight "The air is contaminated and making us sick" he rants looking down at Nikki.

"Ammonia?" Kareem asks searching.

Ray shake his head affirmative with a fixed gaze at Nikki.

Kareem study the ventilation control "The CO_2 filtration cannot cope with that" he mumbles to himself. "Let's get the spacesuits on, at least the air is clean besides we need to move back to the Shuttle" he argues.

"You are right!" Ray stress and haste over to Sabine and Veronica *"Let's go!"* he hurries "Make sure your spacesuits are fully charged, we are moving back to the Shuttle" he instructs firm.

Veronica gaze ignored at Ray as she helps Sabine into his spacesuit. Sabine resist his anger and quietly let her help him dress.

They all five stand side by side in their suits watching the squared cargo door opening with a whining sound letting the pressure out of the cabin. As the door lower down to the ground the first daylight enters reflecting in their helmets.

Nikki, Sabine and Veronica help each other on their way back to the Shuttle, followed by Kareem and Ray dragging the reactor on a makeshift sled.

At the Shuttle Nikki pull her head out of a manhole as Ray and Kareem arrive dragging the heavy sled. "This way" she guides over the voice-comm. "No power, no elevator" she affirms and vanish inside the Shuttle.

Ray stop and gaze at the open escape hatch 'So, the Shuttle is air-less inside' he peculates.

Kareem slap him on the shoulder "Come on *wimp*" he laughs.

They work hard pulling and pushing the reactor past the manhole. Ray feel exhausted as they drag the reactor on the floor over to the Power hold. "Here you go" he smiles at Kareem and walk back closing the emergency hatch.

"We are not done yet" Kareem complain on the voice-comm.

Ray find Sabine in the cockpit and knock at his helmet.

Sabine laugh "I got the radio working on the emergency light supply" he cheers "do you want to call anyone?" he switches the radio to the voice-comm.

Ray get excited "The radio works!" He hug Sabine shoulder to shoulder "You are great, thank you!" he chants "Lets call Bukari."

"Yes..." Bukari answer faint.

"Hi, it's me" Ray reply happy.

Bukari lighten up **"Ray,** how are you? Let me call you back" he rejoices suppressed and disconnect the call.

Ray and Sabine wait quietly watching the sun low in the sky next to the massive Jupiter.

Sabine switch on the incoming call.

"Hello, I'm using the emergency jigger again..." Bukari pauses "there is no image, do you hear me?" he complains.

"We are using the voice-comm" Sabine explains.

"*Oh*, hello Sabine good to hear you are well" Bukari respond surprised.

Ray smile "We are all here plus an intruder" he jokes.

"You are a moron *Ray*" Veronica jeer over the voice-comm.

Bukari stay silent, listening.

Ray check the time on Sabine's pad "We are coming up to you within a day or so" he cheers.

Bukari still don't respond, **"Did you get that?"** Ray blaze inquiringly.

Bukari make a noise "Yes, yes I was thinking" he pauses "better if you dock at one of the old construction ports at the Port-deck. I'll see which one the best and let you know..." he hushes quietly "someone is coming" he mumbles and disconnect.

Ray laughs at Sabine "*It worked!*" he hoots with a large grin.

Sabine look heavy at Ray "**Of course it works**" he booms back.

The control panel light-up. Sabine give Ray a thumbs-up.

"We got power for another four or five years" Kareem joke over the voice-comm as the lighting come back on.

"**yo-hoo**" Nikki salute on the voice-comm.

Sabine switches the particle field on "Charger on" he confirms and tap his fingertip at the field strength meter, indicating 0%

Ray check the air tank 'Almost empty' he concludes. "Keep your suits on, we are out of pressure and its freezing." He leaves the cockpit and look for Nikki, to his surprise Veronica sit at her bedside small talking.

Ray pace indecisive at the same spot struggling to make up his mind if he should walk over to them or not. 'Hmmm what are they talking about? Are they gossiping?' he feels intimidated and turns around and walk over to Kareem helping him to bolt the reactor to the deck.

Walk the Plank

Nikki, Veronica and Kareem are strapped-in waiting for the takeoff. Ray returns to the cockpit closing the door behind him "We are all clear" he confirms sharply.

"It's looking good, we got power charge at 100% and field strength at 100%, all systems ready to go!" Sabine cheers.

Ray feel thrilled as he takes the Shuttle up hovering, gently Sabine add thrust, and they accelerate out of the dusty plum.

Sabine punch the handle "You got full thrust" he affirms as he watches the power indicator ticking down 80%, 79%....

Ray turns the Shuttle to a steep angle, and they climb fast into space.

Sabine stares fixed at the meters "The power keep dropping, but the field stay at 100%" he rejoices as Ganymede's neon-blue aurora glow brighter in the horizon.

Ray feel overwhelmed by the weightlessness 'It feels so good!' he cants as the dark space greet them with myriads of sparkling stars "Welcome to space!" he announces on the voice-comm with a bright grin.

A core of happiness cheers over the voice-comm. The door opens and Kareem flow into the cockpit gazing out the window into the deep space. "We made it" he giggles.

Ray turn and look at Nikki, she waves back at him "Thank you, Ray" she coos sending him a kiss.

They glide silently through space toward the orbit of Callisto. Sabine keep an eye on the power indicator, it's now ticking upward 23%, 24%, recharging from the reactor.

Ray check the navigator "We don't have Daedalus's position locked in, *why?*" he asks Sabine.

Sabine pull his shoulders "We don't have Daedalus's position. Elisabeth commanded the ship to the orbit of Callisto, it's all we know" he nods affirmative.

Ray gets a sudden feeling of uncertainty "Any news from Bukari?" he asks puzzled.

Sabine gaze pensive at Ray "*No...* Let's call him" he hastily establishes the call to Bukari.

Bukari answer the call "Hello Ray! Let me call you back" he stutters.

Ray rush forward "**No, no,** Bukari we don't have time for that" he urges snap "we are on our way up to you."

Bukari pauses "*Um,* we left" he quivers.

Ray lean over the controls "What do you mean you left, you left to where?" he rants perplexed.

Bukari pauses again "Daedalus left the Callisto orbit, we are on our way out of the Jupiter system and..." he quivers heartbroken.

Sabine breaks into the conversation "Activate the lodestar emitter, it will show up on the Beacon Space Network giving us your position" he explains.

Bukari shivers "*But,* they will arrest me if I enter maintenance" he laments.

Ray looks up into the ceiling "And we are running out of oxygen, *dying!*" he agonizes.

Bukari sniffs "Alright I'll switch the tracker on" he mutters.

Ray breath out alleviated "Thank you Bukari, and where can we dock?" he asks waiting for Bukari to answer "Are you there?"

"*Yes...* if you let me think" Bukari protest "there's a construction dock still in use at aft, port 4" he replies and disconnects.

Sabine observe Ray "Will he switch the emitter on?" he queries doubtful.

"If he said he will, *he will!*" Ray nod certain and gaze out the window 'What will await us when we board the ship, will they know we are coming?' he wonders and try to figure out a plan 'We need to free Elisabeth, she is the only one who can bring us home.'

"I got their position" Sabine rejoices "they are off course..." he hesitates and add full power to the field.

After some time, "*Ay*, they turned the emitter off" Sabine laments and turn the navigator on manual. "We will catch up with Daedalus within 2 hours" he hesitates.

Ray nods at Sabine as he unzips from his seat pushing himself toward the door. He feels ready for what's coming and stay hovering in the cockpit doorway. "Listen everyone, we are going to Board Daedalus in a moment, and I need your attention" he charges firmly.

Kareem join Nikki and Veronica at the passenger compartment and Sabine watch Ray from his cockpit seat.

Ray looks around at everyone and begin his speech in a strong voice "We have lived and endured much to find the great answer to a great mystery. We have risked all we have, our home and loved ones for the curiosity of a few earthlings. Now these tellurians want to take away our future and even our lives. I say we are not going to allow that! We are going to take Daedalus back, we are going to fight till we got what is rightful ours!" he reaffirms alert.

Nikki brighten-up "**Yeah!**" she yells applauding.

Ray continues even stronger "And I'm going to tell you how we win. Because know how is what you need to come through, to overcome. Nikki, Sabine and Veronica you go to sickbay, after treatment meet us on the corridor. We will capture and rout out all who collaborate with security from second floor down to the service-deck. Ring-section by ring-section pushing them back to the new-section" he blazes.

"You bet Ray, *let all the traitors walk the plank!*" Sabine rage.

Ray turns at Kareem "Kareem you jam all doors and transporters to the crew section and join with us, *right!*"

"**Yeah**, I'll clip the wings" Kareem cheers.

Ray look gratified at them all "I will free our Captain, and we will all join outside the sickbay" he smiles confident. "Let's board the ship!" he cheers and returns to the pilot seat.

He gazes alert at a faint glow from Daedalus's engines. "Sabine, stay in the engine headwind it will keep us undetected" he chants as they close in on Daedalus.

"**Look...!**, the shield is rotating" Sabine gasps breathless.

Ray squishes his eyes in an effort to see past the ion cloud. "Yeah, the stabilizer engines are turned off, properly the laser communicator too" he mutters and looks back into the passenger compartment. "You need to strap-in. We are getting reversed gravity at docking" he calls.

Sabine steer the shuttle close to the shield, steadily aligning to Port-4 rotating at the speed of the shield.

The centrifugal force pulls the blood into Ray's head, and he feels as if standing upside down, looking down at the ceiling of the Shuttle.

"**Klack**" they hit the docking guide with a quiver and get pulled into position with a loud metallic squishing sound. Sabine give Ray a thumbs-up with a large grin.

Ray strap himself free and fall onto the ceiling, he gets up a bit sour and helps Sabine dawn from his seat. In the cockpit door he sees Veronica unstraps herself as she swing around and land on her feet on the ceiling. She seems filled with the same decisive spirit as he knew from Daedalus. He wonders if that is a good sign.

Ray grab his ice-axe and head for the exit followed by Kareem. Nikki look anxious at Ray "*Are you going to use that*" she shudders pointing at the axe.

Ray shuck his shoulders 'She is getting wimpy' he thinks and crawl into the air-lock. He notices how Veronica smile pitiful at Nikki as Kareem pull himself through the hatch. "Kareem and I first, then the three of you" he booms and close the hatch.

Fresh air rush into the air-lock from the Port-module as he pulls the handle to equalize the pressure. They strip their spacesuits and open the hatch slowly peeking into a large hangar on the port deck. '*No one, it's sealed off*' he remembers and step into the hall. A wall-ladder lead up to the center of the module 'it's to the transporter at the port terminal' he reason.

Kareem crawls up the ladder "*This way*" he indicates confident.

Ray return Kareem a hard smile and follow him up the ladder. Seeing Nikki dragging herself out of the air-lock fills him with an urge to get her into the med-bed.

They all five stand ready as the transporter opens its doors next to sickbay. Two contractors pass on the narrow corridor "**Hey you!**" one of the men yells, Ray throws the axe at the man's face "**Smack**" sending him bleeding onto the floor. "**Wiii**" Nikki screams terrified by the sudden violence.

Kareem hit the other man with a straight punch at his nose, shaken the man take one step backwards. Gaining control the man jumps at Kareem wrestling him unto the floor then strangling him. Ray rush to help Kareem kicking the man till he loosens his grip.

"Let's lock them up at the sickbay" Ray exact looking at the two mauled men on the floor. He picks up his axe and punch the men to move ahead.

Entering the consultancy Dr. O'Barley gaze stupefied "When did you guys get onboard?" he stutters. Seeing the miserable group of Nikki and Veronica supporting Sabine he calls Cathie "*Prepare the med-bed*" he urges.

Ray pushes the two contractors forward "Better lock these two up some-place" he snaps.

O'Barley look hard at the two men "An anesthesia injection will keep them quiet" he rants with a content smile and search for the syringes.

Ray clap Kareem at his back "Let's go." Kareem takes the transporter and Ray walks to the crew-section. Ray finds Elisabeth's cabin unguarded but locked. Without hesitation, he smash the door handle with the axe till the door give in.

Elisabeth looks surprised at Ray's entree "How many are you?" she asks as they rush down the corridor.

"*Five*" Ray cries.

"**Just five?**" Elisabeth shouts as three security guards come running towards them armed with electric-staffs.

Sabine pushes the hand brake closing the automatic door as Elisabeth and Ray run past the section airlock. In the same moment Veronica jump opposite pushing Elisabeth with her into the crew-section yelling to the guards "**I'm with you!**"

"**Dam it!** Now they got Elisabeth" Ray rush, throwing his hands up in the air. He walks down the corridor letting the steam out 'One of the guards was

Ben...' he recalls.

Kareem exits the transporter "All the doors locked!" he cants.

Ray return and notice a skinny man next to Nikki "Who are you?" he asks weighting the man with a glance.

"Its Tom our clerk" Nikki smile posing her arm on his shoulder.

Ray shake his head recognizing him from the crew office. Nikki and Sabine look healthy, just, Sabine still wear a sling on his arm and Nikki look a bit timid holding a broomstick.

Kareem focus at Ray "Now we have lost the momentum of surprise, what is your plan?" he questions.

Ray cross his arms and looks defiant back at Kareem "To fight them from second floor and down. Section by section as planned" he replies sharp.

They walk down the corridor to maintenance. Ray stops in the doorway looking at the empty Command Board and the scattered crew seated at their work desks. "**We are taking Daedalus back!**" he proclaims aloud, they all turnaround recognizing Ray "**Are you with us?**" he shouts looking at each one.

"**Yeah**" they all respond. They turn their heads looking to the side where a contractor enter from the conference room to see what is happening. He gazes stupefied at Ray "*How did you get up here?*" he burst out, he gazes a moment at Ray as Kareem, Nikki and Sabine enters as well. "**Hans, Jacob**" he calls igniting his electric-staff, two fellow contractors enter empty-handed.

Ray look at the three squarely built thugs "What do you think?" he asks Kareem as they scuffle toward the men with Nikki tight behind Ray.

Kareem takes an office chair and roll it in-front of him "If we can fight them one by one we will win" he reassures.

Ray nod and race his axe high as he walks decisive toward the first man. The man step fearlessly forward and punch the rod at Ray's chest. Ray jitters from the electric chock and fall in muscle spasms hurling his axe onto the floor with a reechoing sound.

Nikki smash the broomstick hard down at the man's arm. The stick splinters in two sending the electric-rod whirling at the floor. Furiously the man grab Nikki's arm and throw her through the air into a desk.

Ray lay curled-up on the floor. Gaining strength he kicks the man on his knee with all his body strength "**Clack**" the leg break. The man bent down supporting his knee in pain as Ray kick the electric rod toward Nikki before the second man get a hand on it.

The second man grab Ray just as he tries to get up, he is pinned face-down to the floor, struggling to move. Suffocating from the man's grip his sight begin to blur, the man let go jittering and fall to the side.

Nikki stands with the electric-rod offering Ray a hand. He stands up and look around. One man lay with a leg broken the other man moves a bit and Nikki shock him a second time. Kareem stands with the blood dripping axe in his hand, in front of him lay his opponent wounded and in pain. Ray looks around again "Where is Kei Enatsu?" he wonders.

He walks over to Sabine "Sabine, you take command of the Bridge and Tom you assist sickbay" he nods at the wounded contract workers.

At the airlock they stand discussing how to retake the crew-section "We need more electric-rods" Kareem point at Nikki.

Ray nod affirmative "Only Security have rods" he laments "we have to disarm them."

He looks firm at Nikki and Kareem "I saw Ben with two guards in the crew-section. Let us scare the pants off him" he mutter taking the axe back from Kareem. He stains some blood on Kareem's face and then on himself.

"**Kick ass**" Kareem rage and stand ready for the section-door to open.

As the door open Ray and Kareem step into the narrow corridor. At the left stand Ben with a fellow guard and at the right of the airlock stand another guard with a contractor. They all four wave an electric-rod. Ray turns to the left and Kareem to the right with Nikki following behind.

Ray swing the blood soiled axe in front of him as a warning "Hello Ben, join us, or you die... all your whimsy friends in maintenance are *dead*" he hisses sordidly stepping closer to Ben.

Ben rocks back and forth "*Ray...*" he voices stressed, the guard next to him look perplexed at Ben and take a step back.

Nikki follows at Ray's side "Finish him off, Ray" she demands.

Ray swing his axe up for a blow. Ben ducks in fear "**Wait I'm a crew member**" he cries.

Ray hesitate and Nikki step in grabbing Ben's staff "Disarm your friend" she demands.

Ben takes the guards rod and give it to Nikki, she turns and hand the electric-rod to Kareem. Kareem do not hesitate and punch the rod at the guard's chest in front of him sending him jittering onto the floor. The contractor beside set off down the corridor with Kareem pursuing him.

Ray push Ben down the corridor "Come on, open the door" he command. Ben wave his master-key, and the door opens.

From inside the cabin Bukari look dismayed at Ben and Ray. He leaps out on the corridor hugging Ray gracefully "I knew you would come" he gasps tearful.

With the crew freed they mass into the Bio-section with no resistance. Entering the Hotel-section they hear a continued beating "**BAM, BAM, BAM, ...**" they all stop listening to the loud echoing coming from the main corridor.

Ahead of them stand a formation of Security guards and Contractors in a large column blocking the way to the Saymora Office and the New-section. The guards are dressed in a dark blue battle array of body armor and headgear, shields and electric beating batons. They tap their batons on their shields and stomp their feet in unison, it sounds forceful and frighting.

Ray tries to organize the stupefied crowd into a line without result. They spontaneously run forward breaking off trash bins trowing them at the guards.

Mr. Mark stand in the center of the formation "**Base move forward**" he yells commanding. The first lines of guards charge in a violent outburst against the crew aggressively beating and electrifying anyone in reach.

Ray slam his axe into the shield of the guard in front of him. He manages to wrest the shield free and hurls it back into the crowd. He gets electrified from a guard next to him and step backward in pain.

"**Base open, line two direct support**" Mr. Mark yells, the first line of guards make room for the second line into the front formation. Nikki batter her rod at the head of a guard with little effect. She then punches the rod at the man's neck, and he falls in pain.

Ray and Nikki grab the guard and pull him to the back of the crowd. A fellow crew wrest the shield away and rush back into the fight, another take the baton. Ray see Bukari nearby "Bukari, tie him up" he roars, he stands perplexed for a moment watching the ruthless beating of the crew.

"Line three direct support, line one up" Mr. Mark yells. A new line of guards replace the first one beating the crew harder, forcing them to retreat.

'We are loosing if we don't break their formation' Ray realizes, he watches Nikki and Bukari binding the guard. "Bukari bring a Service-wagons here. I'll take care of this one" he rush and punch the guard unconscious.

"Was that necessary?" Nikki complain.

Bukari comes back with a self-driving Service-wagon "What is it for?" he asks curiously.

Ray lean over and study the scuffed wagon "To ram the guards." He steps unto the rear of the wagon switching it to manual drive.

"You just pull the handle and steer" Bukari yells at Ray.

Ray drive a bit forward **"*Nikki come on*"** he shouts with a large grin. Nikki jumps unto the wagon. Ray speed up and drive fast along the flank of the crowd. He sees an opening and steers head on into the platoon of guards ramming through their formation. The guards jump aside in panic till the wagon tilt and crash. The crowd rush into the dispersed guards in a one to one fight.

Ray stands up, dusts himself off, and to his surprise sees Mr. Mark in front of him.

Mr. Mark look furious at Ray growling some unrecognizable words, as he steps close up and smash his baton hard on Ray's arm. Ray side step from the blow and punch a straight fist at Mr. Mark's jaw sending him a step backward. Ray jump forward for a second stroke, but Mr. Mark parries the strike and aim for Ray's head and connect. Ray looses his hearing as he falls on to the ground.

Ray is dizzy 'I'm done' he thinks and wipes his mouth tasting blood. 'I must find Elisabeth, she is the only one who can get us home.' He gets up on his knees but can't find his balance.

Mr. Mark laugh seeing Ray struggling to get up. He circles Ray "Come on stand up and let me finish you off, **ha, ha, ha**" he rages satisfied and kick at Ray. Ray rolls to the side and avoid the kick. He set off and jump at Mr. Mark pushing him backwards. Mr. Mark taken by surprise stumbles over a man laying on the floor.

Ray grab Mr. Mark's baton and strike him in the chest with the rod. Electric sparks fly to all sides with Mr. Mark laughing, unharmed by his body armor. He moves to get up but fall back jittering onto the floor.

"You have to zap them unconscious at the neck" Nikki say pained, and watch some contractors retreating to the new-section.

The remaining guards regroup into a circular echelon defending themselves against the surrounding crew now better equipped with conquered shields and batons.

Ray feel ail from the brush on his arm and head, he looks up at the black crystal edifice next to them. 'Kei Enatsu where have you taken Elisabeth?' he muses and call out to Nikki over the noise "*Nikki come on let's find Elisabeth.*" They run into the entrance hall of the black glass dice. Seeing Ray's blood spotted face the young man at the reception duck behind the desk.

Ray leaps up the wide stairs and bust into Enatsu's office. The small man seated behind his work desk staring incredulous at Ray and Nikki standing in the doorway.

"*Mr. Barton*, I did not expect you to make it up here." Mr. Enatsu salutes with a half smile as he gestures to the guard to stay foot. "Come and join us" he nods toward Elisabeth and Veronica.

Ray recognizes the fixed gaze of the strong security man next to the door and feels the sore stomach just seeing the man.

"What a coincidence" Mr. Enatsu applauds "we was just talking about the alien artifacts you brought back from Ganymede. Please tell us what you found down there?" he asks monotonously.

Ray stares at Veronica 'What had she told Enatsu? ... Never mind, they are defeated' he concludes. "***The game is over, we have taken out all your guards***" he shouts pointing the electric baton at Mr. Enatsu.

Elisabeth stands-up and look firm at the guard "*Jonathan*, you are a just man, stay that way and arrest Mr. Enatsu" she command.

The man wave from side to side gazing from Elisabeth to Mr. Enatsu, then taking a step toward Mr. Enatsu.

Mr. Enatsu stand up looking disturbed at the guard "You cannot...." he rush out of the office with Veronica following behind.

Ray run in pursuit and see Veronica running down the stairs and Mr. Enatsu the opposite way down the hallway. He set after Mr. Enatsu and reach the end of the corridor where a hatch closes. With a sound of air ejecting the floor jitter. He looks through the small window in the hatch and sees an eject capsule vanishing out of sight into the dark space 'What?' he gasps.

Elisabeth stride out the office building onto the main corridor with Jonathan at her side. She looks sadden at all the people laying scattered around. Along with all the broken inventory from benches, lighting and storefronts. The corridor is stocky from the smell of injuries.

Seeing Elisabeth and Jonathan the fighting stop, and the crowd disperse. They begin to care for their wounded, taking them to sickbay for treatment on the med-bed. The guards walk over to Elisabeth and lay down their shields and batons.

Ray and Nikki find Kareem sitting on a bench, he looks beaten with several electric burn marks on his body.

Nikki bends down at Kareem "Are you alright?" she sighs with a sad smile.

"I'm fine" Kareem nods and straighten up a bit.

Ray feel nausea and sit down next to Kareem. His head and arm ache and hurt. He still feels the adrenaline rushing in his veins as he watches Nikki holding Kareem's hands. 'She looks gorgeous' he muses as he studies her every curve.

Nikki cross her arms "Ray stop goggling at me" she argues and gaze darting down the corridor ... "What happened to Mr. Enatsu and Veronica?" she quivers.

Ray looks down at the floor "Well... Mr. Enatsu left on an eject capsule... can you believe that?" he gushes.

Nikki shake her head "You mean he ejected into space, with nowhere to go?" she marvels jerking her head back.

Ray look heavy at her "**Yeah**, crazy right."

"And, Veronica she ejected too?" Nikki marvel.

Ray stands-up "No, she ran out on the corridor..." He watches the injured in front of them. "Help me get the wounded guards to medical-bay." Ray insists.

The Announcement

In the morning the Pad sounds, Ray takes the call with his whole body still aching *"Uff... yes?"* he laments pained.

"Good morning Ray" Hellman salute, "didn't you have med-bed treatment?" he asks glib.

Ray stiffen "Nice to see you too..." he pauses wondering where Hellman been yesterday, "how are you?" he gushes curious.

Hellman clear his throat "I'm better thank you" he continues before Ray ask more questions "we need to meet at Elisabeth's office at 3:50, I'll let you in on the detail there."

"Right, thank you" Ray hangup, he turn back into bed and embrace Nikki still sleeping at his side.

At the office Elisabeth's secretary salute Ray as usual "They are waiting for you" she smiles.

Ray salute Elisabeth and Hellman, as he takes his seat he notices a scar over Hellman's left eye. 'He looks skinny' he wonders, and the green lamp on the desk is missing.

Elisabeth lean forward "You are amazing Ray, you know that?" she smiles.

Ray smile back a bit uncomfortable as he shakes his head.

Hellman observe Ray seriously.

Elisabeth continues, "Sabine gave us the equipment you retrieved from Ganymede as it is contaminated the bio-section have to study it first. What can you tell us about your findings?" she asks intent.

Ray looks down at the table 'Sabine must have given his statement' he concludes and look Elisabeth in her eyes. "We found the wreck of the Soviet Lander Mars-7 and dismounted the control and radio modules…"

Hellman takes the word "We know the lander separated from the coast stage in 1974 at its rendezvous with Mars. It missed the Mars entry and must have continued to Jupiter where it crash-landed on Ganymede. What we don't know is how it begins to send a coded signal?" he confides.

Ray nod affirmative "Yes, Sabine worked on cracking the encryption, but he needs more processing power" he explains and pause for a moment. "I had peculiar dreams with an entity showing me the ocean of Ganymede…"

"You had dreams…" Hellman interrupts with a tight face.

Ray drag his feet under the chair "Well… that is basically what we discovered" he murmurs gazing at the door.

Elisabeth places her hands on the table "Thank you, Ray. We will talk again after we have interviewed the other two" she round-off and dismiss him with a handshake.

"Come by the office tomorrow" Hellman smile mindfully.

Out in the front office he encounters Kareem waiting, they shake hands "How are you?" he salutes.

The secretary intervenes "You may enter now" she urges Kareem.

Ray strolls down to the park and sit on the bench. 'So, they were going to take testimony from Nikki too' he pictures and breath-in the fresh air. He's relaxing till he receives an alert on his pad. 'Nikki' he intuit and look at the display. 'From the Rover left at Ganymede? Is it Wang?' he wonder and open the message.

>in your time frame wayfarer squatters λ75.33g β22.55g r0.31625 v18.175e- 6 is bound for this system<

Ray glances unfocused 'What an invasive specie, *now it's texting too*' he fumes and switches the pad off. He sits and contemplate a butterfly in the flowers nearby when Nikki cover his sight from behind.

"Hi Nikki" he cheers, she takes a seat next to him and sling her arm around him. "How did it go?" he asks chatty.

Nikki shines "*Aha*, you know…" she chants and study Ray. "I told them all that happened, our dreams too..." she observes Ray's reaction.

Ray nod pensive '*And the message?*' he vexes.

Nikki kiss Ray on his chin "Why worry so much?" she inquires.

Ray shake his head "It just too crazy. The alien singleton on Ganymede has sent me a message using the Rover's transmitter. Just this time it has learned our language" he argues and pull his pad out and show Nikki the message.

Nikki stare incredulous at the pad "*Wow*, you are right" she gasps.

Ray grab after the pad, and it falls to the ground "*You didn't believe me?*" he cries out hurt.

Nikki moves to face Ray "*I did believe you*, it was just a dream... now it's texting" she objects and sit pensive for a moment. "Did it copy your psychology? If it is a billion times smarter than us, how do we know?" she contemplates.

Ray picks up his pad from the ground "It is difficult to know whether it lie or invent things just to please us. This destroys trust between us, and the creature. We need to trust the information we receive, the answers must be verifiable and trustworthy. If the answers are untrustworthy or incomprehensible we need to correct the questions asked till we can trust the answer. Using some kind of protocol..."

"Did you ask it a question?" Nikki interrupts smiling.

Ray jerk back-wards "*No*" he gasps.

Nikki contemplate Ray "Besides, it has lived in a fishbowl for a billion or more years without outside contact. With no idea what it means to be human. It is bereaved of all the quality's that makes us who we are." she smiles witheringly.

"Maybe it communicates with other entities in the universe? If you could see the complete spectra of detectable electromagnetic radiation in each pixel of your view, imagine what you would see" Ray smiles back.

Nikki laugh "Below all the ice?" she then turns serious "but it's more existential than that. It read your thoughts, speak our language and mimics our preconceptions. Who knows what come next?" she hesitates, "Tomorrow I'll study and clean the contaminated equipment from Ganymede, we will see what I find" she looks down at the ground.

"Right, let's go home" Ray encourages and stand-up.

Next morning Ray walk up to Hellman's desk and take a seat in front of him, waiting for him to finish his writing. Ray studies Hellman's scar over the left eye, it is still red round the edge 'he must have got it recently' he concludes.

Hellman looks up "I got the scar doing the mutiny" he brushes the scar with two fingertips.

Ray feels a light blush in his chins as he nods "Was it fiercest?" he asks frank.

Hellman nods as he looks away. He taps at his pad and read a note "Sabine is cracking the coded signal within a few day, he says..."

Ray hand Hellman his pad "The alien entity send me a text yesterday" he interrupts.

Hellman bends over the desk as he read the message "*From the Rover, how can it do that?*" he burst out.

Ray lean in "The entity can manage knotty information, it seemed to understand instantly my thoughts, language, and our technology. It has hyper-technology that is completely incomprehensible to us, our understanding simply cannot grasp it" he reassures.

Hellman gazes at Ray "Has it goals of its own, desires or ethics. If it has, what are they?" he ponders.

Ray race his shoulders in doubt, "Let's see what Nikki find out" he proposes and lean back in his chair.

"Forward that message to me and get some rest, Ray. *We got plans for you!*" Hellman smiles and return to his writing.

At lunch Ray enters the packed Canteen and spot Nikki together with Kareem and Sabine.

At the table Kareem is showing a scar on his upper arm "...if any of these mutineers escape from the new-section. I'll hunt them dawn and drag them back into their cage" he brags with a big laugh.

"Hi big shot" Ray slap Kareem on his shoulder and join table.

Ray look Nikki in her eyes "How's food?" he smiles and notice her eyes shining.

Nikki laugh "Better than protein soup in junk-bags" she giggles.

Sabine side-bump Nikki's shoulder "Don't remind me" he laughs still eating.

Ray bunch up in his chair "Sabine you don't want to be reminded about the code cracking either, right?"

Sabine turns on a knowing smile "Oh yes, the code will be cracked within hours" he pauses "as I have said before, and now I say it again. There is a base of truth in every stereotype and if you are paying attention to the patterns. Then the details will single out by themselves" he cheers lofty.

Nikki widen her eyes "Wow Sabine, what a show-off. What do the message say?" she lavish.

Sabine cross his arms with a grimace "Well, it is alien of nature, mostly cacographic" he dismisses the question, looking away.

Ray lean close to Nikki, studying her face "You are examining the equipment we brought back?" he questions bluntly.

"*Yes*" she drags pensive.

"*And?*" Ray insists getting Kareem and Sabine attentions too.

Nikki zip-up her blouse "The Ocean of Ganymede is poisonous to us. But it got the right chemical elements for *this* alien life-form namely ammonium hydroxide."

Kareem's shake his head "*What alien life-form?*"

Nikki sends a crisped nod toward Ray "The equipment we brought back from the crash site on Ganymede was smeared with an alien life-form of neuron cells. It's basically a large brain organism, a huge self-regenerating fungi culture that lives forever by chemo-synthesizing ammonium. The fungi have immortality by transferring the personality and memory of its individual cells as they duplicate."

Ray, Kareem and Sabine gaze incredulously at Nikki.

She continues, "I mixed ammonium hydroxide in a container and added the dry cells from the transmitter... They came back to life and reassembled as they did I perceived a sense of delight."

Nikki looks round the table and continues, "I found that the cells contain magnetite and organic crystalline structures. It can sense extremely low energy fields. It's swarm mind must be able to do billions of thoughts simultaneously and may have a memory millions of years old. Collectively it processes information millions of times faster than us" she concludes with a small yelp.

Ray looks at Sabine "It is reading our minds. What are we going to do with that thing?"

Sabine look serious back a Ray "We have to dump it into space" he murmurs unsure.

Weeks have passed on their voyage home, Ray have worked on the repairs of the elevator suspension with the maintenance team. The office is quiet and Hellman have been absent most of the time.

Elisabeth comes over to Ray's desk. "Hello Ray" she salutes as she seats down next to him. "We need to talk" she moves closer to Ray. "We have recovered from a reckless insurrection and face tough choices as Saymora Corporation have gone out of business. Leaving us without directions till a new owner emerges." she catches Ray's eyes and nod affirmatively.

Ray nod agreeable as he wonders where she is going with her narration.

Elisabeth fold her hands as she continues "We have decided to take our fade in our own hands and declared Daedalus independent of earth as a sovereign concurrence." She pauses and study Ray's reaction. "We, I and all the department managers are arranging a referendum of a governance body of five elders elected for life." She sits back in her chair looking away for a moment.

"Well..." Ray shifts his feet uncertain.

Elisabeth arranges the pad and papers on Ray's table "I would be glad to have you as manager of the maintenance department?" She looks straight at Ray.

Ray can't help smile as he digests the offer "And Hellman?" he gasps.

Elisabeth smile "Hellman present himself as elective for Counselor" she stands-up and look satisfied at Ray. "You may take his desk right away" she jests and leave.

At dinner Nikki and Ray discuss the new council of elders.

Nikki drop her shoulders "*No, no,* they can only vote on issues presented from a group of crew members. Or race issues for the departments to discuss" she state with a firm look at Ray.

Ray toy with the flowerpot as he shakes his head "*It sounds authoritarian to me...*" he rush and move the Garden Mum flower to the center of the table.

Nikki tighten her hand on Ray's "Sustainable and equity is where the crew give back to the departments as much as they receive. This requires an organization that takes into account all consequences of any decision." she reaffirms.

Ray rubs the back of his neck as he turns on the news channel. The screen show Mars covered in dense muddy clouds with a new uneven ring of debris absorbing the moons Phobos and Deimos. The speaker talk about how smoothly Ceres impacted with Mars. Debunking Earths fears that Ceres impact could jettison so much material into space it would endanger Earth.

Ray point at the screen "Nikki, we can send the alien sponge down to live in Mars's ocean, *look*" he laughs relieved.

Nikki shake her head painfully "No, Elisabeth have told me to keep it alive in a jar, it keeps communicating..." she allures.

Ray look worried at Nikki "What if it adapts to our environment and escapes?"

"It knows too much about our universe, we cannot let it go..." Nikki race her shoulders and smile.

Next day at the office Sabine come by "Ray, Congratulation with the naming" he cheers as they shake hands. "We are having a urgent meeting in the conference, are you coming?"

Ray is happy to see Sabine "Sure, I got the message too" he packs his work aside in an instant "Let's go" he smiles.

Ray take his seat next to Nikki, the conference room is full even with some standing at the back.

Elisabeth wait impatient behind her seat for everyone to settle in. "Good afternoon to everyone! First, the voting of the council tomorrow will take place as planned, we are not here to alter that…" She smiles with her hand on her heart.

"It is to announce to you that a World Government have been formed on Earth. And we have been ordered to apply to their commands. As you all know, by now, we were sent to Jupiter to investigate a foreign signal send from Ganymede." Elisabeth looks at Sabine seating at her side. "Sabine have decoded the original signal and in short it warns us that hostile alien nomads are bound for the solar system. Later we received, yet a message send from Ganymede confirming the first message. We shared the message with UN on earth, and they got verification from the moon observatory. A mass of objects are coming our way" she pauses and look around the room.

"I got an order from the new world government formed in this grave moment, to outfit Daedalus as a battleship. Every drone or ship in space will carry armament" she gazes down at the table.

Ray leans closer to Nikki whispering "We are the breakwater that divide bad faith from hope."